Magnolia Road

THE GRANITE HARBOR SERIES
BOOK THREE

bestselling author
J. Lynn Bailey

One

Bryce

"It'll blow over," my father, Robert Hayes, always says. His go-to saying for every situation the Hayes family is pressed with.

But this isn't a media situation. It is the specific words written in the email that my father received weeks ago from an unknown source that made him uneasy, unsettled. My father isn't an easily threatened man. A life chosen in politics—one I didn't choose to grow up in—is lived under scrutiny. A watchful eye. One misstep, one move out of the ordinary, and the media is down your throat like a thousand knives.

You ate a peanut butter sandwich, Congressman Hayes, not a ham sandwich. Can you tell us why?

Mr. Hayes, your seat belt wasn't completely fastened before you pulled away from the curb. Can you explain why?

Can you tell us why you took public transportation instead of your private vehicle, Congressman Hayes?

So, you're saying your new proposed bill sent to the House has nothing to do with your personal life?

My father's response to all of these? "Give it time. It'll blow over."

I've never seen my father rattled. Except once. *Terrified* might be a better word.

"It'll blow over, sis. I just want to take all precautions to be safe." He's quiet for a moment. "Please."

I hear the sadness in his voice. The sadness no one hears, except the ones who love him most. The sadness that has returned on the 10th of March every single year since I was eighteen.

It's the desperation in his tone that gets me. I'm not one to run.

In fact, that's another thing my father always says. "Don't run. Face everything head-on."

And, in this case, I wouldn't be running. I'd be temporarily relocating, just until this all blew over. Right?

But the bigger problem is, I'm lying. I have a pretty good idea of who's making the threats. And truth be told? I'm scared but not scared enough to tell the truth.

"Lenny's been in touch with the property management."

"Dad, I can do this on my own. I'm a grown woman." I roll my eyes at the phone and pick at my red fingernail polish. "You realize I'm not eight anymore, right? That I handle multimillion-dollar deals?"

Dad chuckles into the phone. "Your mother and I should have named you Tenacious. Bryce clearly doesn't fit."

I smile even though he can't see it.

"Anyway, Lenny will be in touch with the details about the house." He pauses. "And, sis?"

"Yeah?" The smile fades as I look out the window of my high-rise office and watch as the traffic crawls down the 405 Freeway. *I really do hate the traffic in Los Angeles.*

"You're sure? Granite Harbor is where you want to go for the time being?"

No. "Absolutely."

The temporary move worked out great with Stan Reedley at Reedley Literary Agency. I'm a senior literary agent at our headquarters in downtown Los Angeles. We have an office in New York City that I'll check in with to handle office matters that can't be handled from my rental house. Besides, an agent just left, so it will work out fine.

This will be good, I try to convince myself. *I'll be closer to Eli and Alex, Emily and Noah. No, this will be great. No more traffic.*

Granite Harbor is the epitome of everything I've never wanted. Small. Quaint. Lovely.

Growing up in Los Angeles, you get addicted to the lifestyle. Fast-paced. Convenient. Cultural.

I met Alex, my best friend, about ten years ago when she lived in Belle's Hollow, which is five hundred miles north of LA and still in California. Can you imagine driving five hundred miles and still being in the same state? Texas. Texans would understand this. But the East Coasters have no idea how stuck one can feel. One could drive five hundred miles and cover the entire East Coast and a lot of states. Anyhow, when I started taking the flight from LA to Belle's Hollow, the need for exotic food and late nights twisted and turned into a knot and became smaller somehow. The need didn't demand so much fulfilling anymore. Then, Alex moved to Granite Harbor and married Eli Young. That's when I started taking flights cross-country. Maybe I needed Alex more than I'd thought. Maybe that's why I had taken so many trips to Belle's Hollow.

But temporarily moving to Granite Harbor means seeing Ethan Casey again.

"Bryce, listen, I've got to run." He pauses. "And call your mother."

I know what face my dad is making. I know his lips are pursed together in a thin pink line. I know his graying eyebrows are furrowed.

"Her heart has always been in the right place, Bryce."

I let the air escape from my lips as I stare at the high ceiling of my office.

My mother was tolerable until my brother's addiction festered and wrapped around my parents' marriage, crawling between the small cracks that his disease found, getting between them with his manipulative antics.

My mother wants to give love to her son, but that same love is killing him.

"Love you," I whisper into the phone, pushing away the tenderness that starts to form around my heart, and hit End.

Two weeks ago, my father received a rather threatening email. It was simple really. It was an *I hate you for what you stand for* rant.

They're politically driven. That's all. Someone's panties are in a bunch because their political views aren't matched. It's normal.

My father shrugged it off. It's not out of the ordinary for congressmen to receive emails like this. In fact, they're usually harmless, just some crazy person with access to the internet.

But then he received another email that described my parents' home.

Then, another email that gave my mother's license plate number.

Then, another email with a picture of my brother passed out in some dark alley with an unsavory character with a top hat and a dirty face, staring wildly into the camera, clearly unaware he was having his picture taken.

The last one was of me getting into the shower, taken through my window at home. The window I'd cracked just a little bit to let the steam through as I cleaned my body.

That's when my dad drew the line.

If it were up to me, I'd stay. But things at home with my parents are tougher. My dad is the glue that holds this family together. He's the giver. He's the heart. He's the one who picks my mother off the floor when my brother walks out of another ungodly expensive rehab.

So, I agreed to move on a temporary basis to help my dad. To make things easier on him. I'm doing this because he asked me to.

He said, "Pick a place to stay for a bit until this all blows over."

I chose, of all places, Granite Harbor. Besides, what crazy is going to find me there, in a small town on the East Coast?

I walk to my desk and check my email, waiting on a manuscript I requested from a new author. An email from Lenny comes in.

> *Hi Bryce,*
>
> *Here's the address to the house the rental agency provided me with.*
>
> *28 Magnolia Road*
>
> *Granite Harbor, ME*
>
> *There's a key under the mat. I don't know how they can trust that someone won't break in. It's beyond me. Anyway, your scheduled check-in date is September 30. Your flight itinerary is also included. I know; I know, you like to book your own flights because of your superstitions with odd numbers, but your father insisted I do it. I'm sorry, Bryce. My hands were tied.*

You leave tomorrow.

All my best,

Lenny

Leticia Ramos, Assistant to Congressman Hayes

9378 West Monroe Street

Los Angeles, California

Leticia-ramos@losangeles.gov

I let out a long breath. *It's not a superstition*, I want to say to Lenny. But I've tried this conversation with her before, and it never works. It's fact. Odd numbers never bring good things.

September 11, 2001.

Friday the 13th. Because duh.

Robin Williams died on August 11.

My beloved Prince, the singer, died on April 21.

Pearl Harbor on December 7.

Hurricane Katrina on August 29.

Just to name a few.

So, I stay away from odd numbers.

I glance at my watch. Just after five thirty at night. I turn off my desk lamp, slide the box of things I'll take with me to Granite Harbor into my arms, and walk to the light switch. I turn back and look at my office. There aren't art pieces from children that plague the walls or pictures of family. The walls are bare, an off-white, with one frame that hangs behind my desk. A college diploma. That's it.

I won't miss this place while I'm gone, I tell myself.

Though I'll miss the negotiations that have happened behind that computer, the feelings associated with making people's dreams come true. But it's just money made. I've worked here for a long time. Long days. Often nights.

I click off the light.

It's just an office with four walls that held one person who did things, Bryce. That's it.

After I pack a suitcase full of stuff, I grab my broccoli and beef, a fork, a glass of wine, and sit down at my home work desk. A mirror my mother purchased for me when I first bought this place hangs on the wall in front of me. Before my computer comes alive, I see my reflection. My red hair sits around and past my shoulders. My blue eyes have always plagued me, begging for forgiveness when I wrecked my father's car at sixteen. My eyes, trusting yet deceiving my brother's way out of his first rehab when he said they were abusing him.

So, my eyes are not the honest blue eyes you'd find in a child. I believe maybe they used to be. My eyes are the eyes of past regrets, tainted by flecks of some poor decisions.

Like the night my eyes told me that Ethan Casey was *the one*. The eyes that betrayed me when he left the next morning, undetected, as I stared in the mirror that told me I was okay. That I was all right. He just left. No number, no address. No, *Hey, let's go grab a movie.* Just a note that said:

THANKS,

ETHAN

Like I was some booty call.

Sleeping around, one-night stands have never been part of my makeup really.

I didn't know who he was until I made my first trip to Granite Harbor many months later. Not a word was exchanged. I wonder if he even remembers me. Who I was. Maybe he's the one who sleeps around with women in unfamiliar places. It sure as hell isn't a move I pull.

Going back means I'll see him. Most likely, I'll have to speak to him again. There is no avoiding it.

Alex doesn't know. The only thing she knows is, the morning he left, I called her. I told her, with tears in my eyes, that he was the one. He was the one I'd stupidly and naively slept with.

His dark eyes, almost black, had stayed transfixed on mine as he pushed into me. Conveying only silent whispers in my ear, he allowed his body to relax against my flesh. We lay there until just before the sun rose.

That morning, my apartment started to fill with sunlight as my eyes quietly shut. My body exhausted and well cared for the night before, I lay there against his chest.

But we hadn't started in my bedroom.

We'd started at the Los Angeles Convention Center.

There was no way in hell you could miss Ethan Casey. He was tall. His hair was the color of midnight, but I didn't see that the first time I saw him. He wore a Red Sox baseball hat, a dark blue T-shirt, and dark jeans with boots that fit his torso just right. He wore boots but not the type of boots you'd see men in LA wearing; they were work boots. Clean, but still, working boots. Military-style. His face was clean-shaven, not brown skin and not white skin but somewhere in the middle. Like, if he and the sun met on a long, hot day, he'd bronze without sunscreen. His lean jaw flexed every now and then. A dimple just below his mouth appeared when he pulled his bottom lip back through his teeth. He seemed deep in thought. His arms crossed against his chest.

I was in line to get coffee at the coffee truck right outside the convention center. He was still off to the side, reading the menu board, his stance big, confident, and quiet, all at the same time.

I ordered and told the barista that I'd like to buy the coffee of the guy in the blue shirt.

The twenty-something barista whispered back, "I would, too. Is he your boyfriend?"

"No."

Like, duh, wouldn't he be standing next to me if he were my boyfriend? was what I wanted to say.

But this question sent me down the rabbit hole. It was all the barista's fault.

"So, he's single?" she asked another dumb question.

Really, it wasn't a dumb question. It was a question I wished I had pondered before I handed her my cash and made the offer.

I responded with, "I have no idea."

And, immediately, I was embarrassed because I didn't know the answer. He didn't have a wedding ring as far as I noticed. But maybe a girlfriend.

7

Christ, what did I do?

I tried to flag the barista back over to take back my offer, but the steamer was going, and she couldn't hear anything.

My cheeks flushed, I stepped back from the counter and tried to hide.

As I tried to disappear among the patrons, he ordered.

He and the barista exchanged words.

He looked back. Caught my eye. Nodded.

Fuck me. Oh, God. Not like that.

I pretended to be interested in my phone.

The barista called my name.

She called his name. Ethan.

We met at the counter.

"Thank you," he said. His voice was smooth, and it ran the length of my body, creating tiny little bumps along the way.

Then, I said something ridiculous. I finished his velvet-stained statement with, "Thought I'd buy the next person in line coffee. No big deal."

The barista stared blankly and was clearly confused by my reluctance to tell the truth.

Oh, God. Please don't say it. But then she says it.

"But he wasn't the next person in line. He was four back."

Two

Bryce

My phone pings, and it takes me away from my thoughts. It's Alex.

> *Alex: I can't wait for you to get here. I'll pick you up at the airport. What time will your flight get in tomorrow?*

> *Me: Flight lands at 6 p.m. I can't wait.*

> *Alex: Where's your rental?*

I pull up the email Lenny sent.

> *Me: 28 Magnolia Road*

> *Alex: That's right off of Main Street. Thank God, they're even numbers. ;)*

> *Me: Funny. Sarcasm intended. :) Kiss my girls. How are they?*

> *Alex: They're good. They can't wait to see Auntie Bryce.*

Me: You know I'm going to teach them bad habits, right? How to smoke cigarettes. Play poker. Cuss like a sailor. All the important stuff. ;)

Alex: Just get here. Love you.

Me: Love you. See you tomorrow.

This is the longest I've gone without seeing Alex and the girls, and I think it's for two reasons. One, I've needed some space. Time to make my life my own. Sometimes, I feel like I live vicariously through Alex with her beautiful husband and sweet girls. Work has always been my passion. My drive. Men and relationships have always been an afterthought. And, two, it was hard to see Ethan around town. He works for the Maine Warden Service as a game warden.

I've never wanted a family, being raised the way Ryker and I were. Political events. Flashing lights. Security. Campaigns … always campaigns. I sure as hell wouldn't want to put my children through that. And I'm not so sure I wouldn't turn into my mother, who could potentially be the Devil reborn. So, children are off the plate. And husbands? I can take them or leave them.

So, I put all of my passion into my work.

But, now, I'm stuck in Granite Harbor. I want to help my father, clear him from the worry about his family's safety. Why am I being sent away? Well, we can't send my mother away, the steadfast Trudy Hayes, because how would that look at community fundraisers? Events? And my brother, well, he comes around when he's sick and tired. Other than that, we usually can't find him.

I touch my mouse, and my screen comes alive.

I open Google Earth and type in the address, *28 Magnolia Road.*

It's a pink house. Not a bright pink but a soft pink. Pink's not really my color, but it's not a long-term investment either. It's got a little porch that faces the road. Two front windows on either side of the front door. On the corner of Magnolia and Main Street.

My phone starts to vibrate across my desk.

"Shit." I hit Talk. "Hey, Mom."

"Would it kill you to pick up the phone once in a while?"

"Sorry. I was busy watching the Olympics."

"What? The Olympics aren't on."

I know. "How's it going?" I don't dare say, *What do you need?*, or *Why'd you call?* because that would all lead back to three words—*the devil awakens.*

"Your father says you're leaving tomorrow for that godforsaken town on the East Coast. I don't know why you chose to go there of all places." I feel her eye roll and her cheek shake through the phone.

Because it's as far away as I can get from you without having to get a passport. "Because all flights were booked to Africa."

She sighs.

I've never been the daughter she wanted. She doesn't like options that aren't hers or that don't match her beliefs. She doesn't like a sassy mouth or loud noises. She likes her martinis dry and at five sharp. It's a wonder she even had children.

Ryker is the wild one. I am the mild one.

"I don't know why you hate me so much."

"I don't hate you, Mom." I roll my eyes and pick at my red polish again, which reminds me that I need to get a manicure. Which reminds me that I won't have time before I leave. Which reminds me that I need to find a place to get them done in Granite Harbor. *Do they have a salon?* I can't remember. *Christ.* And this takes me back to the phone conversation that I'm having that I don't want to have with my mother right now.

She's talking. But I don't know what she's rattling on about.

"And, at any rate, I don't know why he won't go back to Recovery Life."

Oh, yes. Ryker. "Mom, he's been to that rehab three times now. And you want to waste another ten grand on him? He doesn't want to get clean."

I'm so tired of having the same discussion with her. In the times we do talk, it's about Ryker. Her time to vent. But I'm the dumb one for listening.

"He's being singled out."

"He's being picked on."

"He doesn't have anywhere to go."

"If that facility would just ..."

"If his counselor knew ..."

It's never, ever Ryker's fault.

"Bryce, your brother—" she starts.

No. Just no. "Oh, Mom. Gotta run. The delivery guy is here."

She stalls. "But it's six thirty at night."

"UPS. They work crazy hours."

This is when the conversation gets really awkward. The good-bye.

"I'll see you, Mom."

"You have everything packed, right?"

"Yes," I sigh.

"Call me when you get there."

We both know I won't.

I start to bite my thumbnail again. "Bye, Mom."

"Aren't you going to say *I love you?*"

"I love you."

"That's better. I love you, too. Good-bye." She finishes with a curt tone. It's normal.

She always has to be the first to hang up. Like it's some sort of control thing.

Trudy Hayes has always been of stature. Power. Raised by the real estate tycoon James Bell and her mother, my grandmother, Barbara Bell. God, doesn't that sound like some sort of movie star name? Barb is what she asked Ryker and me to call her. It was never Grandmother, Grandma, Grams, G-ma—nothing remotely related to her age or her authenticity. It's no wonder my mother turned out just like her. My grandfather, James Bell, worked long hours. Drank whiskey under the table but ran a tight ship. Maybe a heavy drinker, but nothing in his life indicated that he was an alcoholic. Grandfather—what he liked us to call him—had money, fast cars, a beautiful home up on the hill with a pool and view of the greater Los Angeles area. Barb swept under the rug the infidelity, the drinking.

My mother swore she'd never marry a man like her father. And she didn't. My dad is everything that James Bell wasn't. Kind. Loving. The glue that holds our family together. The fixer. The worker. The hugger. The nurturer. He'd do anything for my mom, us. The easygoing one.

I think Dad wonders why Ryker ended up the way he did. I think he wonders where he got the disease of addiction. He'll never say it out loud, but I think, deep down, he wonders if it was from Grandfather. My dad's parents were ranchers out of Paso Robles— Tim and Nina Hayes. They worked hard, of course. My dad knows the value of a dollar, but he also didn't have a lot growing up, so he tends to indulge us. But Ryker and I spent summers with Papa and Grandma in Paso Robles. We helped on the ranch. Milked cows, fed horses, killed chickens. I enjoyed the summers with my dad's parents. They'd have the nightly news going as Grandma prepared dinner. The scent of a sweet smoke would fill the air as Papa lit his pipe.

Looking back, these memories are the best memories.

At the end of the summer, Papa would give each of us fifty bucks for our work. Ryker would always blow through his money the second we got back to LA. I'd put mine in my underwear drawer and forget about it.

I grab my phone, stand, and pull up the email that has the flight itinerary for tomorrow.

Jeez, Lenny. I glance at the five a.m. departure time.

If I have to be up by three thirty in the morning, I'd best get my ass to bed. After all, mornings have never been my favorite. I put my gigantic suitcase by the front door, change into my pajamas, brush my teeth, put my retainer in, and slide into my Boll & Branch sheets. The one thing I'll splurge on is expensive bedding. Among a few other things, my mother taught me that.

"Your bedding need no price tag," she always says.

This, this, she is right about.

Scrolling through a few more emails on my phone, I see the manuscript I've been waiting for. I pull out my laptop from my side table, save it to my hard drive, and set the computer down on the floor next to my bed.

I turn off the light and lie here in the darkness. This is the time I allow myself to think about Ryker. Born in 1987, he's the younger between the two of us. Being born the eldest in 1985, I guess God thought I needed the ability to be a natural-born leader; therefore, I've always felt I have to dictate my brother's life.

"Go here."

"Don't do that."
"You can't eat that."
"Brush your hair."
"Get your homework done."
"No MTV. It's past five. Mom will have a cow."
"Get in the car."
"Get out of the car."
"Stop drinking that."
"Please don't put that in your veins."
"Please stop acting this way."
"Please … stop using drugs."

My brother was just like my father. But, at some point, Ryker stopped caring. About himself. His family. The world around him. He started taking on the role of world's biggest asshole. At eighteen, when he left for art college on the East Coast, freshman year, he flew home for every holiday break. Sophomore year, less frequent. Junior year, Ryker who? Senior year, Ryker left college and came back to California. Not on our dad's dime either. The only reason I knew he'd come home was Lenny had seen him at Vons Grocery Store. Said he didn't look good. Said he looked tired. Maybe a little confused.

At first, I gave him everything. I just wanted him to get better. He stayed with me. I fed him. Gave him money. I just wanted my little brother back. But, slowly, I began to realize that what I was doing wasn't making him better. He asked for more money, more often, and if I didn't give it to him, like my gut told me, then my stuff would end up missing. First, it was small things, maybe to alleviate his guilt. Earrings. Shoes. DVDs. My VCR. Seriously, who steals a VCR to support a drug habit? I don't know; maybe they're known as antiques on the black market now. But, when my diamond earrings went missing, the ones that Dad had given me on my eighteenth birthday, I drew the line. Told him he had to leave. He tried to convince me that it wasn't him.

"Someone must have broken in while we were sleeping," he said.

It wasn't until he left that I cried.

Leaning against the doorway, he said, "Fuck you, Bryce. Can't believe you'd turn your back on your own family."

That was when I shut the door, slid down to the floor, and cried. That was also when I found the rubber ties underneath my couch. The ties used by drug addicts to tie off their arms when using drugs intravenously. That was just about the time I met Alex. So, I worked harder. Invested my time where it was useful.

My mom, on the other hand, wants so hard to believe my brother. A mother's heart, I guess. She doesn't know a mother's love won't save her son. She's willing to fight for a battle she won't win.

Bryce

Granite Harbor, Maine, is small, and when the tourists pile in for the summer, the town gets even smaller. There seems to be a lull right now. One that exists between the two seasons, summer and fall, when tourists pack up their summer clothes, their big beach hats, their one hundred proof sunscreen, their money, and head back to where they came from. While the second round of tourists—the leaf peepers—pack their warmer clothes, their cameras, and their inspiration, and drive, fly, or boat in and wait for the spectacular colors to blanket the trees. Fall in Granite Harbor is more than beautiful, if there is such a word.

What I've learned from taking several treks back here since Alex moved here is, Saks Fifth Avenue is a location. Neiman Marcus is Ralph's brother's wife's cousin. And Coach is the guy from *Cheers*. The people of Granite Harbor will take the shirts off their backs to help you even if you aren't a local, but bring up the year that Pittsburgh beat New England or when the New York Yankees beat the Red Sox, well, you might as well pack your things and head west or stay in hiding until the coast is clear and time has passed.

I do appreciate the convenience of the city. The fast pace. Shit gets done in the city. Deals are being signed. Meetings with world leaders are being had. Movies are being filmed. Time moves by the second.

But, in Granite Harbor, you're lucky to get through town on foot and not run into someone you know and get stuck talking for a good seven minutes about Brenda's aunt's cousin's sister's friend, who is named Brenda also. Time runs on the sun. Morning, day, night. It used to drive me insane—the slow pace, the everybody knows everybody—but it's grown on me. I've learned to like that Ms. Ida, the retired librarian—the mother to Ruthie Murdock, mother-in-law to Milton Murdock—knows my name and that Lyn, down at Level Grounds Coffee Shop, remembers my coffee order. And that Boom, the office cat at Ring's Pharmacy, meanders around my legs with a broken meow.

So, yeah, I guess you can say, Granite Harbor has grown on me. It doesn't make me miss the city as much.

"Fall Carnival?" I read the sign as we drive down Main Street.

"You've never been to the Fall Carnival, B?" Alex almost gasps and then smiles. "Well, we're going this year. Emily loves to watch the pie-eating contest."

We pass Granite Harbor Cuts and More—I make a mental note to call and see if Teal has any openings—Harbor Theater, State Farm of Granite Harbor, Granite Harbor Opera House, Merryman's Restaurant, The Angler's Tavern, Ring's Pharmacy, and my favorite, Lydia's bookstore, Rain All Day Books.

We pass the lampposts decorated with fall wreathes.

"Twenty-eight Magnolia Road," Alex says as she puts her SUV into park.

We both lean forward to peer through the front windshield, looking up at the pink house.

"It's more pink in person than it is online," I admit.

"Yeah"—Alex is still staring—"it's pink all right. I heard the new owner plans to paint it."

"Today?" I smile as I climb out of the SUV and open up the back. I grab my suitcase and meet Alex on the sidewalk in front of the pink house.

She puts her arm around me. "How long will you be here for?"

I give her the look. "Until it all blows over."

We laugh.

"The rental agency said the key would be under the mat," I say as we make our way to the front porch. I reach under the mat and find the key.

"Typical Granite Harbor fashion," Alex says.

I unlock the door, but it isn't an easy lock; it's a stubborn lock, and it takes some jiggling before the lock comes free.

We walk inside, and the house is open, which surprises me. From the outside, it looks so small, but the inside, it opens up to a living room, a kitchen, and a back bedroom. I look down at the coffee table and notice three doilies. The decor is dated for sure. A box television sits on a small table against the wall with the front door, next to the window, a sofa circa 1980, a simple dining room table with an old hutch. I can see through to the only bedroom in the back, and on the bed is a quilt, probably handcrafted, that lies flat, untouched, unruffled.

"This isn't bad." Alex takes a few steps into the kitchen. "I mean, green isn't a bad color for the walls," Alex says and then covers her mouth, as if she's trying to convince herself that this place is perfect. "It's a green that's stuck somewhere between forest and mint."

"It's not that bad," I agree. But that's what I kinda like about it. It's quirky.

Alex walks into the bathroom, just off the kitchen. "Jesus Christ."

"What?" I call from the kitchen.

"Uh, well, you definitely have a red bathroom." Alex pokes her head out. "Maybe there was a paint sale down at Sam's Hardware?"

I laugh and walk to the bathroom. "Oh, God." It's bright red. "Is the owner color blind?"

"Guess you'll just have to shower with shades on."

"Don't you think the owner, or the rental company, would have gotten a second opinion on the paint choice?" I run my hand over the red.

"Obviously not." Alex walks out of the bathroom and checks out the bedroom. "Hey, did you ever go on a fourth date with Wes?"

"No. After our third date, I saw an *I Love Mom* tattoo on his lower abdomen. I ran for the hills." I follow her.

"Ew."

"Yeah."

Fourth date is a decision-maker. It either is or it isn't. It's going to work, or it's not. And either way I see it, an *I Love Mom* tattoo is just plain wrong. Especially considering where it is. It isn't on his chest; it's in a place where most women might start to pant, asking for more. It's next to his V.

Deal-breaker. You'll end up dating a mama's boy forever. He'll ask his mom before he buys a house. Gets married. Has a child. Goes on vacation. Wipes his ass.

Definitely not my style.

That's why, when I saw it—even though Wes was beautiful with a washboard stomach and pectoral muscles that were harder than a hot plate—I pushed him off me and told him to leave. I wonder if it creeps out other women. I wonder if Wes thinks it's him. Because it is. I mean, everything is fine until you see the tattoo. I wonder, when his pants come off and women see the tattoo, if they scamper away, just like I did. Change their phone number. Move. Run. Everything looks great on the outside. An attorney. Kind. Extremely handsome. My mom loved him—which should have been my first red flag.

"All right, rest up." Alex kisses my cheek and walks to the front door. "I'll call you tomorrow." But Alex stops at the door. Turns to me. Stares.

"What?"

She shakes her head. "I'm really glad you're here for a while."

I smile on the outside. Really, I am glad to be here. But, somewhere deep down, the guilt begins to push its way up through my throat. I haven't said anything to Alex about Ethan. It's never seemed like the right time. Not that I am trying to keep anything from her. I'm not.

"Me, too."

Alex turns and opens the front door to the sun that's making its descent. That's when I notice the black sedan across the street. Alex pops down the stairs. I don't say anything to Alex about the peculiar car, but it stands out to me.

Blue minivans.

Silver SUVs.

Red sedans.

White sedans.

Travel cars. Family cars. Tourist cars.

Black sedans? Sleek black sedans that look as though they were just pulled off a car lot?

Red flag.

I wave as I watch her climb into her SUV, the one they purchased after the girls were born.

I stare at the black sedan. The windows are too tinted to see who's inside. Coward windows, is what I call them. Coward windows because assholes don't want others to know what they're up to. But I hold my ground and stand on the porch, staring at the dark window that hides whatever's beyond the glass.

Weighing my options, I think:

1. Could be Secret Service. What in the hell would the Secret Service want with me though?

2. Could be a lost tourist. Not likely. Not in that kind of car.

3. Could be part of the death threats my father received. Plausible.

4. Could be the Amazon order I placed two weeks ago that OnTrac said they'd delivered. Wait. Definitely not plausible because, when OnTrac pulls up at your house, you're not sure if it's a serial killer or the pizza delivery guy. Their cars always seem to be dented, running on fumes.

5. Could be someone my father sent to keep an eye out. Also plausible.

I go with options three and five, but I sure as hell am not walking up to the car to demand to know what the hell they're doing because my life is more important than my ego. My stomach grows uneasy. Turning, I pop up the stairs and shut the door behind me, slamming it, hoping that whoever is in the car hears it. I lean against the door and move to peek out the window, pulling back the curtains to see the black sedan.

Still there.

I lock the door. I'd feel more comfortable with a dead bolt.

"Typical Granite Harbor."

I'll ask the rental agency to add a dead bolt tomorrow.

I walk through the living room, taking in the doilies and the eclectic decor, running my fingertips along the wall. I open a few drawers when I make it to the kitchen in search of paper to make a grocery list of stuff I'll need. I find one next to the silverware drawer, and I grab a pen from my purse.

I sit down at the dining room table that seats eight and start my list.

Trying to push the black sedan out of my mind.

There's a knock at the door, and my heart just about falls out of my chest.

Hesitantly, I walk to the door and peek out the hole. Of course, it doesn't work. I roll my eyes and mentally add another item to the list that I'll ask the rental company about.

Cautiously, I turn the handle of the door and pull it open just a bit. I peek out to see that it's Ruthie Murdock, the unofficial welcoming committee of Granite Harbor. She's holding a big container of food. Ida, Ruthie's mother, comes in behind her. Now, Ida, I have a soft spot for.

"Hey, ladies," I say as I unchain the door and pull it open, noticing the black sedan is gone.

"Oh, Bryce! We ran into Alex at Granite Harbor Grocery, and she told us the good news!" Ruthie reaches in for a hug. "We just had to bring you some of Milton's chili, as I'm sure you have nothing in that refrigerator yet."

She hands over the container of chili. "We had some sitting on the stove. He's been practicing for the chili cook-off for the Fall Carnival next week."

"Hey, Ida." I look past Ruthie.

"Ruthie, you know as well as I do that Milton wins every year. Nobody's gonna compete with him." Ida looks at me. "It's good to see you're back, Bryce." She gives me a kiss on my cheek.

Ida is everyone's favorite senior citizen.

"Causing trouble, Ida?" I ask.

"Yes," Ruthie spouts. "Do you know what she said to Leonard the other day at the post office?"

Ida rolls her eyes. "Who was going to tell him his zipper was down if I didn't?"

"Mom, it's all well and good, but when you made reference to his … well, you know, his private area, it just got awkward. And embarrassing."

Ida shrugs. "Oh, you know Leonard got a chuckle out of it."

"And I'm sure his wife, Eleanor, was just a bag of giggles." Ruthie attempts to fix her hair with her hands, more of a nervous habit than anything, shaking her head.

Ida grins ear to ear and looks at me. "There are some things you can get away with, Bryce, and some you can't."

"Noted."

"Well, we'll get out of your hair, Bryce. We're sure glad you're back. We've missed you," Ruthie calls behind herself as she helps her mother down the few stairs.

"Missed you."

I've done a lot of traveling in my life. Seen a lot of beautiful country, both in the United States and internationally. The people of Rome didn't say they missed me when I went back for a book convention. The people of Spain didn't miss me when I went back for a vacation. And, when I went back to Los Angeles, my neighbors didn't know I was gone. Not that I care. Not that they cared even. It's the fact that no one missed me.

But the people of Granite Harbor missed me.

I don't say anything, but I'm moved as I watch Ruthie and Ida make their way back down Main Street.

I stare at the pot of warm chili, and a thought crosses my mind. *I wonder if I can make a better chili than Milton.*

But the thought leaves my mind as I glance down the street and see the black sedan is back.

Bryce

The next morning, I'm heating up Milton's chili while I curse him. I'm not sure what he does to make it taste this good, even cold, but I'm convinced he added drugs. Good drugs. The kind that makes you think it tastes good, so good that it's addictive, and you can't stop eating it.

An email pops up on my phone from an unfamiliar email address.

> *I'll be by today to add the dead bolt.*

Before I went to bed last night, I sent an email about the lock on the door to the property management group. *Why wouldn't the property management group email me back? Who's this email from? The owner? And*, while I'm at it, there's no, *Hello, Bryce*. There's no, *Thank you*. There's no closing to the email. A name would have been nice.

So, I respond.

> *Do I need to be here?*

Almost immediately, I get a response back.

> *No.*

Abrupt. To the point.

The chili starts to boil, so I tend to it, forgetting about the email.

It's just after nine thirty in the morning, and usually, I like to get a quick run in before I get to work, but the black sedan is stuck in my head. So, I opt not to run, just to be safe. It hasn't come back so far this morning.

Could be just your imagination, Bryce.

Could be just your nerves.

Could be. Nor not.

But I lock the door from the outside just for good measure and then shove the key in my pocket. I throw my workbag over my shoulder and head down to Level Grounds Coffee Shop, taking in the cool morning air as I approach Main Street.

When I think of Granite Harbor, I think of nosy neighbors, inconvenience, and the holidays. Nosy neighbors because it's a small town, and everyone talks. The inconvenience because most of the town, aside from restaurants, shuts down at five p.m. Although Granite Harbor Grocery has been open later in past times when I've visited for last-minute items. And the holidays because look at the place. Fall wreaths rest on the lampposts that line Main Street. The fall leaves, as if strategically placed, dance and flip about the street. Something within me loosens. Something deep within me tells me I don't have to be anywhere or do anything aside from be in this moment right now with the small town I've been led back to countless times. I also keep questioning why. Why I come back if I don't enjoy Granite Harbor. Of course, largely, it's Alex and the girls, but I can't help but think about Ethan, too.

"Good morning," an elderly gentleman says while walking his dog.

"Morning," I say.

My phone pings.

It's a text from my mom.

I told you to text me when you got there.

I text back.

I'm here.

My phone rings.
Great way to start my morning.
"Good morning." *Satan.* My voice is chipper.
"Just a text. That's all I asked, Bryce. A text to let me know you arrived in Rock Harbor."
"Granite Harbor."
"What?"
"Never mind."
There's a long, awkward silence. I've always been the one to outwait my mother. She's stubborn, but I'm more stubborn.
"Where are you again?"
"Granite Harbor, not Rock Harbor. Same hard material."
"What?"
"Never mind." I grow impatient, just wanting to hang up the phone. "All right, Mom, I'm here, and everything is good."
Still awkward silence.
"Seriously? You're mad because your adult daughter didn't call you when she landed? Unbelievable. I'm a grown woman, Mom." I wince. *Shit.*
Now, she knows she's under my skin.
"I just wish you'd make your family more of a priority." Her tone is short but crystal clear.
Laughing out loud, I say, "So sorry to disappoint you, Mrs. Hayes, but I shouldn't be the child you're talking to. Why don't you call your son and talk to him about making the family more of a priority? I'm sure he'd love to hear from you."
Click, I hear on the other end of the line.
She hung up on me.
Why do I let her get under my skin? I say to myself as I hastily shove my phone into the side pouch of my bag. *Why do I sink to her level?*
I look up at the clear blue sky and take in a big breath of fresh air as I remember where I was just moments ago—soaking up Granite Harbor.

Running shoes, yoga pants, a light parka, and a double espresso are the simple things I need to get my day started.

I pull open the door of Level Grounds Coffee Shop, and immediately, I'm met with a deep-rooted coffee scent that creeps into my lungs and sits. Asks to stay awhile. There's something about this place that I love. Maybe it's the old photographs that adorn one wall. The old postcards on another wall from all over the world from patrons who sent them when they got back to their home destination. The abstract oil paintings that meander between everything. The music is classical and plays lightly in the background. It's a hole in the wall. A tiny place with two front windows and six or seven small tables.

"Well, well, well, if it isn't our favorite West Coaster." Lyn pushes the rag across the counter. Smiles. Her honey-colored skin and deep, dark freckles match the weight of her smile. "Been missin' you, baby girl." She comes around the counter and gives me a hug. Her scent, coffee grounds and lavender, lingers past long after she's made her approach. Maybe it's her touch, the way her hands are placed on my back, that makes my shoulders come down once again.

"I've missed you, too," I say.

Lyn moves back around the counter. "Usual, honey? Four shots of espresso with some cream?"

"Yes, please." I find my favorite spot close to the window that looks out onto Main Street.

Lyn gets a lot of tourist traffic, which is nice for her because winter in Granite Harbor can be a bitch. Nobody wants to make the trek out in the snow to get coffee. At least, that's what Alex tells me. I've never been in Granite Harbor in the winter. This might be my first.

I open my laptop and start with emails. Just this morning, two hundred emails from hopeful writers, praying that it's their manuscript that blows my mind—or any literary agent for that matter. Of these, unfortunately, I'll maybe ask one for a partial manuscript. Maybe. This isn't the fun part of the job.

I read a lot of words every single day. Words that are beautiful. Words that aren't. Sometimes, I'll go months without finding a manuscript that I click with. It doesn't mean the writing sucks. It might. But it also might not suck. Which is great for me and the writer. Because emailing a dream-chaser with good news? That's *almost* the best part of my job. The most amazing part? Nailing a six-figure contract for the writer. That's when the tears usually come.

That's how Alex and I met years ago. Bellencourt Publishing made the offer, we countered, and the rest is history. I think what attracted me most to Alex was her ease with life. Her ability to take everything at face value and move forward. We'd made the deal with Bellencourt before she lost Kyle. Watching Alex walk through the grief was like inching my way through a slow death. I knew I couldn't fix her. Heal her faster. But I kept showing up.

"Here you go, sugar." Lyn sets down my espresso with cream and two raw sugars.

"Thank you, Lyn."

"Holler if you need anything, baby." Her hand touches my shoulder, soft and gentle. "And don't work too hard," she calls as she makes her way back behind the counter.

I discovered Level Grounds the first time I came to Granite Harbor. It's not a coffee shop that stands out. It's tucked neatly between Ring's Pharmacy and Rain All Day Books. It's perfectly fitting to have a bookstore and a coffee shop side by side. Coffee and books go hand in hand.

I put my earbuds in and click on my work playlist, which consists of Aerosmith, Bon Jovi, Third Eye Blind, and meditation music. I know; I know. Weird combination.

Finally, I make it through all two hundred-plus emails. Unfortunately, I didn't find a winner today, and I'll have to send form rejections to all of them. Some literary agents just don't respond. It's clear though on the agent's website that, if the agent doesn't respond, consider it a pass on the manuscript. I've never been able to do that. My stance is and always has been, if the author takes the time to query me, I have time to at least send something.

I send out the bulk email of rejections.

While I enjoyed reading [insert manuscript title here],
it just didn't work for me.

Next, I open up the manuscript I requested from Shane Swenson. He'd sent me a partial a few weeks ago. My gut told me I had to read more. It isn't the plot that's intriguing really. It's his characters. I had to find out more about Wade Lowe and his draw to poor choices.

Before I dive in, I pour a little cream into my espresso and take a sip. There's something about Lyn's espresso that I can't get anywhere else. Not in LA, not in Rome. Not in the United Kingdom. Not anywhere. Except for Granite Harbor. I watch as a few patrons walk to the counter and place their orders. I watch as a family sits at a far table, closest to the back, with a map, and they plan their next stop.

Inside my head, inside the music, inside my bubble, life is small. My mother has always accused me of being rude.

"You didn't see Delana Weatherby standing by the magazines? You didn't see Brock Johnson at the counter? Honestly, Bryce, I wish you wouldn't be so rude."

It wasn't that I was being rude. I wasn't. I just didn't have my eyes transfixed on others, and, I guess, I didn't care what they thought.

I jump feet first into Swenson's manuscript.

Please, God, let me love this story.

It's just past four thirty when I finally look up. The place is deserted. But Lyn's back in the kitchen with a few of her workers, washing dishes, cleaning up. Level Grounds usually closes at three.

Quickly, I stand and take my cup to the back.

"Well, look who finally joined the land of the living." Lyn smiles and places a hand on her hip.

"I'm so sorry, Lyn. I lost track of time."

"No bother, baby. Get your work done?"

"I did. Thank you. Would you like me to wash this?"

Lyn reaches for the small mug, shaking her head. "No patrons do dishes in my establishment."

"Thank you." I hand Lyn the mug.

I walk back to my place at the front window and gather my stuff. I slip a fifty-dollar bill on the table. I figure the least I can do is give her the money she might have made had I not been working for hours at a table where she could have had at least six to eight paying customers.

I throw my bag on my shoulder. "See you, Lyn. Thanks again," I call to the back.

"All right now, baby girl. Have a good evening."

The door has a bell that jingles slightly when the door is opened and closed.

I don't notice the man when my fingertips leave the doorway, but he catches the door. And what makes me take notice is his swift action.

The man is in a dark suit and taller than most men. His lifeless gray eyes are particularly haunting—and not because they're lifeless, but because the smile behind them feels off.

"They're closed," I say.

I don't move because something tells me not to—and not because of the man, but more for protection for Lyn and the two kids in the back.

He's holding the door open. Staring at me.

I'm standing just beyond the door.

He waits for me to leave.

"Hey, Lyn?" I call out through the open door.

"Yeah?"

"You got a customer out here."

My stare deepens, and the man simply walks away. His steps are quick, calculated, and short even though he's tall.

Lyn meets me at the door.

"Do you know that man?" I motion to him.

Lyn rests her hand on her hip. "Can't say that I do. Why?"

"No reason." I'm not going to explain my suspicions. I am probably wrong anyway. "See you tomorrow." I give her a quick hug and head back toward Granite Harbor Grocery.

Mr. Pete is pricing the lentils when I walk in.

"Well, hello, Bryce. So glad to have you back in Granite Harbor." His thin mustache sits neatly below his nose.

"Hi, Mr. Pete."

"Are you coming to the Fall Festival next week?" he asks.

"Thinking about it." I start to make my way down the aisle as a customer approaches.

"See you." He waves and turns toward the customer.

I look down at my list and continue my shopping.

When I approach my rental, grocery bag in hand, a man in a hunched-over position is on the porch, fixing the lock.

Great, a handyman. Or maybe a locksmith.

"Hello!" I say as I approach.

The man unfolds as he stands. He turns and looks at me with his dark brown eyes. The eyes that tell you he'll stay. Give you what you need. Give you everything that relates to love, and you'll believe he wants it, too. And then he'll run. He'll run and pretend like what happened between you two was all a work of fiction, your imagination. That he wants nothing to do with you. Push you away like a used body. And you'll try to forget him. Tell yourself he's a broken toy that needs fixing. You'll tell yourself he isn't worth it even though your heart is bursting, crying.

The look his icy eyes give me now says, *You don't need me. You're better off without me. Find a man worth fixing.*

You needed more armor before you left California, Bryce. Why didn't you prepare?

My lips dry, I lick them, barely open them, and his name falls from my mouth, just as it did the night we spent together. "Ethan?"

Ethan

M *ove slow. Don't stare.*
The look she's giving me tells me she had no idea I'm the one she's renting from.

"Fixed your door," I say.

Her lips part like she's about to say something. She's holding back. I see it in the way her bottom lip curls under her top teeth. Like the first time I felt her from the inside. The tiny, uncontrollable moan that escaped her lips almost pushed me over the edge.

"The door didn't need fixing, Ethan." Her tone is short. Impatient. "It needs a dead bolt."

I spent too many years in the Marines reading people. It's a sense that I have. Like touch, taste, smell, sound, sight.

I nod, screwdriver in my hand.

Her yoga pants curve around every part of her lower extremities, and it reminds me of the way those long, lean legs wrapped around me as I pushed into her against the bathroom sink. The closet. Up against the wall.

"You shouldn't wear those pants in public." *That came out all wrong.*

I don't want anyone looking at the shape of her ass, how toned her legs are. I don't want anyone to get to see what I saw.

"Fuck off, Ethan," she says as she pushes past me to the front door. The scent that follows her is jasmine. I try not to close my eyes, to enjoy what her smell does to me.

"Is the door done or not? How much longer are you going to be here?" She's standing in the doorway now, arms full.

I turn to her. "Few more minutes."

Bryce taps her foot and looks at everything but my face.

My phone chirps in my pocket.

She walks away, but stops. Turns. "Is this your rental?" She's pissed at herself. Pissed because there are a million and one other places she could have rented, but she rented mine, probably not knowing it was mine.

"Yeah."

"Figures. Well, don't worry; I'll find a new place tomorrow."

No, you won't.

But it's probably a good idea that she does find somewhere else. I knew, in renting to her, it would put us in this spot. But my head told me that it might work. That maybe I might deserve her.

"Whatever you need to do, Bryce."

I bend down and pick up a screw, and she slams the door in my face.

It won't stay shut, not until I tighten the dead bolt, so it swings open, and I see her walking away, shaking her head.

"Seems to me the door isn't fixed, Mr. Casey."

Inside, I'm smiling at the way she's flustered and at the way her body moves when she walks. The way her hips move from side to side.

"It didn't need fixing, remember? Just needed a dead bolt." I gently hand her words back to her.

She doesn't say a word, just proceeds to the kitchen, while I put the dead bolt in and tighten the screws. I'm slow about my work, and I pretend not to notice when she walks from the kitchen to the bathroom.

It's just after five as I put my tools in my truck, and my phone sounds again. I lean on my truck and read the text. It's from my twin brother, Aaron.

Aaron: Beer. Angler's. 15 minutes?

Me: Yeah.

Aaron: You at the rental?

Me: Yeah.

Aaron: So, Bryce knows it's you?

Me: Yeah.

I shove my phone in my pocket and look up at the house just in time to see the front curtain drop. Pretending not to notice, I walk around to the driver's side of my truck and hop in. My phone chimes again, but I ignore it. If my brother wants to talk, he can fucking call me. Hell, I hate talking on the phone, too, but I like it far better than the texting shit.

According to her rental agreement, Bryce will be here for a while. Heard from Alex she needed a place to stay until her father is able to deal with some lunatic who's been making threats to the Hayes family. I knew it was her father's assistant who booked with us. I knew it was her in the house last night when I drove by. It took everything in me not to stop. It works better from afar. I work better, staring at her from a long distance. But, now, she's back, and I'll just have to figure out a way around this.

That night in Los Angeles had my head all messed up. I had to get out. Had to leave before shit got serious. I couldn't allow myself to hurt her. Bryce didn't deserve that. So, I had to get the hell out as quickly as possible.

I'd come out to Los Angeles, as my counselor had recommended, to do things differently. Change things up. But what I hadn't expected was to meet Bryce Hayes for the first time. I sure as hell hadn't expected to sleep with her.

Since the military, I'd been having a harder time adjusting to civilian life. Some PTSD. Loud noises. Crowds. Confined places. But something about her was calming. I focused on her eyes. But it wasn't the color. It was what shaped her eyes. The cradle they sat in, round and wide, quizzical about life.

That night, I lost control. I let her touch me. Run her hands through my hair. I let her kiss my lips and other places. That night, I couldn't control myself. Couldn't gain clarity of the situation. I just did what my body needed to.

I watched her as she sat on top of me and rocked. I watched her eyes as they winced when she called out against me. I touched her from behind and listened to her whimper as the walls closed in on us and the sun rose. Her fiery red hair fell down her back and tickled my thighs as she screamed my name.

James,, my shrink, had said, "Fear of emotions—that's why you're scared of intimacy, Ethan."

I was fucking pissed at James for three weeks before I went back. It's a tough deal to have your ass handed to you in a therapy session—and from a man nonetheless. And therapy was what the military required for my discharge.

Night terrors. Nightmares. Night sweats.

What if I'd lost control in a rage and hurt Bryce? My needs weren't worth it. Needs a man had. Besides, I could live without Bryce, but I couldn't live with hurting her.

That night we'd spent together in California, I hadn't fallen asleep, too scared of what I'd do if my lids closed and the nightmares returned.

You can handle this, Ethan. Just stay away from the rental.

When she emailed Granite Harbor Property Management about the dead bolt, I was in the office with Diane, the one handling my place on Magnolia Road and told her to forward the email to me. That I'd take care of it. I knew I could add a damn dead bolt. I doubt Bryce even noticed the name change on the email thread.

I look up again, but the curtains remain motionless. Good. It's better this way. I put my blinker on and make my way to The Angler's Tavern.

Aaron knows Tuesday nights are slower at Angler's. It's our usual meeting spot. I've gotten better with crowds, but I do it in small doses. Make sure I take my own truck. Make sure I can quickly get in and out.

Before I get out of the truck, I pull my cell phone from my pocket and throw it in the compartment just below the stereo. I don't need another distraction.

I took a month off of work before the winter to do some of the renovation work on the rental. Mostly cosmetic stuff. Fresh coat of paint on the exterior. I had so much overtime, and my sergeant in the warden service told me, if I didn't use it, I'd lose it. I guess, when I came back from the war, it was easier to work. Easier to find structure, no time for my mind to wander.

I'd served seventeen years in the military. A life with structure, being told what to do and when to do it. It was after the military, when I came home to Granite Harbor and finished the Warden Academy, that I struggled the most. I just had more time on my hands to think. I was no longer with guys who understood what it was like to be a jarhead, who had similar experiences, some experiences we'd take to the grave. Experiences I hated remembering. Actions that I didn't agree with but carried out orders to neutralize the threat. Even my own twin, Aaron, didn't understand anymore. I was just different. Separated.

I pull open the door to Angler's. Brad and Adam, two Maine hunting guides, have their usual spots at the bar.

"Warden Casey." They both nod.

"Brad. Adam," I quickly address them.

Aaron is with Ryan and Eli at a table by the door to my right. I order a beer from Felix before I join them.

"There's no way in hell I'm putting my money on the Celtics this year, man," Aaron says.

I grab a chair and sit.

"Don't say that shit out loud," Ryan says, taking a swig of his beer. He looks to me. "What's up, Ethan? You look like you could use a beer."

"How are things going on at Magnolia? Heard that's the place that Bryce is staying at," Eli says.

None of the guys know about what happened between Bryce and me, except my brother, Aaron. And, from what I get from Alex, she doesn't know anything either.

"Changed out the dead bolt today. Start exterior paint tomorrow."

"I can't believe you're missing out on the opening of hunting season to take care of that shit." Aaron shakes his head, setting down his beer.

And that's why Aaron didn't take the house when it was gifted to he and I. Aaron suffers from FOMO—fear of missing opportunity. There are two types of game wardens: those who take time off during the deer season opener and those who don't. The agreement of me taking on the house was, I'd do the updating before winter. We didn't expect to get a renter so quickly. But some things just work out.

"Boys, can I get you guys any food?" Bitty sets down another beer in front of Aaron.

"Think we're good for now, Bitty. Thanks," Aaron says as she takes his empty bottle and sets it on her tray.

"Ryan, how's that new baby of yours?"

Ryan pulls out his phone, and we all groan.

"Here we go again." Eli throws his hands in the air.

"What?" Ryan looks around the table at all of us as he hands Bitty his phone, so she can see his pictures of his infant daughter.

Bitty adores the photos, hands the phone back to Ryan, then walks away.

Ryan looks at his phone. "I've got to run, guys. Early day tomorrow."

Aaron laughs. "Yeah, right. Your wife just gave you the booty-call sign."

Eli grimaces with a mouthful of beer. "That's gross, Aaron. That's my sister."

Ryan stands, stretches, and throws a twenty down on the table. "Later, boys."

Eli stands, too. "Yeah, I've got three girls waiting on me at home."

Eli married Alex some years back, and they have two girls, Emily and Noah.

That leaves just Aaron and me at the table. *SportsCenter* is playing in the background, and there's small chatter from some of the locals. It's been different since I came back from the military. Aaron and I used to be inseparable. Things have changed.

"You talk to Bryce?" he asks.

"Define talk." I take a swig of my beer.

"You say something. She says something. Then, you say something again. I think it's called a conversation."

"Then, yeah."

Aaron smirks. "Why don't you just ask her out?"

"Not that easy." I shake my head.

"Let me guess. I wouldn't understand?"

This has been a bone of contention with Aaron and me since I came home from the military. We try to make things look okay on the outside with small talk and whatnot. But I know it bothers him that I don't talk about much of anything anymore. There's only one buddy from the military I still talk to. And nobody in hell knows I talk with James in Augusta.

"But your buddies in the Corps would, right, Ethan?" he sighs. "You don't talk anymore. To anyone that you used to." He pauses. Peels his label. "I don't care if you don't talk to me, but talk to someone, Ethan."

James's voice plays in my head. *"Fear of emotions."*

I don't answer my brother, and this is usually how it ends.

"I've got to go. You going to hang out?" He throws a twenty on the table. He stands. "Dad call you?"

"No. Why?" I take another swig of my beer.

"Needs some help with a bear trap."

"When?"

"Tomorrow, after I get off."

I nod. "Pick me up at the Magnolia house?"

Aaron stops. Stares. A small smile begins.

"I'm painting." My jaw tightens at the thought of Bryce because I know that's what he's thinking. "Just painting, bro."

"It all starts with some color. Then, it's, *Oh, the toilet doesn't flush? I'll take a look.*"

I shake my head. "Thought you said you were leaving, Warden?"

Aaron laughs. "I am. Later, brother."

Bryce

E than is still as I approach him. My stomach twists into a ball of nerves.

Don't stare at the way his jeans hang from his waist. Don't stare into his eyes. Just don't do it, Bryce. That's when you get tongue-tied and lost. That's when your legs want to fall open and invite him in. Don't you dare do it, Bryce. He left you. Remember that. Now, he won't give you the time of day.

Why the hell is he on my porch?

"Fixed your door," he says.

Are you kidding me? Like he did me a favor. I hold back what I really want to say.

"The door didn't need fixing, Ethan. It needed a dead bolt."

He nods and stares down at my yoga pants. "You shouldn't wear those pants in public."

Wait. What? "Fuck off, Ethan," I say as I push past him to the door.

I hold my breath, so I can't smell his Polo, the cologne he left on my sheets days after he left LA. The scent I wanted to keep on my naked body as I slept in hopes of his return.

Get your head straight, Bryce.

"Is the door done or not? How much longer are you going to be here?" I'm standing in the doorway now, arms crossed.

He turns to me. His defined golden-colored biceps and triceps flex and not as if he's showing off; it's tension. I also see the tension in his jaw.

"Few more minutes."

I'm pissed and confused, all at the same time. I'm so distracted that I don't notice my foot tapping until now. I look everywhere but at his face.

His phone sounds.

Probably another woman. I walk away, but then I stop abruptly. *Shit.* This is his rental. Lenny dealt with the property management team. *God.*

I don't even have to ask to know, but I do. "Is this your rental?" My tone is short.

"Yeah."

"Figures. Well, don't worry; I'll find a new place tomorrow."

"Whatever you need to do, Bryce." Ethan bends down and picks up a screw.

I slam the door in his face.

But that damn thing falls open again. *Un-fucking-believable.* I walk away and say behind me, "Seems to me the door isn't fixed, Mr. Casey."

"It didn't need fixing, remember? Just needed a dead bolt."

Oh, he makes me angry. Gets under my skin. Fuck him. Now, I'm completely frustrated, and I don't know why I came in here in the first place. I have to pee, so I walk to the bathroom, just off the kitchen. I'll hide in there until he leaves.

When I think it's safe, I tiptoe/run to the living room and pull back the curtains to see if his truck is still outside. I watch as he stares down at his phone and then looks up.

I drop the curtains. *Come on, Bryce, you're not a schoolgirl anymore. Stare if you need to stare.*

But I won't dare give him the satisfaction of him even thinking I might be looking at him.

I walk away from the window and retrieve ice cream. *Screw dinner.*

I'm watching *Steel Magnolias*, found from the DVD stash below the television, when I get an email. Now, as I notice the sender's email address, I realize where I went wrong. The email is a thread from a sender I've already been in communication with. *I should have paid more attention.* My head falls back to the sofa. The email I sent to the rental company about the dead bolt was forwarded to Ethan, and he's the one who responded.

> *I'll be by tomorrow morning to start painting the outside.*

I reply.

> *Don't you have to work? You know, do warden stuff or whatever.*

He replies.

> *I'm off for a while.*

Why? But I don't dare ask that. I don't want him to think I'm curious. I want to say something sarcastic, but I can't bring myself to do it. In the film, Shelby has just delivered Jackson Jr., and maybe that's why I'm softer. This part gets me every time. So, I just don't respond at all.

I jump awake to a pounding on the door. I mean, I think I hear the pounding. Maybe it's just the sound of my heart. The television is dark. The house is dark. I sit up and try to gather my thoughts. Slowly, I stand and walk to the door.

I unlock the dead bolt and slowly peer out into darkness.

There's nothing there, except the streetlamp that creates a yellow hue on the porch. But, down the road, I see the black sedan again.

Quickly, I shut the door, the blood rushing through my ears. I've never been scared of the dark, but since our family has been under fire lately, I can't help but think of the threats we've received.

Did someone pound on the door? Or was it a figment of my imagination? Was I dreaming?

Maybe I should mention the black sedan to my father. Maybe I'm being overly paranoid. Maybe I'm just tired.

My heart pounds as my back rests against the front door.

I gather my overactive imagination and my pounding heart, and I quietly walk to each door and window to make sure they're secure and head back to the bedroom.

Once I'm in bed, I try to distract my mind. I check my emails one last time and then set my phone on the nightstand next to the antique lamp that sits on the doily. It makes me wonder about Ethan and his decorating style. Clearly, the person who decorated and painted this house wasn't born in this century. It makes me think of when Ethan acquired the house. *Did he buy it? If so, when? Was it handed down to him from a family member?* From what Alex has mentioned, the Casey twins grew up in Granite Harbor. I guess we didn't get to that the night we met in LA.

I don't hate Ethan. In fact, it's quite the opposite. He just left that morning. Didn't ask for my phone number—a strong indication that he was clearly not interested. And I didn't hear from him again until I make the trek out to Granite Harbor to visit Alex a while back. But what's more is, he didn't even acknowledge my existence, and he hasn't until now. Until we're alone and we're in each other's faces, up close and personal. And he has the audacity to tell me that I shouldn't wear yoga pants in public.

Asshole.

I listen to the adjustments the old house makes as it settles in for the late evening. A foghorn down by the harbor sounds every seven minutes. It gives me some peace. As if maybe I'm supposed to be right here, lying in bed, waiting for the next horn.

I reach for my phone again. I open up the email he sent earlier. You know what? I'm going to respond.

> *You just left. You didn't say a word. You just left that night. At first, it didn't bother me. It didn't. Don't get me wrong; I'm not a booty call. But the more I got to thinking about it, the more I realized we worked. We fit. We'd had a great evening of conversation, wine, and sex. I woke up, and you were gone. And WTF? Then, I find you live in Granite Harbor and are best friends with Eli. You don't*

say a word to me. You don't look at me for two fucking years, and then, once again, stupid call-it-whatever-you-want has ME renting YOUR house. And the first words you have to say to me after almost two years is, "You shouldn't wear those pants in public."

Fuck you, Ethan. Fuck you and your stupid ego.

I wish you all the best.

No, no, wait. I don't wish you all the best. I hope you're chased by geese and roosters for the rest of your life.

P.S. You shouldn't have had sex with me if you weren't going to stay the next morning—or at least, you could have given me your phone number, so I could return your belt.

P.P.S. And, for the record, I don't even like you anymore. I just felt like I needed to send this email.

Have a nice life.

Bryce

I read the email.
I reread the email.
The foghorn sounds.
House creaks.
I hit Send.
Take that, Ethan Casey.
I hastily set my phone back on the nightstand and roll over on my side. Part of me wants a response from him. Maybe an apology with a litany of excuses. Maybe he's in a Witness Protection Program, and he's not allowed to date. He was in the military—something he briefly touched on that night we were together—so it's possible. Maybe he's really an undercover agent for the FBI, and he doesn't want to commit because of travel.
Unlikely, Bryce. And maybe he's just not interested. Maybe he's hung up on someone else.
This thought causes an uncomfortable feeling in my stomach.
My phone chimes.
My stomach drops.

Look.
No, don't look. It doesn't matter anyway.
Look.
I grab my phone from the nightstand, my heart pounding.
Ethan responds.

> *Geese and roosters?*

I reply.

> *Yeah, because they're mean as hell.*

He replies.

> *They're fowl. Their intent isn't to be mean.*

I reply.

> *Of course. You're a game warden. You'll always side with the animals. And, just my luck, they'll flock to you—no pun intended—like you're a god.*

I wait for his response, but it doesn't come. My eyelids grow heavy with the darkness around me, and I let them close, setting my phone down next to me. My last thought before I drift to sleep is of my brother. I'm not sure why, but I at least hope he has a warm bed to sleep in.

Light comes through the handmade curtains, which consist of a piece of fabric that's thick enough where people can't see in but thin enough to let unwanted light in, which shines in my eyes.

The scent of fresh coffee brewing drifts through my open bedroom door.

I don't remember presetting the coffeemaker last night, I think to myself, wondering if an appliance with modern-ish science fits this well-worn house.

I push the homemade quilt and sheets from my body, bunching them at my feet. My silk nightgown clings to my body like sand to the shore, filling in the spots that need touching.

"Good morning," a deep voice sounds from the doorway.

"Jesus Christ!" I jump, and a million tiny needles sting the surface of my skin. My eyes dart to the doorway of my bedroom, of my rental, of my personal space.

Ethan Casey is standing in my doorway, a cup of coffee in hand. "Good news. I wasn't followed by a single rooster or a goose on the way here this morning."

"You can't just barge in the damn house whenever you feel like it, Ethan. I'm a renter, a paying customer." I try not to smile at the rooster comment, and then I look down and realize I barely have anything on, and I grab at the sheet balled up at my feet.

"You're right. I'm sorry. I shouldn't have barged in like this." Ethan sets the coffee down on my bedside table. Looks at me, almost embarrassed, confused by his actions. "For the morning I didn't bring you coffee in bed. For the morning I left," he whispers.

I feel his words vibrate in my chest and ricochet off my heart. *Don't give him the satisfaction of a smile, Bryce. Make him work for it.*

My eyes meet his, and it seems as though there are so many words that he wants to say but can't. There are flecks of darkness but also flecks of light.

I keep the sheet close to my chest, as it serves as a layer of protection against the world, against him, for my heart.

He goes to leave.

"I didn't tell you?" I deflect. "I'm buying a rooster tomorrow. To keep the early birds out."

"I'm sorry, Ms. Hayes, but roosters aren't allowed in the city limits of Granite Harbor. You must have ample space for them to roam," he calls behind himself as he makes his way from my doorway, and I can no longer see him.

Shit.

I hear the front door shut quietly.

A warm feeling seated deeply in my body pushes to my face. My heart picks up pace. I smile.

Dear God, help me.

Seven

Bryce

I decide to stick around, maybe look for a new place tomorrow, and even though I hate to admit it, this is all because Ethan Casey is outside this house, on a ladder, painting, where I can steal glances of his arms and his stomach when he reaches the high spots.

He hasn't said two words to me since he brought me coffee in bed this morning. But I also haven't made an attempt to go outside and ask him if he needs anything.

Should I offer him water? Should I make him lunch?

It's well past four o' clock in the afternoon now, and surely, he's hungry—unless, of course, he brought his own lunch. My mind spins as I sit at the kitchen table, trying to get some work done on Shane's manuscript.

Fuck it.

I walk outside, and he's on the side of the house that faces Main Street, up on the ladder.

Placing my hands on my hips, I ask, "Can I bring you some water or lunch or something?"

"Water would be great," he says without making eye contact as he paints a soft gray over the primer, the pink still barely visible.

I go inside and come out with his water just as he's coming down off the ladder. Ethan pulls at the bottom of his shirt and uses it to clean the glistening sweat that's formed on his face. It exposes his hard stomach and the dark trail that leads to places covered. My face grows flush as I try to distract myself.

Breathe, Bryce.

"I was going to walk downtown to grab a sandwich. Since you're painting the house, I figured you could use one, too."

He drops his shirt, and I can breathe again.

"Yeah, thank you." He stands there. Stares down at me.

Even though we've slept together, I feel like this is all so brand-new. As if he hasn't tasted the inside of me. As if he hasn't put his fingers in places that make me blush.

I stop thinking about his hands, and I look at him. "What kind of sandwich would you like?"

"Turkey." He almost smiles, and his white teeth barely stand out against his golden skin. "Thought I'd stay in line with your poultry references."

I laugh out loud.

More of his smile shows. Though he doesn't laugh, he watches me, thinking.

"Special requests?" I ask.

Ethan places one hand on his hip, the roller in the other hand. "How much time you got?"

I feel the weight of his words, and the intent of his stare settles around me and inside me. I stare back. "I was thinking along the lines of mayonnaise and mustard."

When Ethan Casey smiles—which is not often because, usually, he's got a scowl or a pensive look about him, like he's constantly deep in thought—you'd better remember it or take a picture. A smile tips at the corners of his mouth.

That night in Los Angeles, after we made love for the first time, I asked him what his biggest regret in life was.

His answer was simple. *"Regrets are for those who refuse change."*

Maybe that's what he was doing by making coffee for me this morning—changing.

"I'll take whatever you bring home." He takes the water from my hand and drinks it down, his Adam's apple bobbing with each swallow. Ethan hands me the empty glass. "Thank you." His eyes rest heavily on mine.

As if everyone in Granite Harbor has taken lunch, a break, the world around us pauses, quietly and neatly folding into itself, and all that surrounds Ethan and me is just space.

I breathe. *In and out, Bryce. It isn't difficult.*

I know what this man looks like after he's just made love to a woman. I know what his strong jawline looks like as he kisses a woman's body. I know what self-control it takes for him to pull out right before he orgasms, so he can watch the woman first.

I wonder if he gives other women this look, the look of fear and love.

Breaking free of his stare, I nod, turn, and walk back in the house to grab my debit card. I push away the feelings that start to stir in my stomach and ignore that my heart is now fluttering against my chest.

He made you fucking coffee, Bryce. He didn't buy you a ring.

When I walk back outside, Ethan is on the ladder now, painting, and I quickly make my way past him without a word.

Granite Harbor is everything you'd want in a small town. The people are magnetic and kind. And you have a little bit of everything here. Granite Harbor Opera House, mostly for the tourists and the Bostonians who want a break from city life. Granite Harbor Cuts and More, Harbor Theater. The newish sandwich shop, Oceanside Deli. Rain All Day Books, where I spent countless hours with Lydia, the store owner and a transplant from New Hampshire. Many inns sit on the ocean's coast, including one of my favorites, The Harbor Inn. Ring's Pharmacy. Of course, Granite Harbor Grocery and Level Grounds Coffee Shop.

I peek in the front window and wave to Lyn, who's at the cash register. She waves back.

Maybe making all those trips from the West Coast to Granite Harbor really wasn't for Alex; maybe it was for me. Maybe it was because this little town had grown on me. And, if I'm being really honest with myself, maybe half of those trips were to see Ethan. Check up on him.

"Bryce?" I hear my name from behind.

I turn to see Ryan and Merit and their daughter, Hope, who's fast asleep in a stroller. Ryan's dressed in uniform, which means he's probably on the clock, taking a quick break with his girls.

"Hey, you two!" I walk to Merit and give her a quick hug, and then I do the same with Ryan. I peek in at Hope. "Look at that sweet nugget, just sleeping the world away."

"I heard you were coming back into town but wasn't sure when. Where are you staying this time?" Merit asks.

"Magnolia Road."

"Oh, the Caseys' house," Merit says.

"That's the one."

"See Ethan's doing some painting today." Ryan looks back toward the house.

"Yeah, just running downtown to get some lunch …" I don't finish the sentence as my voice dies down. I don't want to say for us or him because I don't want anyone getting the wrong idea. But what idea would they possibly get that's wrong? Man. Woman. That's it.

"Let's get together for lunch or dinner soon?" Merit says as she pulls me in for another hug.

"Absolutely," I say.

Ryan reaches in for a small hug. "Looks like E's got it pretty well handled, but if you need anything, don't hesitate to reach out."

"Will do."

They go their way, and I continue down to Oceanside Deli where I order two turkey sandwiches with everything. I also grab Ethan three different kinds of chips because I don't know which one he likes best. I'm not sure if he's a soda drinker, so I buy a Coca-Cola and an apple juice.

The sun has retreated back behind the clouds, and the wind picks up on my quick walk home. It is October. The weather is gearing up for a change.

"Gonna be a cold winter." Rick, the pharmacist, takes down an American flag from the front of his pharmacy.

"I haven't been here yet for the winter," I say.

"You're in for an experience that can be both magical and cold as hell." Rick laughs. "See you, Bryce."

"Sounds wonderfully chilling. Thanks, Rick." I have learned though, some businesses close during the winter because it gets so cold, and people really don't go out unless it's absolutely necessary.

Though you can guarantee Warden Young, Warden Taylor, and the Casey wardens will be out and about, saving people's lives, pulling cars from ditches, and being ruggedly handsome, all at the same time.

When I approach the house, Ethan is down off the ladder, cleaning his hands, and my stomach flips inside out and upside down. It's the way he's cleaning his hands, the way he pulls the towel from each finger. Like he's a pro painter, painter extraordinaire, and he's just finished his own personal *Starry Night*.

"Here's your sandwich. Turkey with the works and a few other things." I hand him his bag of food.

"What's all the other stuff?" He grabs the Doritos.

"Wasn't sure what you liked. What I gave you, Ethan, were options." I walk to the porch and take my seat, embracing the wind against my face. I take my sandwich out of the bag.

Ethan wanders over to me and sits down next to me, about two feet away.

A good, safe distance for both of us, I agree.

The wind begins to pick up. Tendrils of my hair flick around my face.

I take a bite of my turkey sandwich. Chew. Swallow. "Not bad."

Ethan sticks his hand in the bag of Doritos. Chews, swallows, and says, "Oceanside has a mean turkey."

I laugh. "Maybe one that chases you around town, only to catch you and gouge your eyes out."

There's a still silence around us. The wind stops momentarily, as if waiting for his response.

"Sorry about that," I say and take another bite.

"Never be intimidated to eat in front of a man. Men like women who eat food," my brother used to say—until the drugs dictated when he woke up. If he slept. If he went to work. If he lived.

Ethan is still eating the chips, his sandwich untouched.

"You eat the chips first?"

Ethan nods, his fingertips cheesy and orange, at his side. "I was wondering why you don't actually."

"Who eats their chips first? That's like a side dish to a meal. You always start with the main course." I take the last bite of my sandwich.

"Not how we do it in Maine." He shrugs, cleaning his hands with his napkin now and then opening the wrapper to his sandwich.

"So, wait, you guys eat the chips first, sandwich second?" I grapple with this idea.

A smile begins at the corners of his mouth, and his lips part; he almost, almost laughs.

"Pulling your leg, Hayes." He looks out across the street.

I look down the street as the wind begins to pick up once more and notice the black sedan again. I think better of saying something to Ethan. I don't need a man anyway to keep me safe. Last minute, when I packed, I shoved the Mace my brother had given me into my suitcase.

The wind howls.

"Hell of a storm moving in," he says before he takes the last bite of his sandwich.

Somehow, I have a feeling the black sedan is up to no good.

Ethan

When I put my tools away outside, she's standing at the doorway on the porch.

You should go, Ethan.

"Do you want to come in and wash your hands before you go?" Bryce asks.

No, I should go, Bryce. I should.

I nod and follow her in as she shuts the door behind us.

The wind kicks up, and I casually use my fingers to pull back my grandmother's old curtains and look outside, trying to distract myself.

My hands are sweaty, and my heart is pounding out of my chest. I see Bryce walk to the kitchen and dump our trash.

"So," she calls from the kitchen, "when did you buy this place?"

I let go of the curtains and walk back into the kitchen, leaning in the same doorway I've stood in since Aaron and I could walk.

"Few years go." I put my hands in my pockets, so I don't reach out and touch her.

Go, Ethan. Leave.

She reaches up to the top cupboard to put something away, and I can't help but take in every part of her body as she does. Remnants of that night in LA blow in and out of my head.

Her mouth on mine.

My mouth in places it's missed since that night.

Her naked body in front of mine as I gave her what she needed.

What we both needed.

It was just one night, Ethan.

I thought she'd get over it. Hell, I never thought I'd run into her again, and the situation, her, me, us, would be easy.

"Ethan?" Bryce is staring at me.

"I'm sorry. What?"

"Why'd you buy it? I asked." She opens the fridge and puts the milk inside.

"Investment. But, really, I couldn't see it leave the family. It's a house we've had since our dad was little. Our grandmother's house. When she passed away, it was written in the will that Aaron and I split it, but he didn't want it, so I bought him out."

Bryce leans against the fridge, crossing her arms. "Because you have all this time to fix up houses? Don't you work, like, ninety hours a week?" She bites her lower lip.

"Took some time off to work on the house. Just cosmetic stuff." I stand from my lean, keeping my hands in my pockets, and look up at the interior of the house. "Structurally, she's sound. The pink had to go though."

Bryce laughs. When she does, my heart slows down, and I stop breathing. Just for a moment. Her laugh is genuine, and the sound runs through my veins. I don't dare allow her to see me smile when she does. She can't get attached. I can't go there. Not with her. I'm no good at this.

Fucking James's voice plays in my head again on repeat. *"Fear of emotions—that's why you're scared of intimacy."*

"Is Grandmother Casey also the one responsible for the bathroom color as well?"

"She was color blind."

"Oh."

She's biting her lip again, and I try not to smile.

"Nana was proud of it. She was also cheap. Hence, the paint color."

The wind screams around the corner because the whole house takes on the gust, moving and creaking.

She jumps.

I smile. This time, I can't hold it back. "Scare you?"

"Caught me off guard, is all." She grabs the back of her neck and rubs. Looks out the window.

That night, as her breasts rested against my side while we lay in bed, I ran my fingers through her hair.

I don't do long-term. I don't do relationships.

Ethan, you need to leave.

"I should go."

Bryce looks up at me. "Okay."

Nodding, I turn, hands stuffed down deeper in my pockets, just to be cautious, and I walk to the front door.

Another blast of wind whooshes around the house as it moans with the uncomfortable adjustment.

I stop and look back toward the kitchen to see Bryce standing there.

I want to explain. I do. But I can't. It's better this way. She won't get hurt in the end.

"I'll come back tomorrow. Finish up the paint," I say from the doorway.

Bryce wears a wall. She doesn't allow people in too often. She comes off as the tough one, the brave one, for others to lean on. I saw that in LA. And I see it right now. What drew me to her was the wall. I wear the same one. I put the same one up, so I thought the beginning of the end of us would be easier. Something happened that night that I still can't explain. I think it's true for both of us.

James will be pissed. But he doesn't have to face Bryce. He doesn't have to look her in the eyes when he's fucked up. When he's screwed things up.

"Good night, Bryce."

"Good night, Ethan."

I drive to my house up on Monty Street, on a hill. I chose this house just for the view. The house was a shithole, but I've done some work on it.

Making my way inside the house, I flip on the light to the kitchen and set my wallet, phone, and keys down. I throw leftovers in the microwave and jump in the shower.

The hot water sinks into my skin, and it burns at first, but the longer I stand here in its stream, the more accustomed my body grows. I guess, if you stay anywhere too long, you grow accustomed to it. Get used to it. Just like living without, you grow into it. It might not be perfect or what you want, but eventually, you'll settle down.

I take myself in my hand and stroke just like I watched Bryce do to me as she looked in my eyes and witnessed my body crumple before hers.

With each stroke, I told myself this was just a woman with needs.

With each stroke, I told myself she'd be gone in the morning.

With each stroke, I told myself that the look in her eye was lust; it wasn't love. Love took time.

But, when she stopped because she couldn't take it anymore and she slipped on top of me and put me inside her, I almost lost it.

And, when she whispered in my ear that she needed me—maybe it wasn't for everything in life; she probably needed me for the physical—I pulled her off of me, tucked her beneath me, spread her legs from behind, and buried myself in her. I found out that night that she liked this position. I loved watching her hips as she squirmed. I loved grabbing her breasts from behind and listening to her moan as her back rested upon my chest.

I'd never in my life felt so helpless, so not in control of myself. It scared the shit out of me. The fucking shit out of me. I'd been with women in my life. Slept with women in different cities with the travel I did with the military. But never once had I felt like I couldn't walk away. That was the easy part. But, with Bryce, I'd entered a whole new, unfamiliar territory.

I finish myself off, turn off the water, grab my towel, and dry off. I put some athletic shorts on and grab my dinner out of the microwave.

Before I leave the kitchen, I see an email has come in on my phone.

It's Bryce. My heartbeat picks up, and I set my plate of food down and read the email.

Dear Ethan,

I'm really sorry about the bird comment in my last email. I come in peace and wish no harm on you.

And thank you again for the coffee this morning. Thank you for your service to our country. I feel like an asshole now.

Good night.

Bryce

I smile and hit Reply.

Dear Bryce,

You're not an asshole. You're anything but an asshole.

Good night.

Ethan

I try not to get my hopes up that she'll respond, but I take my phone and my plate of food to the living room and turn on the television to the hunting channel. Something my brother and I used to enjoy a lot together. Something I've had a hard time getting back into since coming back from Iraq, but I go because I get to spend time with Aaron. Somewhere along the way, I lost the passion for hunting.

In the war, we had to make split decisions that changed people's lives. Changed our lives. Changed what we'd thought and how we thought and if we thought. I had gone over there with a platoon of eighteen guys. The first tour, we came home with twelve. The second tour, we went over with twenty-two guys and three women. We had come home with nineteen.

Although I'm not ordered to see James anymore, I do. Just seems to help get things out a little better, I guess. Makes it easier on my parents, my brother. I'm not the same man I was when I left for the Marines at age eighteen. I don't regret the decision. I will always be a Marine. But I saw things and did things that changed the course of my life.

An email notification pops up on my phone.

It's from Bryce.

> *Dear Ethan,*
>
> *I'd like to offer a truce. I'll cook dinner. Tomorrow night at six p.m. My house. Wait, your house, the one I'm renting. The pink, now half-gray one.*
>
> *Please RSVP because dinner for one won't work. Or the conversation might get a little one-sided. Lol.*
>
> *Bryce*

A half-smile spreads across my face, but then it fades.

I can't. I can't go. I want to go, but I can't.

But what if you can go?

You can't.

Expectations come with dinner, Ethan. Expectations you will never be able to fill.

I don't respond yet. I need to think on it, and I can't tell her I need to think on it because I don't want to hurt her feelings. That's the last thing I want to do. But, by saying no now, it might allow her to adjust and maybe find someone who's not me. Someone who can be the man she's looking for. I can't be that person.

I respond.

> *Dear Bryce,*
>
> *I'd like to eat dinner with you, but I can't. I have plans.*
>
> *Rain check?*
>
> *Ethan*

My phone rings. It's my mom.

Fuck.

My mom has the ability to call at the most inconvenient times.

"Hey," I answer.

"Hey, honey. Did you get the leftovers I put in your fridge today?"

"I did. Thanks, Mom."

It's quiet for a minute, just the low hum of two televisions in the background—my father's news on one end and the hunting channel on mine.

"How was your day today? Did you get the painting done?"

"Until the wind kicked up."

It's as if my mom calls to check on me every evening to be sure I'm all right. It's not like I've ever flipped out or anything. She's just noticed the change in me since I came back, just like my brother and dad have.

"Do you need me to do any of your laundry?"

"I've got it, Mom."

"I have time to do it, Ethan. It's really no big dea—"

"Mom," I interrupt, "I've got it."

"Right,' she sighs into the phone. "I know you do." She says this as if she's trying to convince herself that I'm okay.

Some days, I have to convince myself that I'm okay.

"Listen—" She coughs, her attempt to remove the wobble in her tone. The worried tone. "The Murdocks are coming for dinner tomorrow night and bringing Milton's niece. She's in town for a few days. Thought you might want to meet her."

No, Mom. But I can't tell her no on this because I can't stand the worry in her voice. "What time?"

"Six."

"I'll be there."

"Oh, good. You need a nice girl in your life, Ethan."

Here we go again. I roll my eyes and run my hand over my face. "Mom, I'm tired. Just need to get some sleep."

"Okay, honey. See you tomorrow night."

Nine

Bryce

"The Marines?" I say to Alex, who's on the other end of the line.

I had known Ethan had served, but I hadn't known it was the Marines.

"Eli said he doesn't talk about it much. But he did two tours in Iraq. Eli said he volunteered to go back for the second tour."

I called Alex because I wanted to hear her voice, but I also wanted to get more information on Ethan. I was tired of hiding behind the bush. Tired of not asking questions, for fear that someone might find out. Who cares? Who cares that we slept together? But I can't slip anything past her. We're quiet for a moment.

"It's kind of obvious," Alex breaks the silence.

"What is?"

"Come on, B, you know I see the way you look at him."

"With disdain and hatred?"

She laughs into the receiver. "Everything but."

Alex waits for me to elaborate, but I'm not ready to share our night together with anyone. I keep the memories of our night together tucked away behind the cookie jar, and at night, when I'm desperate for his touch, I reach for the memories and allow myself to get lost in the feelings they bring.

Flash: Me against the wall. Him holding me in place with his middle, pushing into me with slow, controlled thrusts.

Flash: Us as we lose ourselves in each other.

Flash: Him between my legs, using his tongue to make me arch off the bed.

"You know?" I ask.

"I don't have to know anything to read my best friend."

"How come you didn't ask?"

"Wasn't my place. I assumed you'd tell me when you were ready."

"I'm not ready."

"I know, B." Alex pauses. "From what Eli says, Ethan is a really good guy. Messed up from the war but a really good guy."

Messed up from the war, are the words that float on the loose ends of web strings, attaching themselves to anything to stop the free fall. This notion I can't accept.

The night we spent together wasn't a night that was messed up. It was everything but. It does somewhat explain his abrupt departure that morning. It might explain some of his odd behavior. But what I refuse to believe is that he's messed up. Different, yes. A changed man, as he should be. War changes people. He's not used goods. Unsalable goods. He's a good man who's seen a lot of death. Sadness within despair.

I hear a baby's cry in the background.

"All right, it's bedtime for the Young girls."

"Love you. Give the girls kisses."

"On it. Love you, too," she says and hangs up.

I hold my phone in my hand, daring myself to email Ethan. *You're not a child, Bryce, for God's sake. You're a grown-ass woman. If you want to email a man, email him.*

So, I do.

Dear Bryce,

I'd like to eat dinner with you, but I can't. I have plans.

Rain check?

A rain check? Plans? Right. Of course he does. What if he has a girlfriend? Oh, God, Bryce. Ethan seems private, so of course, Alex or Eli wouldn't know if he had a girlfriend. Shit. How could you have been so stupid? So forward?

I roll my eyes and toss my phone on the coffee table.

I decide to watch *Steel Magnolias* again. I bite my thumbnail because of the damn email I just sent to Ethan, cursing myself under my breath, and when my teeth meet the quick, I instantly regret the last bite.

My phone sounds. It's a text from an unfamiliar number. I look down at my phone and open the text.

> *Unknown Number: Does dearest Daddy know what you did, Bryce? Taking things that don't belong to you is always a no-no.*

Immediately, I grow hot, light-headed. My stomach begins to twist and turn and move.

Taking things from people that don't belong to you is always a no-no.

> *Me: Who is this?*

I play into their game. I wait for a response, and my eyes dance back and forth between the movie and my phone screen as I fight the nauseating feeling building in my throat.

There's no response from the unknown number.

What does he know? She know? This is a secret too well hidden for anyone to find.

Immediately, I text my brother and don't think about the fact that I haven't spoken to him in a long while. Don't wonder if this text will come out of the blue. Hell, I'm not sure I will even get through. Sometimes, his numbers work; sometimes, they don't. I have a total of seven phone numbers for him, labeled as Ryker 1, Ryker 2, Ryker 3, Ryker 4, Ryker 5, Ryker 6, and Ryker 7. Being the addict that he his, things like phone numbers and mailing addresses are always in limbo.

His excuses:

"Lost my phone."

"Working on getting a new one."

"Moving."

"Roommate trouble."

Ryker knows Mom would take him back again, back home, where he'd have a clean bed, toothpaste, a toothbrush, warm food. But he'd never move back home. We both agreed, when we turned eighteen, we would move out and never return to living with Mom. Because that was like living with an Apache helicopter. She's always hovering. Mothering. Smothering. And, if you didn't abide by her rules, answer her incessant questions, well, that was fine, but you'd better pack your shit because she'd send you on the biggest, all-expenses paid guilt trip of your life.

I text each number.

> *Me: It's your sister. Call me. It's important. Someone knows.*

From each number came an alert.

> *Message Not Delivered.*

"Shit."

My heart picks up pace as panic sits in my throat.

The night, just a year ago, is fuzzy. Hazy. The memories will never fade from my mind. I did what I had to do. What I had been tasked to do. That night still haunts my mind, invades my unconscious thought.

"Regrets are for those who refuse change." I remember Ethan's words like a memory that I'd rather not cling to.

I turn down the movie just a bit, so I can think, praying Ryker will get my text somehow, because all this was done to protect them after all.

I'll need to take a Benadryl tonight; otherwise, I won't sleep.

In life, I think we all question our decisions. Right. Wrong. Indifferent. Still, I know it was the right decision. The right action. Even though it sometimes doesn't feel like it.

In my makeup bag in my purse next to the couch is a little container of pink Benadryl. I take one and turn off the movie, and everything is dark. I embrace the darkness, allowing it to consume me, quiet my racing mind. I breathe, curling up, and pull the afghan that sits neatly on the back of the couch to drop it over me.

I wait for morning.

And, with this text, I know who's been threatening my family.

It's the smell of coffee that rouses me, calls my eyelids to open. But it's the racket outside that makes me jump.

Up on the couch in the sitting position, I wait for the noise again.

I stand, gathering my location and the date, and I walk to the window, pull back the curtains, and watch as Ethan carries the ladder to the side of the house where he was yesterday, most likely touching it up. I quickly realize that red is Ethan's color with his Red Sox hat, and the way his chest and arms fill the black T-shirt makes my body feel things I probably shouldn't. When he notices me, I pull away, drop the curtain, and step back.

"Shit. What time is it?" I look to the clock on the wall. Just after ten. I slept later than I wanted to.

Ethan must have made coffee. Ethan must have seen me sleeping.

Shit!

Quickly, I run to the bathroom and clean up my face, brush my teeth, and jump in the shower.

The hot water feels good against my back from the awkward sleeping position on the couch. The water beats down on my body, and I wait for it to wash away the worry.

He's back. He's back because this is his house, and he's doing the painting. Of course he's back.

He also wants a rain check on dinner, Bryce. Remember that?

I put my head under the steady stream and feel it as it falls down around me.

There's a knock at the bathroom door.

My head flies up. "Uh, yeah?" I ask.

Ethan opens the door. He's looking at me through the fogged privacy glass. My body is most likely unclear, blurry.

I cover my breasts and my area below. "Can I help you?"

The water still streams against my back.

"I've seen you naked before, Bryce," Ethan says.

This statement pisses me off. As if it's his right to see me naked now. Part of me wants to turn off the water, get out, and stand before him, naked, just to see what he does. Just to watch him squirm uncomfortably.

Besides, I don't get him. One minute, he's giving me the cold shoulder, and the next minute, he's making coffee.

I turn off the water. "What do you need, Ethan?" My voice echoes off the shower walls. I close my eyes as the mention of his name has me visualizing his hands in places, touching me, loving me.

He clears his throat in the quietest way possible. "Do you have sugar?"

Pulling back the shower door, I keep my hand over my breasts but allow him to see part of my nipple. Why? I'm not sure. Maybe a reaction. To show feeling. To see what he wants from me.

Ethan's grip on the door is hard because I can see the whites around his fingernails.

"No," I say.

Ethan's eyes are on me. His stare intent. He drops his eyes to my exposed nipple. "No what?" He looks back up at me.

Internally, I smile at this. He's forgotten his question.

"No, I don't have sugar."

"Right. I'll run down to the store and grab some. I need some for the coffee. Tried it last time without and it tasted like shit."

I nod, biting my lower lip.

"Do you need help?" he asks.

"Help with what?"

"A towel?"

Shit. I forgot a towel. "Yes," I sigh.

He walks into the bathroom, and on the other side of the toilet are the towels. As he passes, I take in his smell. Polo. The scent I didn't want to wash from my sheets for days after we let our bodies tangle, feel. I remember wishing he'd left a shirt at my place, so I could wear it against my body.

Ethan hands me the towel, and I let go of my chest—on purpose—to grab it.

I hear him exhale as his eyes beat down on mine, then drop to my chest, and then come back to me again.

"This isn't anything new, Ethan. You've seen them before," I barely whisper, unable to catch my own breath, holding the towel to my chest. "Thank you."

He turns and walks to the door, almost unwillingly.

"Ethan?" I ask.

He doesn't turn but instead looks up toward the ceiling. "Yeah?"

"Why'd you come in here?"

Silence hangs in the bathroom with steam from the shower.

"For sugar."

Then, Ethan leaves for the store.

Ethan

You fucking idiot. You just had to go in there, I think to myself as I try to remember what the hell I'm going to the store for. *Sugar.*

It's not her body. It's the freckle that she has just above her ass. It's the way she holds her breath every time I touch her. It's the way she has a witty response to things I say. It's the way she defends herself and doesn't hold back. It's the way her body fits perfectly next to mine. It's the way she pulls out my words. I've never met a woman like Bryce Hayes. I've tried to forget her, bury her deep in my memories, keep her at arm's length.

"Ethan!" A familiar voice interrupts my thoughts.

It's Rick's partner, Charlie. He walks to me.

"Will you be participating in the Fall Festival's hot dog eating contest?"

Fuck.

Every damn year, somehow, I get talked into doing the hot dog eating contest.

"After all, you've won every year since you were a kid. Except the years you were gone." He bounces up on his heels. Bruce is average height, rounder in the stomach. A clean-shaven face with round cheeks.

"How many people do you have so far?"

"Counting you? One."

"So, I'd be competing by myself?"

"No, I'll get a few more entries before the day's over."

A car passes along Main Street. Silence drifts.

I don't want to do this.

"Great, I've got you down!" Charlie turns and walks back toward Ring's Pharmacy.

I return with sugar to the house on Magnolia Road and find Bryce on the couch, sipping coffee, clothes on.

Thank God. I've never been more thankful for clothes in my life.

"Hey." I shut the door behind me. "Sugar."

"Thank you." She gives me a half-smile, stands, and takes the sugar from my hand and into the kitchen.

"Gonna go start painting." *Maybe dump cold water down my pants.* I pull my hat on tighter, adjust it, and walk out the front door.

My phone starts to ring as I hop down the steps and to my truck. It's my mom.

"Hey," I say, resting my phone between my shoulder and my cheek as I grab some gear out of the back of my truck.

"Hey, sweetie. Don't forget about dinner tonight."

Fuck. "Yep, haven't forgotten." *Totally forgot.*

And this reminds me that Bryce invited me for dinner, and I said I couldn't. She didn't sic chickens on me or turkeys or roosters, I note.

"You're really going to like—honey, what's the Murdocks' niece's name?"

"Tessa? Chelsea?" I hear my dad's voice in the background.

"No, no. I think it's Bethany," she sighs into the phone. "Your father is losing his mind. Okay, honey. Six o' clock tonight. Our house. What is her name?" I hear my mother ask my father again.

"Yep. Got it. Bye, Mom."

I'm almost done for the day, and I'm cleaning up when Bryce comes outside. I haven't seen her most of the day, and I've tried to convince myself that it's a good thing.

"Hey, stranger. Get some work done?" I ask, putting the last of my paint things in the back of my truck.

"Yeah, I did actually. Finished editing a manuscript and sent it back to the author."

"I have no idea what that means, but it sounds like a good thing."

She leans against the post on the porch, crossing her arms. "It is." She grins. "You headed home?" A piece of her hair falls to her face.

"Yeah, and then dinner with my parents." Technically, I'm not lying.

When Bryce initially asked, I didn't have plans. I just didn't think it was a good idea for us to be alone in the house. Together. I don't trust myself.

I open my truck door and throw my phone on the seat. I shut the door and turn to her.

"Well, have a great time." She tilts her head. Her eyes meet mine.

"You have plans?" I ask.

"Alex is coming over. Going to grab dinner at Merryman's."

I nod and pray she doesn't wear something too revealing. Pray that a man doesn't walk up to her, ask her to be his wife, and they live happily ever after.

Why? Because you're gonna man up and ask her yourself? Grow a pair, Ethan.

"Be in by curfew." I give her a smirk and walk around to the other side of my truck.

She's still standing on the porch, watching me.

I lean across the bed of my truck. "Hey, the whole town shuts down at five p.m., so make sure you're in by then."

"Thanks, Dad. Will do."

I smile.

"You're something else, Warden Casey." She walks down the steps. "Heard you were the reigning champion for the most hot dogs eaten at the Fall Festival for the past million years."

I cringe. "Something I'm not proud of."

Bryce nods. "I was thinking about entering my chili in the chili cook-off."

"Whoa. And go up against Milton Murdock?"

"Guess so." She shrugs.

"Good."

She backs away from the truck before I'm ready for her to leave. "So long, Warden."

I pull in the driveway behind my parents' SUV. The Murdocks are already here. I debated on coming.

Fake a cold. A fever, Ethan.

I'm doing this to appease my mom. I walk around my truck, follow the walkway to my parents' front door, and walk in.

"Oh, there he is," my mom, Helen, says. "In the kitchen, Ethan."

"Hey, son," my dad, Bill, greets me as I walk into their kitchen with a hug.

My dad has always been a hugger. Give him one too many drinks, and he'll give you several. This is the kitchen where Aaron and I spent many mornings falling asleep in our cereal before school on Monday mornings because of our hunting excursions on the weekends. The same kitchen table we sat up late at night, getting homework done.

"Ruthie, Milton." I lean in and shake their hands.

"This is our niece, Elizabeth," Ruthie says.

Elizabeth? I think. *Not even close to the names my mom mentioned on the phone.*

"Nice to meet you." I give her a handshake.

Her hands are cold. Her eyes are blue. Her hair is brown. "Beth," she smiles, "for short. Your mother tells me you're a game warden."

"Guilty."

Awkward silence.

My parents talk to the Murdocks.

"I write ad copy for Nike."

I try to look interested. "What brings you to the East Coast?" I ask, reaching for a green olive my mom put out.

"I've always wanted to see the changing of the colors," she says, also reaching for an olive.

"Won't happen for a few more weeks, according to the foliage report."

"Guess I'll need to kill time before then." She smiles.

"Let's eat, shall we?" my mom says, turning to the table. "Moose steaks, mashed potatoes, and cauliflower."

I take my usual seat at the table, politely pulling out Aaron's old seat for Elizabeth.

"Thank you," she says.

It makes me think of the time when Aaron and I were kids, and he pulled my chair out from under me when I went to sit down. Just as I fell, there was an end table waiting to go to a new home next to us. I busted my forehead on it. Blood went everywhere.

Mom freaked.

Dad went to get the first aid kit.

Aaron told me that I'd better pull my shit together if we wanted to go hunting that weekend, so I did. Convinced Mom and Dad that it was just a cut. Heads bleed a lot. That it didn't hurt and that I wasn't seeing double even though I was.

When we went to bed that night, I told Aaron, if I didn't wake up, it was his fault.

I look over, and Beth's lips are moving and then sipping a glass of wine. She's looking at me, bringing me back to the present moment.

"What?" I ask.

"So, you're a twin?" she asks again.

"Guilty."

"What's it like? Are you identical or fraternal?"

I take a bite of my mom's moose steak with the special seasoning. Chew. *What does she mean, what is it like to be a twin?* Chew.

Think of a nice response, Ethan. Don't be rude, I hear my mom's voice in my head.

I can't answer the first question without being rude, so I say, "Fraternal."

"I guess you wouldn't know anything different, I suppose?" she says with a smile.

I stop. Look at her. *Right. Yes. Now, we're getting somewhere.* Sex with Beth would be easy. She's attractive. There are no strings attached because I don't get the same feeling when I look at Beth as I do with Bryce. I wouldn't lose control. I wouldn't feel the need to stay the night with her.

Time passes. Conversations take place.

Me to Beth.

Mom to me.

Me to Dad.

Ruthie to Beth.

Milton to Dad and me.

"Oh, shoot," Mom says. "I forgot to throw the cobbler in the oven." She throws her napkin on the table and stands.

"Don't worry, honey. Why don't we just go to Get the Scoop downtown? That new ice cream shop?" Dad says.

Mom looks at the Murdocks.

"What a fantastic idea," Ruthie says. "Though I was looking forward to your cobbler, Helen. That reminds me; please tell me you're entering your berry cobbler into the Fall Festival?"

"Oh, Lord, here we go," my dad says. "She's been on the fence about this for weeks, Ruthie. Perfecting a new recipe, she says."

Mom laughs and touches Dad's arm. I've always admired their love. Maybe not as a kid. But as I've gotten older. Their relationship. How one plays off the other. Where Mom stresses, Dad's calm. Where Dad's forgetful, Mom remembers. Where Mom's efficient, Dad's at a turtle's pace.

Like my mom says, "He'll be running late to his own funeral."

And it's not that he doesn't leave on time; it's living in a small town. He'll stop by Sam's Hardware to pick up a few screws or weed or feed and talk to Sam. Dad has a hard time ending a conversation because he's got to be somewhere. So, he stands there, listens, engages, and eventually, he'll get to where he's going.

Dad stands from the table and starts collecting dishes. Ruthie and Milton stand, too.

"No, we've got the dishes. You two just sit back down and relax," Dad says.

"I've got it, Dad." I stand and clear the table. Then, I start the dishes as Beth engages in conversation with the others.

It's just after seven in the evening when we walk down to the ice cream shop. It's one of the few businesses that stays open later. It doesn't take us any longer than usual because Ruthie and my parents were raised in Granite Harbor. They know everybody. Milton came to Granite Harbor by way of Texas.

"Do you plan to stay in Granite Harbor, Ethan?" Beth asks as we walk.

"It's home," I answer.

"Yeah, but can you see yourself raising children here?"

I won't have children, I want to say but don't. I don't for several reasons. But the first one is, I don't want to have to explain why I don't want children.

"Yeah, I guess." I open the door for Beth.

When I hold the door for our group, I turn and see Bryce with Alex.

I see the face she makes when she sees me.

I see the face she makes when she sees Beth.

I make a face when I remember telling Bryce that I couldn't have dinner with her. A face asking Bryce to read between the lines. *This isn't what I want.*

Fuck.

This isn't what it seems.

I follow our group in and swallow the huge lump in my throat that has just formed.

"Well, hello there, Alex, Bryce." My mom reaches in for a hug, followed by Ruthie. "So good to see you both."

Alex keeps the conversation going, but Bryce is quiet.

My heart pounds against my chest. See, this is already complicated. I made coffee, and now, it's all fucked up.

I squeeze behind our small crowd in the ice cream shop and lightly touch Bryce's elbow. I put my lips close to her ear, so she's the only one who can hear me.

"Can we talk outside?" The last thing I want to do is hurt her. *This isn't what it looks like.*

I see the hesitation in Bryce's eyes, but she concedes.

She follows as I take the lead and open the door for her on the way out. Maybe it's because we slept together or the fact that I made her coffee that I feel the need to explain.

She walks a few steps ahead of me and turns, crossing her arms. "What'd you need to talk about, Ethan?"

Bryce bites her lip, and I've resolved the fact that this action, her biting her lip, is due to nerves.

What I want to do and need to do are two different things. I want to tell Bryce that Beth is no one and that I just did what I had to do to keep my mom from worrying. But that means opening up about things I can't. What I need to do is take Bryce behind the building and show her how I feel.

Do I lie or tell the truth?

Eleven

Bryce

My shoulders are tight, and I try to ease them down from my ears by crossing my arms. I try not to allow Ethan to read my eyes. "What'd you need to talk about, Ethan?"

"It's not what you think," he says.

I shrug. "You don't owe me an explanation." This is my best attempt to show Ethan that seeing him with the other woman means nothing to me. "We had sex a long time ago. You made coffee for me. You didn't put a ring on my finger, Ethan. Come on. There were no *I love you*s exchanged."

Ethan hesitates. "My mom worries."

"About what?"

"Me."

"Why? Are you—is that … a smile, Ethan Casey?"

"You treat me different."

He smirks, and I dance in the middle of mustard plants. His smile is perfect and imperfect, beautiful and broken.

He runs a hand over his neck.

"How different?" I ask. *Push away your feelings, Bryce.*

Ethan's looking at me. Watching my mouth. My eyes. Maybe he's waiting to see the lie. The lie that takes root around my conscience and dissolves into nothing.

No trace of a voice I had just moments ago that said, *Tell him how you feel.*

Maybe this, too, is a barrier I put up to protect my heart from loss. I lost my brother to the needle, the drugs, lost my family in a sense. My dad delved into his work. My mom delved into my brother's addiction. And there I was, standing, waiting on the corner for my time to grieve. But I didn't. I just promised myself I wouldn't allow my heart to hurt that much again.

"My mom worries that I'll fall off the deep end." Ethan hesitates but then gently takes me by the elbow, so we can walk toward the harbor.

"Makes two of us." I laugh.

"How so?" He's inquisitive, his face displaying a curious look. He's back to serious Ethan.

"How much time do you have?"

"Enough."

I look out over the dark harbor as we approach. The distant foghorn blows. The sun has long since left the sky. Seals bark.

"My brother, Ryker, got hooked on heroin. He's been to rehabs before. My mom tries to continually save him. Makes excuses for him. Making him sicker. My father gets lost in his work to avoid our issues. And I come here."

We're at the edge of the water.

I feel the moistness of the air against my face. I take in the silence, and I try to pull out the differences of our childhood.

"What about you?" I ask.

Ethan crosses his arms. Sighs. "Robby and I met in boot camp when we were eighteen. Just young. Fresh out of high school. Clean-cut, small-town boys looking to serve our country. He came from a good family. Had a wife and a baby on the way. We did our first tour together in Iraq. After we came home from our first deployment, Robby struggled just a little bit. His wife had had their first child while we were over there. He'd lost his sergeant right in front of him. Lost friends. Had to make big choices in life-threatening situations. Decisions we weren't comfortable making. Then, we did a second tour." Ethan pauses. "Tore him up emotionally. He came home. They gave him painkillers for the wounds on the outside. He was supposed to see a therapist for the wounds on the inside, but he didn't. Had no trouble taking the pain medication though. Got hooked. Six months later, he was discharged from the military. His wife left him. He lost housing. He lost everything."

A seal barks.

The foghorn sounds.

"Robby's mom called me a while back. Went down to Brookline to see if I could help him."

He's quiet. He shoves his hands in his pockets. Looks down at the million tiny rocks that sit against the harbor's edge that we can barely see.

"What happened?"

"There was nothing I could do. He was long gone. He sat. Rocked in his chair. Tapped his head with his fingers. Counted. Ducked for cover every time a car drove by."

I catch my breath somewhere in my throat. It's the sister in me, the daughter in me, that wants to keep Robby safe. Like Ryker. I wish I could scoop him up and put him in a bubble, keeping him safe from the world.

Ethan's eyes meet mine. "Robby's a real good guy who saw some real bad shit and did some real bad shit to make everything go away. The bombs. The gunfire. The screaming."

My heart begins to chip away.

Did Ethan experience this? Did he live through this? How did he come out on the other end of things? Why is life so unfair to some people?

"Where's Robby now?" I whisper.

The foghorn sounds again against the dark sky.

"Not sure. His mom doesn't know. Talked to her the other day. Like to check in with her once in a while."

I nod. "Why would I have more compassion and empathy for a man I don't know than my own brother?"

"Love." Ethan drags his eyes away from the Atlantic, the vast, strong body of water that can overpower ships and take lives, and looks at me. Looks through me. "You love your brother, that's why you're angry. You can't be angry at a man you don't know because his addiction doesn't directly affect you."

And, for the first time in a long time, I feel like someone sees me for the person that I am. The truth of my character, sometimes ugly. The truth of my downfalls, sometimes beautiful.

"Love," I whisper just so I can feel the way the word tastes in my mouth, letting it settle.

"Ethan?" a woman's voice sounds from behind us. "There you are."

We both turn to see Helen with Bill, Ruthie and Milton Murdock, Alex, and the woman Ethan showed up with standing just outside Get the Scoop.

This just got real awkward, real quick.

Ethan walks, and I follow his lead. I look up at him, and he's looking down at me. His eyes say, *Don't leave,* so I don't.

"Beth, this is my friend Bryce."

I stick out my hand—not for her, but for Ethan. "I'm his girlfriend. He just doesn't know it yet." I wink at Beth—and not in a snide or condescending way.

I said it, so Helen would stop worrying. I said it, so Ethan would stop trying to appease his mom. I said it, so I could buy some time with Ethan. I don't dare look at Alex, for fear I'll laugh because she's probably giving me *the look.* The smug one that says she's about to laugh at any moment.

Beth, caught off guard and embarrassed, makes me feel awful.

"Don't worry, Beth. He didn't know he was my boyfriend until just now."

I look over at Helen, whose jaw is on the floor in the most elated way. Bill smirks, and Ruthie is speechless.

Milton says, "There goes the neighborhood."

"Well, it's nice to meet you, Bryce. I was worried why a man like Ethan was still on the market. For a moment, I'd lost faith in women."

I reach back and intertwine my arm with his, and I feel Ethan's body tense. I place my thumb on the inside of his wrist where no one can see it and gently slide it back and forth.

The tenseness in Ethan's body loosens.

"Ethan and I go way back. Just wasn't sure who was going to make the first move. It all started back in LA," I tease, knowing he'll stop me soon.

"Beth, I'll walk you back to my parents' house."

I linger on Ethan's arm for just a moment, savoring his skin beneath mine, letting him know that I'll be all right on my own while he's gone.

But, in the corner of my eye, I see headlights are moving toward us fast, weaving all over the road.

Ethan sees this, too, because, in one fell swoop, he's able to push all seven of us to the side wall of Get the Scoop as we hear the car come squealing closer and closer and closer.

The screeching gets louder.

A loud bang.

I brace for impact because the sound of the car is so loud now.

The black sedan comes flying by, the taillights zigzagging toward the end of town.

Ethan's already on the phone. Immediately, we hear the police sirens.

"North on Main," Ethan says.

Granite Harbor PD stays at a safe speed down Main Street, going through town, passing us, following the black sedan that we can no longer see.

"Is everyone all right?" Ethan asks.

We nod awkwardly, wondering what the hell just happened.

The black sedan is back, is all I keep thinking. *Was he gunning for me? I should say something.*

But I think about the text I received earlier. I think about the awfulness that could cause if I breathed a word to anyone. I think about Robby and what Ethan would do for him.

"Dad, Milton, get Beth, Alex, Mom, and Ruthie home. I'll send Eli for Alex and Officer Lent if he has any questions."

Bill nods at his son. Beth, Ruthie, Helen, Alex are still shaken.

I reach out for Alex and give her a quick squeeze, and we both give each other a knowing nod.

We separate from the group. Ethan takes my hand, and we begin to walk down Main Street.

"We're looking to see if anyone's been hurt or injured." His step is purposeful as I lag a step behind.

But he stops mid-stride.

My mind is spinning.

He turns and takes one step back to where he's in my personal space. Grabs my face with both hands. His breath is minty and ice cold.

"Are you all right?" I think he whispers, his eyes expectantly searching mine.

I try to nod but can't, and I'm not sure if it's the shock of what just happened or the fact that Ethan Casey is inches away from my face. His eyes wild, he blinks several times, as if trying to gain clarity in his head, of the situation.

He turns, grabs my hand, and pulls me like a toddler, searching through storefronts with his flashlight from his phone.

It's a bit chillier now.

We hear trucks before we see them. Ethan pays no mind to their thunder. Two game warden trucks and a personal truck park in the middle of Main Street, blocking off the nonexistent traffic. Aaron, Ryan, and Eli stalk toward us.

"Looking for people hurt. Not sure if the asshole hit anybody," Ethan calls to them, gripping my hand.

I think the shock on their faces isn't for the situation at hand; it's the fact that Ethan Casey is holding hands with a woman.

Ethan realizes this a second after I do.

He holds tighter.

"I'm going to take Bryce home, and then I'll be back," Ethan says to Aaron.

Aaron nods.

"Eli, Alex went with my mom and dad and the Murdocks back to my parents' place," Ethan says. "I said I'd send you over when you got on scene."

"We've got this. Go get Alex," Ryan says to Eli.

Eli does a quick turnaround and heads back on Main toward the Caseys' house.

I pull myself closer to Ethan, taking two steps to his one.

Silence lies in front of us as my thoughts begin to tick.

1. I claimed Ethan as my boyfriend but purely to convince his mom that he has a woman who will watch out for him. That was my only motive. Right?

2. The same black sedan I've seen in front of the house on Magnolia Road for the past few days has just hurled past us. Why? Trying to kill us? Me? Who was behind the wheel?

3. Ethan is still holding my hand.

"You can let go now," I whisper against his shoulder, looking up at him.

His breathing is heavy, he's deep in thought, and he acts like he didn't hear me. Something flipped in Ethan. From quiet, tight-lipped Ethan to Ethan the dictator.

"Are you all right?" I ask.

Still, no response.

"Ethan," I say louder and stop our pace.

"What?" he snaps. His eyes still wild.

"Are you all right?"

"Fine. Let's get you home."

We walk up the steps to the house on Magnolia Road, the nearly gray one now with specks of pink.

"Ethan, wait. Can you just stop for a second?" I don't budge anymore.

He stops. His back to me.

"Ethan," I whisper, "we're safe. Everyone is safe." With my other hand, I reach up and touch his shoulder.

Ethan sighs. Turns to face me. I see fear in his eyes.

Ethan

As the black sedan barreled right for us, I'd envisioned a death, another funeral, and life without one more person. The way I acted with her was so protective. I saw one color, and that was red. Touched her in public like that. Held her hand. I couldn't help it.

Gunshots.

People screaming.

Dying.

Blood.

Lots of blood.

That is what went through my head, what I saw, but I know it didn't really happen. Something flipped inside me. As if we were on the field again, and I was directing men into war. Setting them up for death, not knowing the outcome but praying for the best.

We're standing on the porch, and she's telling me we're all right.

Bryce is focused on me.

"Come inside." She pushes past me because, now, I'm the one who needs help.

The insanity of the moment has shifted.

She opens the door and gently tugs on my hand. I shut the door behind us.

"Sit down," she says in the dark house as she reaches the lamp and turns it on.

I do.

Bryce goes to the kitchen, and I lean back on the couch, closing my eyes, trying to gain some clarity. Nothing like this has ever triggered me at work. Ever. I've done a lot of work with James to keep the mild case of PTSD at bay. The only difference between work and this situation are Bryce and my parents.

You're in too deep, Ethan. You need to nip this in the bud now.

I hear the microwave ding and cupboards opening, closing.

Bryce comes back into the living room, carrying a mug, and sets it down on the coffee table in front of me. "Give it a few minutes to cool." She sits down next to me, resting her head against the back of the couch, her eyes straight ahead.

Quiet hangs in the air like the first breeze of fall. It's calming. I take a big breath in.

We both stare at the wall, resting in the moment.

"Wonder how Robby's doing. You should try to get a hold of him."

"You call Ryker, and I'll try to reach Robby. Pinkie swear?" I say, giving her a sideways glance.

She wraps her pinkie around mine. "Pinkie."

I smile. I learned this from Robby's daughter, Madalyn, when she was about seven. I don't remember the promise she made me make, but I remember her toothless grin and her bright eyes.

We keep our pinkies entangled as we slowly let our hands fall to the couch.

"I need to tell you something." Bryce hesitates.

I wait.

"I use sarcasm to piss off my mom."

"Why?"

"I have no idea. I guess because it's easier than dealing with her shit." She waits.. "You seem to treat your mom really well. Don't ever tell my mom I admitted that, okay? If you ever meet Trudy Hayes."

"Promise."

My pinkie tightens around hers, but she wiggles loose.

"Drink your tea," she says.

I walked into the house on Magnolia Road, hyped up, unable to see straight with what had happened earlier, but Bryce did something. She didn't cradle me, baby me. She kept the lights dim, ordered me to sit down, made me tea, and told me something about her life. For whatever reason, this helps. Brings me back down. My heart rate has slowed. I'm not on edge.

I pull myself forward to sip on the tea. "This tastes like shit." I set the tea down, the bitterness of it still resting on my tongue.

"It should. It's expired. Apparently, the owner of the place didn't update the stash."

I laugh out loud. For the first time in a long time, I allow myself to take part in something I watch others do every single day, most likely without thinking about it.

I look over at Bryce, who's grinning. Not laughing but instead watching me laugh.

"Thank you," I say.

"For what?" she whispers, still watching me.

"I don't think I've laughed like that in an extremely long time." I shake my head, clasping my hands between my legs, leaning back against the couch. My head falls back again to match hers.

"I like your laugh," Bryce says, not looking at me, focused on the ceiling now.

Every inch of me wants to reach out and run my hand along her lean jawline, touch the collarbone that runs the length of her shoulders. Put my lips on them. Something I've done before, something I've missed.

I could pull her to me, put her on top of me, and she'd go along with it—and not because she wanted to, but because she knew I needed it. My heart begins to pick up pace.

The sourness of the tea still lingers in my mouth. "The owner needs to buy new tea," I say, trying to push away what she does to me.

She smiles again. "Definitely leaving a one-star review on the website. Tea is shitty."

I feel the smile begin to form.

We both laugh until we're done.

"Can I turn off the lamp by the door?" she asks.

That would make it dark.

"Yes," I say, trying not to think about the things I've done to her in both the dark and the light.

Bryce stands and walks over to the door and locks it.

Chill the fuck out, Ethan.

Her yoga pants hug her hips, her ass, everything in all the right places. What's more is, the attraction I have for Bryce goes much further than her body. This is at the exact moment I panic. This is the exact moment my rational thought leaves, and my need for her changes. It becomes carnal need, not a want.

The light is clicked off.

I hear her slide off her parka, and through the window's light, I see her silhouette.

Oh, fuck.

I don't move a muscle.

Bryce walks to the back of the house and comes back with a pillow and a blanket. My eyes have fully adjusted to the dark.

"Can you stay here tonight?" she asks through the darkness.

"Yeah," leaves my mouth before I can think.

"Lie down," she says, tossing a pillow to me.

I take off my shoes as she does the same. Then, I turn and extend my legs down the length of the couch.

Lightly, she crawls in front of me, putting her backside against me. Her scent fills me as I close my eyes and allow her body to adjust to mine.

She pulls the blanket over the top of us as my heart begins to slam against my chest. I close my eyes and swallow, trying to regain my thoughts, praying to God she doesn't feel my heart betraying me. Once she's adjusted, my arm has no place to go but around her waist, so I gently rest it there and feel it everywhere.

"Is this okay?" I ask.

"Yes."

She reaches up and pulls her hair tie from her hair, and I let out an unexpected and quiet groan.

"Are you all right?" she asks.

"Yes."

My head rests inches behind her.

Don't fucking move your ass, Bryce, please. Because it's pushed up against me. *You can't lose control, Ethan.*

"Ethan?"

"Yeah?" I swallow, counting all the different types of snakes in my head to distract me.

"Let's get some tea tomorrow."

"Yep," I breathe.

"And, Ethan?"

"Yeah?" Taking my hand from her hip, I run it over my face. "Good night."

I breathe in her scent. "Good night, Bryce."

I know I won't sleep tonight because I'm too terrified of what I might wake up to. The nightmares or her.

It's just after six in the morning, and I haven't slept. I'm tired. But there was no way I could leave her last night.

Maybe, in a weird sort of way, it was what we both needed. I listen to her breathing, slow and steady; she's asleep. Quietly, I pull myself from behind her, replacing my body with the blanket. She gently turns over.

In the bathroom, I wash my hands, rinse my face with cool water, and then pad back into the kitchen and make some coffee.

I pull my phone from my pocket, knowing I have an appointment with James today in Augusta. Though we only meet every other week now, it keeps my head right.

The coffee starts to percolate as I rest my body against the counter, checking my phone. *I should just go. Things got too close last night. I should really go.*

"You're still here." Bryce's voice is low, tired. Her steps almost unheard. She smirks. Her tank top and black yoga pants are still in pristine condition against her body.

"Made coffee." I shove my phone in my pocket and lean against the counter with my hands, trying not to stare at her body. "Sleep okay?" I know she did because I heard her quiet, small breaths for most of the night.

Bryce nods. "More than okay."

I feel it in my chest first; it's warm, and it spreads like ooze to my stomach. It's something that makes my chest want to explode and simply contract at the same time.

If I said something like this out loud, James would say, "What does that mean?"

And I'd say something like, "What do you mean, what does it mean? How the hell do I know? That's why I keep coming back here." Then, I'd think on it because he became stoic and quiet. I'd say, "It's a good feeling. Something I enjoy."

I play James's question game with Bryce. "What does that mean?"

Though she just crawled out from the couch, probably with a kinked back and maybe a sore neck, her red hair rests perfectly down her back. Her eyes are bright with promise, made a little apprehensive as she steps closer.

"It means, I like the way you feel when the hands reach every second of every hour on the clock. It means, I like waking up with you. It means, I'm glad you're still here." She pauses. "And what I'm most thankful for is, the black substance leaking out of that contraption on the counter." She smiles and pulls her hair up in a ponytail.

I don't know what to say to that, but the feeling she gives me in my chest and stomach sets my body on fire.

"I'm going to go shower now," she says.

I can't answer her, so I don't say anything.

The bathroom door shuts behind her, and I finally exhale, walk to the cupboard, grab two mugs, and pour some coffee.

Once I hear the shower going for a minute, I bring her a cup of coffee. I don't knock because something tells me I don't need to, and this makes it all the more dangerous in combination with what I feel in my chest, the ooze still spreading to places it shouldn't.

"Bryce?" I call.

The shower's water runs hard.

"Yeah?"

"Here's some coffee."

She pulls back the shower door enough to show her face dripping with water, her once-fiery-red hair now dark hidden, strands matted to her head. "Thank you." She pauses. "Are you going to shower?"

Wait. What? Right now? With you?

Every fucking bone in my body screams yes. But it would go too far. I'd kiss her. Feel her with my fingers. Explore her body with my hands. Touch her breasts with my mouth, just to watch her come unglued like our night in Los Angeles.

"Come here," she says.

I'm by the sink, and immediately, nerves build. Good ones. Not so good ones. I feel the ooze spread to my face as I visualize her body dripping wet.

You shouldn't do this, Ethan. You shouldn't fucking do this.

I take a step forward and then another.

I'm to her, standing outside the shower, and she pulls the shower door to show me her body. The steam from the shower rages behind her as my eyes bury into hers. Then, they slowly make their way down her shoulders, breasts, stomach, hips, the hair that protects what I've tasted with my tongue.

The ooze spreads to my mouth where I remember what she tastes like.

My face is on fire when she says, "Can you get me a bar of soap?"

Soap. I should know what that is. Soap.

All I can think about is the way her hips fit perfectly against mine as she called my name, her face when she reached her peak three times that night.

I had done that to her. I'd made her body do things and reach places she'd never reached until me.

She asked for soap.

Can you tell me what it looks like? I want to ask because I can't fucking remember what soap is.

I can't handle it anymore. I can't.

Give her what you both need, Ethan, my head says. I don't hear my voice of reason; it's fucking gone.

With both hands, I lift her out of the shower and feel my adrenaline begin to surge.

The color red, the color of her hair, blurs my vision as I gently put her down in front of me, so we're both facing the mirror.

She's biting her lip, staring back at me. She doesn't say a word but gasps when I grab her hips and hold her against me, so she can feel what she does to me.

With two fingers, I hold back the lips that protect the one place I need access to. I slide another finger against her and feel how wet she is.

I watch her reflection in the mirror as she slightly leans forward, placing her hands on each side of the sink, spreading her legs for me.

"Ethan, I need you." Her voice is breathless already.

I get lost in her as I slide my finger inside her, and she moans.

"What do you need, Bryce?" I push harder. "Tell me what you need."

"You."

I remove my fingers and gently push on her center with only a little pressure.

Red.

Blurred vision.

I can't control myself as I hear her soft whimpers again and then, "Ethan."

My hardness rages against the confines of my pants.

Gently pulling her head up, I watch her face in the mirror as my fingers do this to her. Bryce says my name again, this time more shallow and between controlled breaths.

I watch her breasts start to bounce, as she moves against my fingers.

"I'll stop once you come."

Her eyes narrow as her mouth stays open.

A painted red mural with a mix of only shades of red, I see shades of passion, feel her panting against me, and I need more. The more panting, the more colors in my mural.

"Oh my God." I hear her say as my fingers slide up against her again and back inside her. She grinds her hips hard against me as she screams my name, "Ethan!"

My vision is blurry with shades of red still reaching my mural, and then they slowly fade away as I feel her body fall forward.

I don't remove my fingers. I keep them there as she pulses, allowing her to come back down.

Slowly, I pull my fingers from her, and my body goes rigid, hard, cold.

Why did you let it get to this point? You should have handed her the soap and left.

I place my hands on her hips as I drop my head against her back, trying to regain whatever control I have over my actions. Her breathing is still ragged.

Bryce doesn't turn around. She stays put, maybe for fear that I'll walk away again. Maybe to save herself. I drop my hands from her hips and walk out, leaving her there to clean up the mess that we seem to keep making.

Bryce

Last night, I wanted to tell Ethan about the black sedan. Instead, I told him about my mother. Our relationship. The unease of it all. Maybe, if I had told him about the black sedan, things that happened between us this morning wouldn't have happened. How would the story have changed things? I'm not sure.

It's now late in the afternoon.

I'm at Granite Harbor Grocery right now, in the lentil aisle, staring at the dry chili beans, trying not to remember Ethan. The look he gave me. A look I've seen only twice from him. A look of no control. Fear.

Need. Something we both saw coming.

Touch. Something that we both desperately needed.

Onions, I think to myself. *I need onions.* I attempt to shake myself from the confines of thought.

Our foreplay was good. Hot. I feel my cheeks grow warm. I wanted more of him. He just stopped. When my body came to its conclusion, he just stopped. Walked out of the bathroom. He hadn't let me touch him.

Stop, I tell myself. I feel my face flush again.

"Hello, Bryce." I hear a gentle voice behind me. A voice that doesn't mix well with my thoughts at the moment.

I turn to look toward the voice. "Hi, Helen." Ethan's mother.

"They have the best lentils here, if you ask me," she says, grabbing bags of pinto beans. "Did you hear that Granite Harbor PD tracked down the black sedan? It had gone off the road just past town, and nobody was in it. Can you believe it?" Helen shakes her head.

I can believe it because whoever was driving the black sedan is probably more sinister than we think. Immediately, I think of Ethan and how he went into preservation mode. Hero mode. Making sure everyone was accounted for, safe.

There's silence between Helen and me as we stand here.

She's holding her basket, looking between the items in her basket and me. "I hope I'm not being too forward, Bryce, but we'd really love to have Ethan and you over for dinner." A warm smile spreads across her warm face, blue eyes. "Ethan … Ethan hasn't introduced us to a girlfriend in an awfully long time, and I must say, I'm elated that it's you."

I want to tell her that the girlfriend thing isn't real. That Ethan hasn't asked me to be his girlfriend. But I also don't want Helen to worry about Ethan. I want Ethan to be okay.

"Well, you raised a good man, Helen"—I pause—"an extremely good man."

"Ethan came out like that. Though"—a concerned look she wears now—"when he came home from his second tour, things changed. He grew quieter. More withdrawn. But I still see the same magnetic spark in his eyes as I did when he and Aaron were just boys." Her voice grows lighter.

"We'd love to come to dinner. What day and when?"

Helen looks at the chili ingredients in my basket. "Are you making chili?"

Shit, caught. I was going to enter my chili into the Fall Festival but under an alias. "Maybe." I eye her.

Helen covers her mouth. "Are you entering chili into the Fall Festival against Milton Murdock?" She eyes me back, and a smile starts to form.

"Maybe."

"I'll help."

"You'll have to take an oath of secrecy, Helen. I have a secret recipe," I whisper, leaning forward.

"You have my word. Fall Festival is tomorrow. When should we get started?"

"Meet me at the house on Magnolia in twenty minutes," I say.

"You've got it," Helen whispers back.

And then we separate.

I grab the rest of the ingredients and am able to think clearly without Ethan popping into my head.

"Thanks, Bryce," Mr. Pete says, waving as I leave. "You know, if I were keeping tabs on chili ingredients, I'd say you were prepping for battle with Mr. Murdock in the cook-off tomorrow."

What the hell? How does everyone know I'm making chili? It could be stew. Stew can have beans sometimes.

"Bye, Mr. Pete. Thanks again." I wave and make my way outside to the fall weather that's beginning to take shape.

I stop and grab a coffee at Level Grounds just to say hi to Lyn. We chat for a minute, and I'm back on my way to the house on Magnolia.

Ethan's truck is outside.

Heart, don't freak the hell out.

Stop.

It starts to pound.

He's walking back out to his truck from inside the house.

Be cool, Bryce.

"I'd say come in, but it looks like you've already been doing that," I say as I approach.

Although caught off guard, he, too, tries to act casual as I watch his defined arms reach for a paint bucket.

"Just finishing up the paint on the outside," he says. As if he didn't have his fingers inside me this morning. As if he's unaffected by what happened.

You gave him what he needed or what you both needed, Bryce. Let it go.

I stop at his truck, watching him put the ladder up over his head as his jeans rest lower against his hips, exposing a piece of his washboard stomach.

Totally doesn't affect me. I try to convince myself. "Look, I'm having a friend over in fifteen minutes, so you'll need to be gone by then."

Ethan gently sets the ladder down against the house and stops. Looks at me.

Part of me wants to see how he deals with this. Part of me doesn't.

"Besides, isn't it a bit late to get started with paint?"

"Who's coming over?" He walks back over to his truck.

"Why do you need to know?" The stubborn Bryce comes out, the one my mother wrestles with when she calls.

Ethan walks over to me and stands in my personal space, making me wish I had gum in my mouth right now just in case he decided to kiss me so that I'd be ready. If he tried to kiss me, my body would crack into a million pieces.

He shrugs. "If your friend is a man"—he leans in so that his lips are close to my ear, too close for me to gain any rational thought—"does he know my fingers were inside you this morning?" His lips brush my ear.

I feel his words, his tone, vibrate in my chest. I swallow against sandpaper. "No," I say breathlessly. *Why can't I have the same wit with Ethan that I do with my mother?*

He pulls back so that he's staring at me. His jaw tense, his look long, staring.

Pull your shit together, Bryce. "It's your mother."

I watch relief spread all over him like a blanket.

"I highly doubt she'd want to know that." I smile. *There she is!* I tell myself. *There's Bryce.*

Ethan's shoulders relax. His words are still spinning in my head like a Ferris wheel.

"What's she coming over for?"

"Top secret." My legs, like jelly, make their way to the porch. "If I told you, I'd have to kill you."

"You are anyway," is what I think I hear him reply.

"What?" I ask, turning to see him at his truck.

"Nothing."

"Did you just say something?" I walk down the steps of the porch and toward his truck. "Did you just say I was killing you?"

Ethan turns to me after I reach out and touch his arm. He flinches.

I immediately pull back.

His back to me, he sighs. Ethan's broad shoulders move with a big breath in.

"Ethan …" I hold my breath, my best effort to hold back the words on the tip of my tongue, but it doesn't work. "You're the one who put your fingers inside me this morning. I was taking a shower. You, not me, were the forward one," I try to whisper and get my point across at the same time.

He places his hands on his hips, his back still to me.

"At least look me in the eye, Ethan."

Ethan slowly turns around. Gives me the same look he did this morning.

"Am I interrupting something?" Helen calls, making her way toward us on foot.

Snapping out of my confusion with Ethan, I turn toward Helen. "Not at all." I swallow, taking several hard steps back.

"Mom." Ethan nods, turns, and stares at me.

Helen looks between the two of us. "I'll meet you inside, Bryce." Her hand touches my shoulder as she walks inside.

I've never wanted anything more than to reach out and run my fingers across his lips. My hands to touch his bare chest. For my heart to heal his wounds that I can't see.

Take what you need from me, Ethan, I want to say. *Take what you need, and we'll fix the rest later.*

"I'm sorry, Bryce. I'm not who you think I am. And I can't be the man you need."

He doesn't wait for me to say anything. Besides, it wasn't a question. Ethan Casey was giving me a statement. Is the statement true? He thinks it is. Do I think it's true? Not a chance.

"You don't know me well enough to know what I need, Ethan. You don't get a say in that."

Ethan takes a step toward me. "You're right; I don't. But I know myself. I can tell you what I'd like to do to you, but I won't. I can't. The price you'd pay for my selfish ways would never be worth it."

All the air that surrounds me now, I can't seem to breathe it in. My skin breaks into chills. "Who says we both can't be selfish? Take what we need." I find pockets of air that I take in slow and steady, trying not to let Ethan know that he has this effect on me.

"You can't agree to that, Bryce."

"Nobody tells me what I can and can't do, Ethan. Nobody."

A smile barely touches the corners of his mouth, and then it fades quickly. His stare has me transfixed.

"It won't be fair, Bryce," he whispers, taking steps closer to me.

"I'm not asking you to be fair."

His stare turns to sadness when he's mere inches away from my face. Maybe he has feelings he can't help. I have them, too.

Toward Ethan. Toward my mother. My brother. Maybe he has wants he can't help, too. We all do.

He pulls at his short hair; it isn't long enough to do anything with, but it's enough to show his frustration. He breaks eye contact with me.

I reach out and touch his hand as it leaves his head and falls to his side. My fingers intertwine with his, and my mind flashes to this morning. He wore a coat of armor around his heart, keeping it between us, protecting himself.

"What are you asking?" he says.

"Give me what you can." *What the hell are you doing, Bryce?*

Like a drug I've never had, he's the sweet taste in my mouth. He's the euphoria I get when he touches my body. The intoxication that seeps into my veins, giving me the release that I need. Crave.

With the wall, his wall, still between us, he lets go of my hand, taking the rest of the space between us. Gently, he pushes my hair back, so he can get to my ear. Looking forward, I try not to close my eyes. I take in a deep breath because I know I'll need it.

"I'm a complicated man, Bryce," he whispers into my ear. Then, he pulls back, quickly walks to his truck, and leaves.

I watch as he drives away, unsure of what I just signed up for. Unsure of where this will lead us. Unsure of the end result. But one thing is for sure; I know what I want.

I walk into the house, and Helen is thumbing through a travel magazine at the kitchen counter. She looks up when the door shuts behind me.

"Ready to get started?" She's pretending that what she saw outside wasn't complicated. Maybe because she doesn't want to meddle in her son's business. Maybe because she doesn't want to know.

Either way, I wish Trudy could be more like Helen. Trudy would be the hawk. Swooping down, using her talons to pick up and lose information. Giving her opinions when they weren't wanted.

That reminds me; I should call her.

"I am." I walk into the kitchen and put the grocery bag on the counter.

I don't have the complete secret recipe to my chili written down. I do have several scraps of paper with changes I've made to the recipe over the years scattered in my recipe folder, but I know it by heart, even the changes.

"Do you want to cut the onions while I rinse the beans?" I ask.

"You've got it," Helen says as she looks in the bag. "May I?"

"Yes, absolutely."

This question of hers makes me feel like I'm private. That, by looking in the bag, she's invading my privacy, but she's not.

Helen grabs the onions from the bag and gets a cutting board and a knife while I get the big bag of pinto beans and rinse them.

Helen chops the onion.

After the beans are rinsed, I grab the whiskey.

Helen stops. Looks at me. "I've never taken you for a whiskey drinker, Bryce."

"It's the secret ingredient. That, and"—I pull another small bottle out from the bag—"fish sauce."

Helen stops altogether. "Whiskey and fish sauce." Her eyes bounce from the ingredients and back to me. "I guess I'll need to take your word for it."

She continues to chop while I grab the rest of the ingredients and shove the brown paper bag underneath the sink.

I grab the garlic, another cutting board, a knife, and begin to chop.

"You know, Ethan wasn't the man he is today," Helen says. "Wasn't as quiet, wasn't as serious. So … removed. I guess that would be the right word."

Chopping the garlic, I listen.

"When the boys were little, Ethan was always the cautious one. Aaron was the more outgoing one. More of a risk-taker." She stops, thinks, and stares at the living room ahead, lost in her own memories.

"When he came from the war for the first time, came home for a visit, he was all right. I assumed the small change in him, the way he didn't smile, the way he was more withdrawn, was the war. What they had to see over there. Do." Her voice grows quiet. "I tried to keep things normal for him at home. The way they always were. Something familiar. There's nothing normal about war."

She stops cutting the onion for a moment. "When he came home and told Bill and me that he wanted to enlist in the Marines, it took us by complete surprise. Ethan has always had the softer heart, the old soul of my boys. Ethan was the one who would bring injured animals home and try to rehabilitate them." She smiles at the memory, laughs.

"There was one time when he brought home a wounded bird from the woods. He and Aaron were about ten years old. Anyway, he put it in this big blue container, and on the outside, the bird didn't look wounded. Ethan said he just couldn't fly. The bird had survived the night, so Ethan took it to share at school the next day. He said, when he pulled the bird out of the container to share with his classmates, the bird's head dropped to one side. The bird had died." Helen covers her mouth to stifle a laugh. "I shouldn't be laughing, and of course, I didn't laugh at the time when he told me. Instead, I consoled him, his wounded heart. Made him some hot chocolate, and we buried the bird in the backyard. We have somewhat of a pet cemetery in the backyard for the animals that Ethan couldn't save. Which weren't very many. He saved many animals."

Helen's voice grows quiet. "So, you can see why he went into such a protective mode last night when that car came at us." She grabs another onion and begins to cut again.

We chop and listen to the silence.

"Just because there aren't any wounds on the outside doesn't mean he's not dying inside."

I meet Helen's gaze.

"You have given Ethan a smile that I haven't seen since he came home from his second tour, Bryce. I really enjoy seeing his smile." Tears come to Helen's eyes as she chops again. "Damn onions."

I enjoy Ethan's smile, too.

My phone sounds.

I grab a dishrag and wipe my hands. "Excuse me, Helen. I'll be right back."

In my purse, I grab my phone and see that it's my mother. I hit Ignore and begrudgingly make a note to myself to call her back when Helen leaves. I shove my phone back in my purse and walk back to the counter.

Fourteen

Ethan

I sit across from James, my leg bouncing up and down, slouched, comfortable in the space that I'm in.

"Why is your leg bouncing, Ethan?" James asks, his hands folded casually in his lap.

It makes me think about our first year together and how he'd sit, pen and notepad in hand, waiting for me to give him my life story.

I pull my body forward, placing my elbows on my knees, contemplating whether to tell James about Bryce. My leg stops bouncing.

I'm no longer ordered to come see James. I do it on my own.

His office is clean. The dark, thick hardwood floor is protected by an off-white area rug. Bookshelves line the length of one wall. *Love and War. A Separate Peace. Waking the Tiger: Healing Trauma. To Kill a Mockingbird. One Flew Over the Cuckoo's Nest. War and the Soul.* I wonder why James houses fiction books in his office. I come up with reasons in my head, never asking him for the true answer. Why? I don't know. Maybe my curiosity is the answer I'm looking for. Maybe it's the one I want to believe. Because life is easier lived if it isn't your own. A make-believe world is just that. You can walk away at any time.

"You're nervous. Care to discuss it?" James reaches forward and takes a sip of his water. Folds his hands back in his lap, crossing one leg over the other.

"There's a woman," I say, leaning back. Knee starts to move up and down again.

James nods. "Bryce?"

My mouth falls open. "How do you know about her?"

"I'm a trained listener, Ethan. She's the only woman you've ever brought up."

I nod. "She's back in town again for a while." I stall.

"Have you asked her to dinner?"

I pull back my lip to a snarl and give him a look. "No, why?"

James shrugs. "That's what you do when you find a woman you'd like to spend more time with, Ethan."

"James"—I shake my head—"you know how I feel about that shit. I can't ... I can't just ask her out."

James frowns. "Remember the circle we did a few years ago? I asked you to draw a circle. And all I asked you was to put where you were in relation to the circle. Remember?"

I nod.

"And remember when I asked you to add the important people in your life in relation to the circle and you?"

Fuck.

"And you drew you on the inside, and everyone else on the outside. Helen, Bill, Aaron, Ryan, Eli." He pauses. "What's changed since then, Ethan?"

Leg starts to bounce again.

"Where would you put Bryce on the circle?"

"Outside."

"And why?"

I let out a big breath. "Because, James. You know why."

"Say it out loud."

My eyes narrow. *Fucking A. Why do I pay this man one hundred dollars a session?* "You know why."

"Say it out loud," he says again.

"Why? So, it feeds your ego?"

That's the thing with James; I've never been able to get under his skin. Ever. No matter what I've said to him in the past, and I've said some pretty harsh things—not because of him, but because of who I've become and fought so hard not to be.

"You don't pay me one hundred dollars a session, so I can feed my ego; trust me, Ethan." James smiles and takes another sip of water. "Why would you put Bryce on the outside of the circle?"

"I'll hurt her if she's on the inside."

"Why do you say that?"

"Because I know, all right?" I lean forward because I want to stop the shaking of my leg.

"You aren't giving yourself the chance to hurt her, Ethan. Your fear of emotions—"

I interrupt the sentence I've heard him say a thousand times to me. *"That's why you're scared of intimacy, Ethan."* I mimic his voice, his tone, his gestures, but I partly smile as I do it.

"Is ... is that a smile from Ethan Casey?" James asks.

We both know he's right about my fear of emotions. Commitment. Love. Intimacy.

"What are you going to do about this fear?" he asks.

There's a long-drawn-out silence between us and outside his office. Not even the song sparrows sing.

"Fear can keep us from happiness," James says. Lays it out on the table like it's rye bread or a perfectly acceptable statement. His eyes narrow. "Fear comes up in different ways, Ethan. It might not always show physically with shaking, sweating, not eating. But it can also certainly be in decisions we don't make or situations we walk away from because we can't face them. It can be sex relations, ambitions. Self-esteem—you're fearful of how Bryce will make you feel. What, maybe vulnerable?" James stops talking for a moment, waits, eyes me from his chair.

"I need to go," I say and stand.

"Did you ever stop to think that maybe life might work out for you?" James says and stands also.

"No." I turn toward the door.

"And why not?"

"Because death is always inevitable, James. Always. We come into this world one way, and we get out one way. It's that simple." I open the door and shut it behind me.

I throw my keys on the table beside the front door. I need relief from all this shit that's going in my mind.

I grab a bottle of Maker's Mark along with a small glass from the liquor cabinet and listen to the glub of the bottle as I pour it, adding some ice from the freezer.

The booze slides down my throat, burning, and explodes on my empty stomach as I slam the glass down on the counter.

I wait for the poison to reach my brain and lift the feelings that inundate me right now.

Everything slows down.

Words in my head aren't so loud anymore. Thoughts don't spin so fast.

I pull off my shirt with the intentions of a shower.

The doorbell rings.

I finish the glass of whiskey. I'm not expecting anyone, but it could be my brother or my mother. Which would be weird if I answered the door with my shirt off.

But it's her hair I notice first behind the door.

I pull it open.

"Hey." A small exhale escapes her mouth as her eyes involuntarily drop down to my bare chest and shoot back up to my eyes.

When I see her, I can breathe better. More clearly. Maybe it's the whiskey, too. My stomach gets tight, and I think it's nerves.

I've had liquid courage. This can go so right and so wrong.

"Your mom gave me your address. I hope that's all right. I need you to try this chili. I walked up here."

I realize she's holding a small container in her hands.

"Have you eaten?"

"No."

Bryce holds out the container.

I take it. "Come in," I say, knowing I'm asking for a situation that might not be right, but my heart is overruling my head right now. Also, the whiskey.

She steps inside, and I breathe her in. The scent of her shampoo, citrus, combined with her body way too close to mine make me realize I need to move. I shut the door behind her. Bryce spots the Maker's Mark on the counter.

I walk in front of her, throwing my shirt on the counter. "Care for a drink?" Small metaphorical red flags go up for me.

There's a short silence before she answers, "I could use one, yes." She sits at the counter while I stand on the other side, creating distance between us. "Give me your honest opinion about the chili," she says, watching me as I make her a drink.

"Anything with the Maker's?" I ask.

"No."

"Straight?"

"Yes."

I slide the glass across the counter after I drop a few ice cubes in it.

I pour myself another small glass and take a sip. I watch her.

"What?" she says. "Never seen a woman drink whiskey straight before?"

"Just Dani Leroy. In high school. Watched it come out of her nose, too." I feel the grin begin. Maybe it's the booze. Maybe it's Bryce here, in my house.

"Ouch."

"Yeah."

She puts her glass to her lips and sips. It's so quiet that I hear her swallow. Bryce's lips form a thin line as she sets her glass down.

"Can I tell you something?" She sweeps her finger across the brim of her glass.

The whiskey has definitely reached my head because flashes of her meet the forefront of my mind—from this morning to our night in LA. These memories seem to drown out the bad ones. The ones I don't talk about. The ones I only share with James.

"All ears."

"I think I'm going to enter my chili in the Fall Festival tomorrow."

"Is that why my mom came over?"

"Yes. But why would you assume it was for the chili?"

"Helen Casey makes the best chili in the state of Maine. Aside from Milton Murdock."

"But ... she didn't say anything. She just cut the onions, the garlic. Helped with the secret ingredients." Bryce looks dumbfounded.

"She probably wouldn't." I shrug. "Wait, how'd you know where I lived?"

"Played dumb with your mom. I figured your girlfriend should know where you lived, but I played it off as the new girl in town. 'A left on what street, Helen, to get to Ethan's?'"

I've got to take a cold shower, I think to myself as we both put our glasses to our mouths, attempting to relieve the tension between us. Not the bad tension. The sexual tension I know I feel. But does Bryce feel it?

"I should go. Let me know if the chili is good enough to beat Milton's?" Bryce stands, taking her glass to the sink.

I don't say she shouldn't go. I don't ask her to stay because we both know it's a bad idea. Not a good mix. Booze and sex.

"Yeah," I sigh as she walks past me. Still, my shirt lies on the counter, and I grab for it, but she beats me to it, swiping it from the counter before I do.

"Like I said, I'll take what I can get."

Fuck. I don't care what she takes. I'll give her anything, except the dark places my mind goes when life seems to get hard. *Cold shower, Ethan.*

There's nothing to say to that, except, "Okay."

She walks to the door, and I follow in her wake.

I pull the door open, but she turns, looks at me, doesn't say a word, but hands me my shirt back. I want to say something profound. Deep. But the words don't come. *What would James say in this situation?* Hell, I'm not even sure he likes women.

Hesitantly, she takes her hand and gently touches the spot on my chest where my heart is. "I can't fix this. I wish I could." She reaches up and touches my temple. "I wish I could fix your memories. Only the bad ones." Bryce allows her fingertips to slide from my temple to the side of my face, down my chest, and lets her hand fall next to her. "Good night, Ethan."

Bryce walks outside.

Am I driving her home? I can't. I've had something to drink.

And I can't seem to fucking catch my breath. My body is full of need, surging with energy.

Let her go, Ethan.

Let her walk away. Her house isn't more than two blocks downhill.

Why can't you be strong enough?

Let go.

I wait seventeen seconds, and something inside me tells me to fucking run after her.

I'm outside and reaching for her arm. I flip her around and not so gently push her back against the truck. I grip the sides of her face and smash my lips to hers with everything I have. My tongue searches into her mouth as she opens wider for me. Our eyes stay locked as I allow my body to press up against hers. I feel myself harden, and I want her to know what she does to me without words.

Her hands slide to my ass, and she pulls me closer to her, wanting this just as much as I do.

My tongue probes her mouth as I feel her body relax, and this makes me think of how tight she was in my mouth until she finally relaxed when I made her come.

I pull away, catching my breath, and I watch her chest heave in the moonlight, her stare hard.

"What do you want, Bryce?" I take my hand and slide it over her covered breast.

"Whatever you'll give me," she pants.

Think rationally, Ethan. For fuck's sake. "What if it's just this?"

She nods and takes a big breath in. "I'll take it."

But I see the truth in her eyes. She'll want more.

Despite that, my lips crash down on hers again.

Bryce

He pulls me inside, and I'm drunk on him. Maybe the whiskey, too. He leads me to his bedroom with power. Force. A force not used against me, but for us.

If it's just sex, will you be all right with this, Bryce?

My question goes unanswered because he moves me to the end of his bed. The only light in his bedroom is from the moon outside.

Ethan removes my sweatshirt and T-shirt.

A woman never comes to a man's house, whom she has feelings for, without shaved legs and a sexy black bra with panties to match. It's just code.

He admires me, dropping my sweatshirt and T-shirt to the carpet. In a trancelike state, he slides off my pants, too. Ethan steps closer, a half an inch from me, taking my face in his hands, searching my eyes for the answers about right and wrong. Maybe sex is the right answer. Just sex. But we've tried this. For some reason, it comes back to this.

His mouth takes mine. At first, slowly, sensually, his tongue probing my mouth with thought, using it as a tool of measurement.

How far do I go?

When will I stop? If I stop.

What happens when my hands reach her breasts and brush against her nipples, and they harden? Then, what?

He does this. He takes two fingers to my back and unhooks my bra with one snap, and my breasts release with a jiggle. Ethan slides my bra off as his lips reach my neck. My nipples grow hard against his chest, and he groans at this. He pulls away and looks into my eyes first, as if asking for the go-ahead. The signal that all of this is okay.

I reach down and undo his belt but not without admiring his body first. "Is it a job requirement for game wardens to stay in shape?" My eyes scan his body.

"No. It's just part of the job." He stoops down and toys with my mouth.

When his belt is off, I undo the button on his jeans and slide them down. His unit at attention, I slide his underwear down, and he reaches out, gripping my wrists, pulling me back up to him, my body sliding against his on my way up, coming alive with every inch of his.

Ethan pulls my hair back with one hand, searching my eyes once again.

"What are you looking for, Ethan?"

"I haven't let a woman kiss me on the mouth in a long time."

"Why not?"

He shakes his head. "Just not the way I operate."

"Then, why do you let me?" I hold my breath, and his lips barely graze mine as he closes his eyes.

He shakes his head again. "I don't know."

I grab the back of his neck and allow us to blend together as my lips, my tongue find his. We fall against the bed, and my legs spread, asking for more. As he trails kisses down my chest, his body moves to the side, and he uses his eyes to look me over. Look after me. Ethan's eyes meet mine again as he takes my breast in his hand. My nipple hardens beneath his touch as I clench my legs, wanting more of him. He moves over to my other breast, this time acknowledging my budding nipple between his fingertips. My feet up on the mattress, I use them to push my hips up to meet his touch.

Ethan's hand moves down my stomach. My head drifts, and I have to close my eyes. His hand slides further, dipping under my black lace panties.

"Ethan," I say in a whisper, opening my eyes to see his hooded look. "Please."

"Please what?" His fingers reach my opening, and he stops.

I pant. I watch him.

"What do you need from me?" His fingers touch my middle, and I call out beneath his mouth when it crashes down on me.

I grab my own breasts and arch my back from the mattress, pushing my middle closer to his fingers.

"Bryce, you're so wet." Ethan pulls back and watches me as I begin to unravel underneath his touch.

"I can't …" Ethan's voice changes. "I can't give you any more than this, Bryce."

Wanting more, I push harder against his hand. He groans, falling against my neck.

I put my hand in his underwear and take his length in my grip.

"Fuck," he whispers in my ear, pushing himself into my hand.

In one swift move, I push myself on top of him.

Ethan grips my hips hard as I feel his length between my legs.

"Take your underwear off, Ethan," I demand.

"No."

"Ethan, take your fucking underwear off right now."

His eyes narrow as he stares up at me. Bewilderment, frustration, curiosity burn through the look on his face. He reaches down, me still on top, and effortlessly slides off his underwear. As my middle falls to his hardness, we both groan.

I start to move, sliding myself on top of him. Skin against skin.

He pulls.

I push.

He sits, taking me in his arms, pushing himself to the side of the bed, as if I were a rag doll, his muscles contracting beneath me. He stands, my legs wrapped around his middle, his hands around my ass, breasts against his chest.

"Where are we going?" I ask.

"Kitchen."

"Kitchen?"

He reaches my lips with his and slides his tongue between them. I wrap my hands around his neck and enjoy this feeling he brings me.

Ethan carries me to the kitchen and slides me against the counter. It's darker in the kitchen. Less moon. He leaves me on the counter and goes to the refrigerator. He opens it and stands there, the light hitting his body in all the right places, his manliness still standing at attention. I marvel at him, stare.

He leaves the refrigerator open and walks to the cupboard.

"What are you doing?"

"Getting hydrated." He grabs two glasses.

Ethan walks back to the refrigerator and pours two glasses of water. He walks back to me and hands one to me. "Drink."

Ethan eyes me as I watch his Adam's apple bounce with each swallow.

I put the glass to my lips and tip it back, feeling the coolness fill my mouth. I swallow.

Ethan is close enough to me where I see the conflict in his eyes, the storm that rages between bouts of clarity.

"What?" I ask, setting the water glass down next to me.

I realize just how naked we are. Clothes don't hide our flaws, our insecurities, what we do to make ourselves feel better, our need for purpose. Clothes hide our external wounds, our trouble spots, our outwardly strength.

Ethan stands next to me. "I need to walk you home."

I already knew he would say this. I saw it in his eyes, the way he swam the sea of regret to get to me. Pushed himself to touch me amid the war that waged behind his eyes.

"I know." Gently, I slide off the counter, eye-level with his bare chest. I take his lean hips between my hands. I gently kiss his chest, the dusting of hair touching my lips. "I know," I repeat.

And, with that, I leave him in the darkness of the confines he's created to lie down with himself. Sleep with himself. Rest uneasy with the decisions he's made to protect others from his own hurt.

I come back out of the bedroom dressed, my hair retied tighter against my head, making myself feel more in control.

Somehow, Ethan is clothed, which makes this all the more harder, although, I'm not sure why. Perhaps a wall created to keep out what hurts and nurture what doesn't in order to keep the heart intact.

Ethan opens the front door for me. "After you," he whispers in the same voice he did moments ago in his bedroom. When I walk past him, I catch his scent, and it almost consumes me. Secretly, I wish I could sleep with one of his shirts to keep his scent close to me, so I wouldn't forget the way it made my heart feel when he touched me. Ethan Casey seems to trigger my senses and rights the wrongs of life.

Next time, I tell myself.

Late evenings in Granite Harbor are colder. Something Los Angeles never experiences. Late evenings in Granite Harbor are my favorite. The peepers call out, expressing their concern for the change of weather.

I match his pace, two steps to his one, we walk down the hill to Magnolia Road in the silence of the world; the only interruption is the painful reminder that we can't go back.

After a few short minutes of silence, we reach the front of the house that used to be pink; now, only the eaves are patiently waiting for their new coat.

He stares down at the ground, most likely looking for the right words to tell me or excuses of why he stopped. I should tell him not to explain. I should tell him that I don't have expectations, but secretly, I do, if I'm being honest. So, I don't say anything.

We walk to the door, and he stands far enough away so that I can't touch him.

"I'll see you, Ethan." Like this is good-bye. Like we've made an agreement that it's better this way. That we can't let things get out of hand.

But why? Why not let them get out of hand?

Because, I say to myself, *you saw his eyes. The conflict. The remorse.*

And then I remember it. In Los Angeles, right before he entered me, the same look, both wild and unreachable.

I look at Ethan. He's ruggedly handsome, so beautiful, both in character and to the eye. It's as if God graced him with perfect muscular facial structure. I want to ask him if the storm rages behind his eyes just with me, but I'm too scared. Too scared to hear the words that will most likely drive me to heartache.

"Good night, Bryce." He meets my eyes.

I nod, opening the door to Magnolia Road. "Good night, Ethan."

He doesn't move until I step inside and turn back toward the front porch.

Ethan turns to leave.

"Ethan?" I ask. *Don't do it, Bryce. Don't.*

"Yeah?" He turns to face me again, this time from the bottom of the steps of the porch.

"The storm that rages in your eyes, is it just for me?" I nervously wait for his answer.

He looks down at the sidewalk and then back to me. Ethan knows what I'm talking about it. He might not see it, but he feels it.

"It's always just for you, Bryce," Ethan whispers loud enough for me to hear his words that are crystal clear.

And this makes my heart shatter into a million tiny pieces that fall to the cement walkway like feathers. If I'm responsible for the storm, I'm also the maker of the wind that moves the storm. Until he rights himself, we can't work, and I'll just have to accept that.

Sixteen

Ethan

I need to clear my head. Gain some stability.

Last time we were together like this, she made me feel things and do things that were unfamiliar territory. And the feelings drifted into days, weeks, months after we were together in Los Angeles.

I push us to the edge of the bed, her on top of me, and put whatever feeling she gives me into my touch as I stand, wanting her to know it isn't her; it's me.

"Where are we going?" she asks.

"Kitchen."

"Kitchen?"

I take her mouth and own it as if it were mine. As if I could selfishly take it anytime I pleased. When she wraps her hands around my neck and kisses me back, I feel her legs tighten around me, and I almost lose my shit.

Oh, fuck.

I recite the only creed that kept me sane, distracted, from what was around me in war.

This is my rifle. There are many like it, but this one is mine. My rifle is my best friend. It is my life. I must master it as I must master my life. My rifle, without me, is useless. Without my rifle, I am useless. I must fire my rifle true.

I must shoot straighter than my enemy who is trying to kill me. I must shoot him before he shoots me. I will.

My rifle and I know that what counts in this war is not the rounds we fire, the noise of our burst, or the smoke we make. We know that it is the hits that count. We will hit.

My rifle is human, even as I, because it is my life. Thus, I will learn it as a brother. I will learn its weaknesses, its strength, its parts, its accessories, its sights, and its barrel. I will ever guard it against the ravages of weather and damage as I will ever guard my legs, my arms, my eyes, and my heart against damage.

We reach the kitchen, and I slide her onto the counter. I walk to the refrigerator in my nakedness; for some reason, I don't care when I'm with Bryce. I open the fridge. Something about her gives me a piece of freedom. A small slice of hope buried somewhere in the ramblings of who I've become since I came home from war and transitioned to civilian life.

Glasses. I need glasses. I walk to the cabinet and grab two glasses.

"What are you doing?" she asks.

"Getting hydrated." I walk back to the refrigerator and pour two glasses of water. I hand Bryce one, trying to contemplate my next move. "Drink."

I watch her as she drinks. Her breasts need kissing. Touching. The way God outlined her body in this moment is as if it's for me and only me. I wonder if he created Bryce just for me. That would be a perfect world. But he wouldn't create something so perfect and just give her to someone who'd most likely hurt her.

You don't deserve a heart like hers, Ethan. You'll see. It's just a matter of time before you break her heart. Save her the ache.

"What?" she asks, setting her glass of water down on the tiled counter I installed last winter.

I know what I need to do. Know what the right decision is. The best decision for her. The best decision for me right now is to take her up against the wall right now and let her know how badly I need her. Want her. But morning will come, and I'll feel the need to disappear again.

I meet her eyes with mine. It's as if she knows what I'm about to say. She shouldn't trust me when I can't trust myself.

"I need to walk you home."

"I know." Bryce pushes herself off the counter.

She puts her hands on my hips, and I feel the lump in my throat grow. When she kisses my chest, the act is so innocent, so transparent, that, for the first time in a long time, I want someone to see what I've seen, and it's almost as if she has. I control the groan that wants to explode from my throat. It isn't a sexual groan, a way of wanting; it's an emotion.

"I know," she says again and walks to my bedroom to collect her clothes.

When she leaves the kitchen, I breathe deep, resting my hands on the counter in front of me.

I throw on a green warden sweatshirt and other clothes from the dryer.

When Bryce comes back out from my bedroom, I envision we just made love. And, after, I'd give her a slow, open-mouthed kiss and pull her to me. Whisper in her ear that I'd like to do that every night to her. But, right now, the reality is, we didn't make love, and I need to take her home.

I walk to the front door and open it for her. "After you."

After I walk her home, my mind wanders on the trip back up the hill. When she asked about the storm that raged in my eyes, what I didn't tell her was that I love her enough to leave her alone. I love her enough to protect her, to keep her safe from men like me. I have tasted her, longed for her, and I'm not willing to allow her to love a man who can't give her what she needs.

I watch her through the crowd of people gathered on Main Street for the Fall Festival. She's with Alex and Eli, holding the hand of their oldest daughter, Emily.

My mother has always found the Fall Festival to be both fun and wondrous. Her words, not mine. I find it to be confining and suffocating. But I do the hot dog eating contest as part of my role of game warden which is to entertain the kids and be a part of our community.

"I just don't know how you ate one hundred and twenty-two hot dogs last year, Ethan," Ruthie says, her mother, Ida, next to her.

Ida was our librarian in Granite Harbor as long as I can remember, and retired about ten years ago.

"One at a time," I answer, following the fiery-red hair as she moves through the crowd.

"Anyway, I think that Bryce Hayes is going to give you a run for your money, Milton," my dad, Bill, says, taking one last bite of his chili.

My mom smiles. She probably doesn't know that I know she assisted with Bryce's chili.

Aaron's watching someone, too. I know he's had a thing for Lydia since the minute she moved to Granite Harbor from New Hampshire some years back, but when Ryan swooped in on her—Aaron walked away. Truth be told, I don't think Lydia cared at all for Ryan. She saw right through him, knowing he loved someone else.

"Fiery redhead at one o'clock," Aaron whispers as we walk with Mom, Dad, Ruthie, and Ida through the crowd, watching kids bob for apples, play games. Other community members and groups sell pies and win chili contests.

Don't panic, I say to myself as I watch her walk closer to us, more Eli leading the way than Bryce.

Ryan and Merit approach with them, and their daughter, Hope, is in some sort of contraption that holds babies close to their parents, hands-free.

"Eli, Ryan." Aaron and I each extend our hands.

Ever since we were kids, we've met down at the Fall Festival every year. But, last year, it seemed like we all had to work. And I never took leave in the military, so I missed some years.

Ida approaches Bryce. "Don't tell my son-in-law, Bryce, but your chili won in my book. And, if you tell a single soul, I'll swear I never said it and shove carrots in your ears when you're sleeping."

Bryce doesn't know whether to laugh or run, but she manages a smile. "Well, I'll take that as a compliment, Ida. Thank you."

Ida nods matter-of-factly. "You're welcome."

Ruthie looks to Eli, Ryan, Aaron, and me. "Whatever came of the person driving the black sedan, boys?" She takes another bite of chili from a small cup.

Eli chimes in, "GHPD found the car, but there was no one in it. Ran the plates, and it came back to Steven Williams out of Portland, Maine, who reported his car stolen three nights prior."

Ruthie shakes her head.

I notice Bryce changes. It's subtle, but she grows stiff.

"If you ask me," Ida says, "it's probably that serial killer from Rio de Janeiro."

Ruthie looks at her mom, a befuddled look. "Mom, what are you talking about?" Ruthie rolls her eyes. "I thought I told the staff at the senior living center not to allow you to watch *Dateline* anymore."

"Ruth Ann Murdock, I'm a grown woman, and I can watch whatever I damn well please." Ida crosses her arms.

I catch Bryce's eye and watch as the corners of her mouth turn up. She motions with her head that we move away from the group, that she'd like to talk.

I follow her lead, and we slip away from the group to a bench between Ring's Pharmacy and Level Grounds Coffee Shop. We don't dare sit on the bench together because, in the Granite Harbor gossip mill, you're most likely to end up pregnant or married just by sharing a bench together. I think I'd be fine with that though.

"Hey." She leans in and whispers as we watch the festivities.

"How are you?" I whisper back. It's been almost twenty-four hours since I took her home.

"I have an itch."

"Where?" I look down at her.

Her eyes meet mine. She swallows. Her face is full of trepidation.

"What's wrong?" I turn to her, concerned.

She swallows again. "Ethan, everywhere." She's careful with her words. Her mouth partly opens as she stares up at me. "I can't do half measures. I need all or nothing. We either need to be friends or together. But not this." She motions her hand between us. "And I'd like your cell phone number. Just in case of emergencies."

"My number's 207-223-4689," I say. "I thought you said you'd take what I can give you?"

"Offer is off the table." She looks away from me, biting her lip.

I glance over at our group of people, wondering if they're still in deep conversation. Every single one of them is staring at us, but they flip around like they weren't staring. Some pretend to be engaged in conversation.

"I can't give you what you need, Bryce," comes out of my mouth.

"All right, folks. Gather around, gather around," Mayor Thissel says from a podium set up in front of the chili tables. "Time to announce the winner of this year's chili cook-off."

"I know," Bryce whispers. "Friends?" She sticks her hand out.

No. Fucking no. That's not what I want—and it is what I want, all at the same time.

I slip my hand in hers, feeling her warmth even though the temperature is beginning to drop. "Friends."

Our hands stay intertwined. We hold on. Hold for each other maybe. Hold on for times that will get rocky. That's what friendships are, right? Through thick and thin.

"We should walk back over before people start to notice," Bryce says.

Bryce and I walk to meet the rest of our group, moving toward the podium.

While Mayor Thissel talks with the Fall Festival chairman, Tom Sullivan, I watch Bryce. What I expect to see is a smile. But I don't. I see what she's doing. She's putting on a brave front. Her words try to cover up what her heart feels. I see it. I'm not stupid. I think about the vulnerability she shared with me last night, her breasts bare, her body open to me, as she sat on my counter and drank my water. Maybe it was confidence. But I think it was bravery, courage, intimacy.

My face turns flush, hot. Instantly, I need to know the answer to this question.

I turn my body toward her, move in front of her line of sight, bend down, and whisper in her ear, "Have you sat naked with a man, uncovered, and allowed him to look at you the way I did last night?"

I pull back only a little to see her eyes; they are wide with fear, not with the confidence they reflected moments ago.

She shakes her head. "No."

I nod, staring, willing her to know, feel, the complexity of my ways. Things I don't understand. Being with her, seeing her on a daily basis, makes it harder to be strong.

Mayor Thissel takes to the microphone.

Seventeen

Bryce

"Well, well, well, I had to double-check the count to be sure, but we have a new winner for this year's Fall Festival chili cook-off," Mayor Thissel announces to the crowd.

"You're out, Milton. Time for new blood," Ida says with laugh.

"The winners of this year's Fall Festival chili cook-off is…Bryce Hayes and A. Helper."

The town of Granite Harbor is shocked as silence pushes through the crowd like quickly pooling milk, and all eyes turn to me.

This is really awkward. I look up at Ethan as Aaron collects cash from Eli and Ryan.

"Told ya she'd win."

Ethan bends down and whispers, "They want you onstage, Bryce. Go on." He smiles only slightly. "I'll be crowd control."

It's silly that a town chili cook-off can cause this much of an uproar. I look away from Ethan as the crowd moves like water to clear a path for me to the stage. I look to Helen—aka A. Helper—and she gives me a thumbs-up.

It's a stupid chili cook-off, not the Academy Awards. I've been to the Academy Awards when Alex's book was made into a movie and nominated.

I walk quickly to the podium, trying not to make this a big deal. Mayor Thissel places a medal around my neck.

"This isn't necessary," I say.

"Oh, it is. And"—he winces—"we thought we'd jump ahead and get it engraved just because Milton Murdock had won every damn year, so, uh, it has Milton's name on that, but don't worry; I will order you a new one with the correct name."

Mayor Thissel places a hand on my shoulder as we pose for a picture for the town newspaper.

Thissel takes to the microphone again. "We will have the hot dog eating contest next. Ethan Casey, are you here?"

The crowd moves to a table lined with a white tablecloth and four plates sitting at each place.

Ethan doesn't break eye contact with me, and I don't join him back in the spotlight either. His turn to be awkward in front of the crowd.

Just like me, he hates it. I smile as he wants to crawl out of his own skin, and I know this because his right shoulder moves in a circular motion once. He did this when we first met in Los Angeles. He tries to casually talk to Aaron next to him as Mayor Thissel goes on and on about how many years Ethan has held the crown of hot dog eating champ. Just like me, he doesn't much like the crown that Granite Harbor has bestowed upon hum, but he takes it.

I slip back into the crowd next to Alex. I take my phone out and snap a picture of Ethan taking his seat at the table along with Eli, Ryan, and Aaron. *Wait. They all do it?* They smile, bumping elbows, laughing.

Alex slips her arm around me. "You won!" she whispers. "Watch out Rachael Ray."

I feel a hand on my back from the other side of me. "Congratulations, sweetie. I knew you had it in the bag," Helen says.

"Couldn't have done it without you."

"I just cut the onions and garlic." She winks.

"'Bout time someone threw Mr. Murdock off his throne, Bryce," Ruthie says and smiles, standing next to Helen.

"Remember," Mayor Thissel says through a megaphone now as Tom Sullivan sets down huge plates of hot dogs next to each contestant, "you have thirty minutes to eat as many hot dogs as you can. Are you ready, Wardens?"

Ethan, Eli, Aaron, and Ryan don't answer but assume a position—bending over their plate, chair slightly pushed back—and they look at the mayor.

"Go!"

All four wardens begin the process and take two hot dogs at a time.

I smile when I see Ethan smile as he looks down the table at Aaron. Although all four men seem different and life has taken them on separate journeys, this is something they can come back to. Reflect on. They laugh as if no one is watching. Talk among themselves as if sitting at Angler's Tavern over a beer instead of a plate of hot dogs. I realize instantly this is why Ethan continues to do this. He doesn't do it because he wins. He does it because this is the one thing that strings these four men together. It's the familiarity, the bond, that draws on the strength of their upbringing together. It just so happens that Ethan is the best among the hot dog eaters.

I see Ethan smile again as he slows his process.

"Seven minutes left, men," Mayor Thissel says through the megaphone.

The wall Ethan has built to hide what he saw at war is slowly cracking, and I know this because of each new smile from him.

"Two minutes," the mayor says.

Tom brings Ethan one more plate of hot dogs—his fourth plate, to be exact—while Eli, Ryan, and Aaron slow. Hit a wall almost. Ethan grabs two more dogs and puts them into his mouth. The other wardens just don't have it in them.

"One minute." Mayor Thissel leans down, so Tom can say something in his ear. "Two hundred and two hot dogs for Ethan Casey, beating his old record of one hundred and twenty-two."

Our small town erupts into cheers as Ethan shoves the last hot dog in his mouth.

"Two hundred and three hot dogs!" Mayor Thissel calls into the megaphone.

My phone chirps, signifying an incoming call. I pull my phone from my back pocket.

I hit Talk and walk to a quiet spot away from the crowd.

"It's about time you called me back, asshole," I whisper into the phone.

Silence on the other end of the line.

"Ryker?" My heart begins to pick up pace as I think of all the unimaginable places he could be right now.

"Yeah, hey, sis."

"Don't *hey, sis* me right now, Ryker. I think Luke knows."

"Nobody knows."

"Ryker, someone knows." I look down at the screen and see *Ryker 4*, the number he's called me from. It's all confusing as I thought my text messages didn't go through. They said undeliverable. "Did you get my text?"

"No, I didn't. Sam did. Sold him my phone. Said you sent a text message a few days ago."

Silence hangs on the line.

"I'll take care of it, Bryce. Chill the fuck out, okay?"

"Do you have any idea I'm all the way in Maine, Ryker? Seriously, is your head that far into your veins with your addiction that you can't see what the hell is going on?" I'm trying not to pace on the sidewalk as I watch as Ethan takes the podium, the bib still hanging from the inside of his collar.

"You're in Maine?"

Fuck off, Ryker. I hit End.

This makes me think of my mom and the way she's always fiercely protected my brother from the world. From himself. From my father. From me. God forbid, we ever say anything critical of my brother. She infuriates me just as much as he does. I should call my mom, maybe to mend fences a bit, but I just can't do it.

My heart is slamming against my chest. I have a heavy secret that I just want to come clean with, and the only other person who knows is strung out on heroin and only God knows what else.

Dad is the only sane one other than me. I want to call him. I want to tell him, but I'm afraid, if I do, he'll give up our secret. He'll want to protect Ryker and me—rule with the Dad heart, not the leader heart.

It's easy to set it to the side when I'm busy, but when my heart feels happiness and joy, the secret pushes it aside and says, *You don't have the right to feel this.*

The only thing my dad has always ingrained in our heads is to speak up. Do the right thing even if fear sits in the middle of the room, asking for another ten minutes of your life.

This time, together, Ryker and I, we're doing the right thing even if we're lying to our father. Keeping secrets from the people we care about, even if it's at the risk of them getting hurt—which is where most of my guilt sits—is killing me.

"Hey," a voice calls from the shadows.

I look up just as tiny needles prickle my skin. The crowd has disappeared.

Ethan comes into view. "What are you doing over here, in the dark?" His hands shoved in his pockets, he takes some steps closer.

My phone rings.

"It's my dad. Hang on."

Ethan nods.

"Hey, Dad."

"How's my little girl? Granite Harbor treating you well?" he asks.

"Always. Listen, have you heard from Ryker lately?"

"No." My dad tries to hide the disdain he has for Ryker. Not for Ryker, but for his disease, what he's doing with his life. My dad believes that you can turn addiction off at any time. Make it disappear with just a simple choice. Something changes in his voice. Concern. "Is Ethan with you?"

Wait. What? How does he know who Ethan is? "What?" I ask.

Silence sits on the end of the line.

"How do you know who Ethan is?" The words fall out of my mouth.

Silence.

"You've talked about him before, B."

I've never known my dad to be a liar. A family man, a decent man with respect for himself and others. Not a liar.

"I have?" I don't remember ever talking about Ethan to anyone. I look to Ethan, who's standing in front of me, who has no idea what's being said on the line. It's the stress that's causing me not to remember things. It has to be.

Besides, my father has never given me a reason not to trust him. Ever.

"Remember when you were flying out, and you mentioned that he'd help you settle in?"

I think on it. It was a stressful time. Maybe I did say that in mere hopes. Maybe. My dad isn't a liar, so it must be the truth.

"Oh, that's right," I lie.

"Anyhow, it's going well out here. The security team has a few leads on who's been sending the threats, so I'll let you know when I know something, Bryce."

"Okay."

"Love you."

"Love you, too, Dad."

I hang up and stare at Ethan.

My dad is in politics.

His security knows everyone we interact with.

Since we were kids.

But, if that's the case, why didn't he just say that?

When I look at Ethan, I forget about what transpired with my father and my brother. I see the medal hanging from his neck, and I laugh.

He smiles. "What? This?"

He takes the medal in his hand. Then, he looks at Milton Murdock's medal hanging from my neck.

We both laugh.

I forgot I still had the thing on.

"At least yours has the right name." I laugh through my words.

He moves closer, pulling me to him. "I can't believe Bryce Hayes beat Milton Murdock."

Eighteen

Ethan

When I can sleep, I do. Taking every last minute of it if I can. Sleep has been a rare commodity, a luxury, since coming home and transitioning to civilian life. But it's the incessant ringing in my ears that makes me think real life is calling.

I grab my phone from my nightstand. "Hello?" I say, my eyes adjusting to the darkness.

"Ethan? It's Maria, Robby's mother. I'm so sorry to call you this early."

It's still dark out. *What time is it?* "It's fine, Mrs. Rodriguez. Is Robby okay?"

Please no. Words I've patiently waited to hear. Predicted I'd hear.

"Ethan, it is not good. Robby tried to kill himself last night. The hospital contacted me." There's no shake in her voice. No mistake in her words.

Hispanic women—wives and mothers, sisters, nieces of the military—somehow, God made them better. He built them a bit differently to withstand heartbreak—with more strength in their hearts and in their bones.

I don't say anything. I'm not sure I can. I want to ask if he's all right, if he pulled through, but I'm too scared to know the answer. My stomach grows nauseous.

"He's alive. There is swelling on his brain," she says, "so the doctors are keeping him sedated."

Another long silence.

"I just thought I should call you and tell you since you and Robby were so close in the Marines."

"Should I come out?"

"No."

"Really, Mrs. Rodriguez, I'm on vacation from the warden service. It won't be an issue."

A long pause.

"Then, maybe."

Another long pause, as if she's waiting for the tears to pass. Holds them back. In many of our long conversations about life, about Robby, with Robby, for Robby, I've never once seen Mrs. Rodriguez shed a tear—and not out of lack of love, but because she is the strength in the family. Helped take her husband to his final resting spot when Robby was a boy. Raised four kids on her own. Walks to work as a maid at one of the motels close to where she lives, where Robby grew up. Robby talked about his mom often when we were overseas. Admired her strength.

Massachusetts is where Robby and his family are from.

"I'll take the train," I say. "I'll be there soon."

"That will be fine, Ethan. Good-bye, Ethan."

"Good-bye, Maria."

It's six in the morning, and my mind wonders how Robby's ex-wife and daughter are doing. *Do they know yet?* I didn't think to ask Maria.

This makes me think of Bryce. *This is why, Bryce. This is why we can't be together.* The war fucked us up. Made us different people.

My voice of reason chimes in, *You've never tried to kill yourself, Ethan. You've drunk yourself into oblivion, yes, but never tried to take your own life.*

I think that's why I've stuck so closely to James.

I think about my mom and dad, too. Aaron. What would happen if I decided that life was just too much? To end it all? I couldn't do it. Couldn't be the cause of their heartbreak. Although pieces of me died, left overseas on the sands that took my sanity.

My family didn't choose me. They're stuck with me. But Bryce has a choice.

I debate on calling James and leaving a voice mail on his work phone. I should. Just to let him know what's going on. But what's he going to do to help the situation?

"Yeah, James, it's Ethan. Robby tried to, uh … take his life. That's all I know. Going to Brookline on the nine o'clock train this morning. Just thought I'd let you know. I'll reach out when I get back." I've talked many times about Robby. Mostly the good times. Some of the bad. Some of the real bad.

I jump in the shower to try to wash off the news, the feelings it brings, but it sticks with me like a bad habit. After the shower, I get dressed, pack a bag, lock up the house. *Shit.* I don't want to pay parking at the train station. Maybe I'll have Bryce drop me off at the train station, and she can use my truck while I'm gone since she doesn't have a car here.

Fuck. I didn't get her number. She has mine. But I didn't get hers. I glance at the clock—*7:05.* She's probably awake. I drive down to Magnolia Road.

You could go in, Ethan. You have a key, I tell myself as I wait outside in my truck. *You've done it before.*

I could make her coffee. *Just friends,* thinking about the way my hand fit into hers last night as we shook on our agreement. Our *just friends* agreement.

Would a friend stop by another friend's house at seven in the morning for a ride? Yes.

Would a friend stop by and make coffee this early? Questionable.

Would friends go as far as we did the other night? No.

Outside in my truck, I notice there's a small light on in the kitchen. Probably the one just above the stove. I put the truck in park and wait. If I'm going to make the nine o' clock, I've got to act soon.

You could drive your truck to Brookline, Ethan.

And deal with all the traffic? Fuck that shit.

Robby's mom's house is two blocks from the station. I can walk there and get a ride to the hospital. And it'll be better for Bryce. She'll have something to drive. Not that she needs a vehicle in Granite Harbor, but it will be nice to have the choice.

I get out of the truck, quietly shut my truck door, and walk to the front door. Three small knocks, not wanting to startle her, and I wait.

The door pulls open, and she's awake, coffee in hand. "Hey. You look like hell. Are you all right? Come in."

I walk past her and run my hand over my face. *Fuck, I forgot to shave.* That's when you know I've got my mind busy on other things. I follow her to the kitchen like a lost puppy dog.

She pours me some coffee and pushes it to me.

"Thank you."

"You're welcome. Are you going to explain why you're here so early and why you look like death?"

I barely smile, feeling the weight of Mrs. Rodriguez's words. "Robby tried to kill himself last night, and I'm headed to the hospital in Brookline," I say with no emotion.

What I like about Bryce is, she never overly concerns herself with things. She's methodical. Logical. And it isn't because she doesn't care; I know she does. But she also knows kind words won't change a fucking thing.

"What hospital?"

"Didn't ask."

"Who called?"

"His mom."

She nods. Puts her coffee cup to her lips. Thinks. "When are we leaving?"

I jerk my head up. "What?"

"When are we leaving?"

"I can't ask you to come with me, Bryce."

"You didn't. I'm telling you. I'm coming with you. When do we leave?"

"Bryce, that's not why I came here."

"Then, why did you come here, Ethan?"

"To see if you'd give me a ride to the train station. You can use my truck while I'm gone."

Bryce nods. "That's really nice of you." She's being sarcastic. "One of the things I've learned about being a friend is that you're there during the really shitty times, too." She pauses. "I could just say, *Let me know if you need anything,* or *Call me when you get there.* That's a part-time friend. A shallow friend. As much as you hate to admit it, Ethan, you don't want to do this alone, and I don't want to let you do it alone. But the truth is, you're scared to ask for help, especially from me, seeing as we've had sex, but I won't let you say no to this because good, long-lasting friendships don't survive on *let me know if you need anything*s and *call me when you get there*s. They survive on the really shitty times, too." She pauses. "So, what time do we leave?" she asks again, sipping her coffee.

"Train leaves at nine."

"Why don't we drive?"

"I hate city traffic."

"Well, the good thing for you is, I'm from Los Angeles where we take up residence in traffic on our daily commutes. I'll drive through the traffic."

This time, I take a drink of my coffee. The drive from Granite Harbor to Brookline is about three and a half hours. We'd have our own vehicle, which would be nice.

"Can you leave your work?" I ask.

"I can work from anywhere."

I nod. "This is good coffee."

"I know." She takes one last sip, turns, walks to the sink. Rinses her cup. Puts it in the dishwasher. "You finish your coffee, and I'll quickly go pack a bag."

What in the hell just happened? "Okay."

While she packs, I finish my coffee, rinse the coffeepot, take out the filter, and put it in the trash. Take out the trash. And, while I'm coming back around to the front, I notice an unfamiliar car parked outside—not in front of the Magnolia Road house, but off to the side and across the street. The hair on the back of my neck stands at attention. Why I notice this specific car, I have no idea. It's a black two-door. Tinted windows. I walk to the porch and watch the car, letting the driver know I see him. Or her. I mentally remember the Indiana license plate. For all we know though, it could be a tourist, a leaf peeper. Maybe someone visiting family.

I walk inside and lock the door. Bryce is at the counter, going through her wallet.

"Do you know the black two-door coupe outside?" I ask Bryce.

She looks up. "I don't think I noticed." She walks past me and peeks out the window. "Far off from Indiana, huh?" She looks back at me and then back to the window, pulling the curtains back just enough to see the car. "Never seen that car before."

I see the split-second pause before she says, "I have something I need to tell you, Ethan."

The rev of a car engine gets my attention. "Is that the black car?"

Bryce looks back out the window. "Yeah. It just left."

"We're going to stay here until I know the car is gone, and it's not watching the house." Something about this seems so off. "Tell me what?" I ask.

Nineteen

Bryce

You've opened the can of worms, Bryce. You need to tell him.
Perhaps it was my body's way of preserving itself by speaking those words. Preserving by trying to alleviate the worry, the fear, the constant looking over my shoulder, the stress that plays on my body.

But Ethan's phone begins to ring, interrupting us, and I'm not sure if it's fate deterring me from telling Ethan or truly an accident.

"Hello?" he says.

I look back out the window to be sure the car is gone. It is.

"Hi, Mrs. Rodriguez." Ethan looks back at me. He motions for a pen and paper.

I retrieve a pad and a pen from a drawer.

Thank you, he mouths as he takes down an address.

"Got it." Silence. "How's he doing?" Another pause. Waiting.

If Ethan is giving Robby this kind of dedication, his mother this kind of time, Robby has to be someone who is worth every minute.

You agreed to go with Ethan—no, you told Ethan you were going along with him to Brookline, Massachusetts.

As friends, I can be there for him. This is exactly what he needs. Maybe someone outside the box. An outsider who hasn't known him since birth. An outsider who doesn't know Ethan

Casey as he was before he went to war and came back a different man.

Be this for him, Bryce. And how dare you want to free your mind from worry when Ethan is going to be by his friend's side. Don't you dare unload your fears on him.

He hangs up.

"I assume Maria is Robby's mom?"

Ethan nods. Tears the piece of paper from the pad and shoves it in his back pocket.

"How is he doing?" I ask, grabbing the ends of my elbows, pinching at the skin.

When Alex lost Kyle, I watched her. Held her as she cried. Held her when she didn't cry. Was present for her. Though I've never lost anyone close to me. Not like that. So, watching Alex, I learned how to be a better friend. But Robby isn't dead yet. He's still alive.

He sighs. I see the frustration in his face, the way the stripes run across his forehead, creased, like a fan. The short lines from the corners of his eyes tell me more than he's giving me with words.

Friends don't touch each other. They don't reach out and touch in romantic ways. But they hug.

I pull him to me by way of his hand, and he moves toward me as if he needs this more than he thinks he does. I put my arms around his middle as my head falls to his chest, and I listen to his roaring heart. I push my ear as close as I can. He finally puts his arms down over my shoulders.

Thump.

Thump.

Thump.

Thump.

I can't tell him this will all be okay because I'm not sure it will. I can't tell him this will pass because it might not. It will linger. This hurt. It will stay awhile. It will come back on some days. Hurt more. I know this from watching my brother destroy his life. What did this to Robby was brought on by a heart that couldn't deal with what he had seen, what he'd had to do in times of war. It was a heart that just couldn't take the sadness, the wreckage. A heart and a head that couldn't agree upon what's right, what's wrong, and just plain coping with life. Ryker, too, did have a pure heart, but somehow, we lose ourselves. We lose sight of what's important.

Addiction can be a byproduct of circumstances. Addiction can be a byproduct of a pure heart. Addiction is a byproduct of heartache. Robby is the end result. We have two ways of living. One is with the addiction, feeding it, loving it, and hating it. Nurturing it by giving it what it needs. The second way of living is fighting for life. Admitting we need help. But some people have too much baggage to look back. Too much destruction. Too much self-hate that they continue to feed their addiction in hopes that what's left of their mind, their heart won't ache anymore.

When Ethan says, "You ready?" I realize he never answered my question.

But it doesn't matter. It doesn't matter if I know whether Robby is okay or not. I realize, for the first time in a long time, that I'm right where I'm supposed to be and what will be will be.

I don't want to pull away from his chest. I want to listen to his heart in hopes that it will tell me the stories that he's not ready to share with me. In hopes that, one day, it will beat differently—and not for me, but for him.

"Yes." I unlatch my hands from his back, and his arms leave my shoulders. I stare up at him.

"What?" he asks, nervous under my watchful eye.

I've been naked in front of this man, unclothed, exposed, and he's never once flinched under my gaze. But, right now, I see a piece of vulnerability somewhere in his eyes.

"I like the sound of your heart, Ethan. It's pure and strong. Don't ever forget that." And I say this not because I'm undeniably attracted to him. I say this because I want him to know his heart is true. I want him to believe what others say about him and not what his head tells him. I see the fear. That he'll turn out like Robby. "Everyone is different, Ethan. Every single one of us. Have faith in that."

He breaks eye contact with me, and I leave the room to collect my things.

Ethan's at the door, looking out onto the street.

"I wonder if people wonder."

I try to walk past him with my bag, but he takes it from my shoulder and follows me out to his truck.

"About what?"

"About my truck here at all hours of the night and morning."

"Why would anyone care?" I open the truck door as Ethan sets my bag down in the bed of the truck.

"City girl." He gives me a half-smile as he walks over to his side of the truck, and we climb in.

"Who cares what people think, Ethan? We're two friends who might have had good times together, but more importantly, we're friends first, doing what friends do for each other."

He laughs. "I don't care what they think, Bryce. I don't care if they know we've fucked."

For the first time, I notice how neat it is. Something I didn't notice about his house—not that it wasn't. I just didn't look around to take notice. Maybe because it was dark. Maybe because I was more focused on Ethan without a shirt on. "Is your truck always this neat?"

"Organized? Yes." He flips on his blinker.

"Your house, too?"

"Guess so."

"Why?"

He smiles again. This time, he looks at me. "Do you not like organization, Bryce?"

"No, I appreciate organization." I look in the back seat to see a cluster of bungee cords, color-coded and put neatly into a side compartment. "What if someone took those bungee cords and rearranged them?"

"Nobody ever has."

"Well, I guess I have some work to do." I smile and place my hands in my lap. I sit back, listening to the low hum of the tires against the road.

Maine is beautiful in the fall. There's representation of bright yellows, deep reds, shades of orange, and every variation of these primary colors. It's an overcast day in Granite Harbor, and I watch as the sea follows us out of town, wishing us well.

Ethan has one hand on the wheel. His gigantic watch sits on his left wrist. What is it with game wardens and big watches? Eli, Ryan, Ethan, and Aaron all have these watches that can probably cook dinner, fold out into some sort of rescue floatation device, and answer all questions that Google can.

"Do you miss work?" I ask.

"I do. Had too much overtime, and they basically tell you, use it or lose it. Guess it gives me more time to get other stuff done."

"Like what?"

"Work on the house. Fix some fence. Help my dad on a few projects. Fish a little." His sunglasses fit his face just perfectly. They curve with the slight bump of his cheeks.

Ethan's jaw is tense, and I know he's worried about his friend, so I'm going to ask him another question, but before I can, he asks me one, "So, you're a literary agent. What does that mean exactly?"

"How did you know my exact title? Not everybody knows the words *literary agent*."

"Google is a very powerful tool." His face is still stoic.

"Basically, I'm the middleman between the author and the publishing houses. I sell books in a sense. Authors pitch their stories to me, and I'll bite off on the ones I think I can sell to the publishers."

"So, you read a lot."

"I do."

It's quiet for a bit. I take in the scenery, the ocean, the changing colors, and the lies I tell myself. *This isn't awkward at all. The only reason you came along is to help out a friend. You're not in love with Ethan Casey.*

"What's your favorite color?" I ask.

Ethan's lean face and long jawline make every muscle in my body want to reach out and touch him—not because of desire, but because I want to know what he feels like under my touch when his face is this still. When he thinks. What his strain after life gets to be too much feels like under my fingertips. I want to feel his heartbeat against my own chest again to see if we match beat for beat, and if we don't, I'd rather it be that way because different is more important than the same.

"Blue."

"Why?" I respond all too quickly. Nerves getting the best of me.

Again, he's quiet. "It was the name of the dog I had, growing up. An Australian shepherd named Blue."

I expected him to say something like, *I had a blue truck that ran forever*, or, *Blue is one of the colors on the American flag.*

"I like that name."

We pass another body of water surrounded by red maples and sugar maples. The vibrancy of the colors almost takes my breath away.

In Los Angeles, we don't have trees. Well, we do, but it's not often that we see them. We don't have the beauty, the home that Maine has. It's as if we were built on an escalator, constantly moving from point A to point B. In the scuffle of life, we don't slow down, for fear of not meeting a goal, a deadline. Life here is much simpler, much slower-paced. And more beautiful than I've ever seen. I didn't realize I needed simplicity in my life.

"Are you scared to see Robby?" I whisper, feeling the weight of my own fears. Fears that didn't generate from the present moment, but fears that had generated when I first saw my brother strapped down to a hospital bed.

I look at Ethan as he tries to find the answer he's looking for.

"More scared for his family," he says and then coughs to clear his throat. He doesn't like sharing this with me. The vulnerability of it all because he does the shoulder-pull-back move. Like he's got to stretch, so he pulls it back in a circle only once.

That was an honest answer. I wish my family had had an Ethan looking out for them when Ryker overdosed. Especially the third time. How your brother—a once charismatic, fun-loving, smiling, well-raised boy—could turn into a pile of ninety eight pounds with open wounds on his face from incessant scratching, worry, and paranoia, only proves addiction doesn't care who its takers are. How a young man in his freshman year of high school, who had plans to graduate from high school early and be a doctor, allowed the poison to eat through his veins, turning him into the devil, I wish Ryker would have chosen to walk away instead of taking his first hit.

Ethan

S cared.

Scared is the way I felt when we made our push into Fallujah, Iraq, in the dead of night, waiting for the underbelly of our Humvee to explode.

Scared is the way I felt when Blue was hit by the car.

Scared is the way I felt when I first made the call to James's office, when I knew I couldn't fight this war inside my head alone.

Scared is the way I felt the morning I left Bryce wrapped up in her own sheets, terrified I'd never see her again but even more terrified of what I'd do to her if I stayed.

But these doesn't compare to this moment right here—petrified that I'm falling in love with Bryce Hayes and I can't stop.

"Listen, Ethan, if we're going to be friends, there are some things I need to know about you." She pauses. "Ten yes or no questions. Are you ready?"

"You're up first."

Bryce clasps her hands together. "Are you a late-night snacker?"

"No."

"I totally took you as a late-night snacker." She shakes her head. "I mean, don't get me wrong; you're definitely in shape—

everywhere—and your endurance is unmatched, but I just thought you'd slip an Oreo in after nine o' clock."

I want to laugh, but I don't. Maybe because I just want her to continue to make that face, one of surprise.

The road begins to narrow, going from two lanes to one. I adjust my hands on the wheel. "Have you ever cheated while playing a game?"

"Come on, everyone has."

I shake my head. "Yes or no answer, Hayes, I don't need an explanation."

Bryce rolls her eyes in a joking fashion. "Yes."

If I took a dollar for every time I cheated my way out of checkers with my brother, I'd have an IOU with interest to pay back to the Checker Cheaters of America. But I don't tell Bryce this. I let her fester in her own moral dilemma.

She smiles. "Have you ever cheated on a test?"

"No."

Bryce rolls her eyes again. "Are you kidding? Next, you're going to tell me that you're really Jesus Christ. Seriously, haven't you ever done anything immoral?"

"I slept with a married woman."

Her mouth falls open. "You did not."

"You're right; I didn't. But it came pretty damn close."

It's as if her mind is catching up with the momentum of the conversation. "You kissed a married woman."

"I didn't know she was married. Not until, well, much later."

Bryce turns her head and stares at the road. She opens her mouth to speak. Closes it. Opens it again. "Sure beats my cheating at Monopoly."

"Have you ever dated someone more than once?" I ask.

"No."

"Same question," she says. "Wait, let me guess … the married woman?"

"No."

"Do you have regrets?" she whispers out of turn. Her lips almost pressed against the window.

"Yes. Same question."

"Yes." The tires glide now across the road. "Have you ever slept naked with more than person?"

"No. Just you."

Bryce uncomfortably adjusts herself in the seat, the corners of her mouth pulled down. "I'm sorry. Friends don't ask friends those questions."

I reach over and put my hand on her thigh before I realize what I'm doing. *This is a bad idea, Ethan. She asked for friendship.* But something in me knows she needs my touch. I want to say, *Friends don't touch each other like the way we've touched each other,* but I don't. There's nothing said about it.

What I would give right now to be in a bed, it doesn't matter where, in the sheets with her, my skin pressed against hers. Her breath against my mouth. Her thirsty cry for me. The way her eyes close just before she climaxes with me inside her.

I push the selfish thought away as she asks another question with my hand still on her leg.

"What's better—"

But we're interrupted because her phone begins to ring.

I watch her shoulders rise as she looks at the screen.

"It's my mother."

"Take it."

"I don't want to."

"Why?"

"You don't know my mother."

"I know you, and if you don't take it, you'll feel bad as soon as you hit the Ignore button."

Bryce pulls back her lip in a snarl. "You think you've got me dialed in, don't you, Mr. Casey?"

"No, actually, I don't."

She gives me the evil eye. "Hey, Mom," she answers, sticking her tongue out at me. "No, I fell off the face of the planet, but thankfully, I was returned by the Millennium Falcon just yesterday. I was getting ready to call you and tell you about my amazing trip around the sun." She's quiet for a minute. "It was a joke, Mom. Mom, stop. Stop. It was a joke." Again, silence. "Ryker's always MIA. Nothing new to my ears." She rolls her eyes and stares at the ceiling of the truck. "Wait. What? You had him at the house? What did Dad say?" Listens. "If you continue to save him—give him a clean bed to sleep in, food, a warm shower—why the hell would he want to get sober? He has the best of both worlds."

There's a tightness to Bryce's voice. One I've heard directed at me. Rightfully deserved. When she came to Maine to visit Alex and all I gave her was a nod. Which is probably the path I should have continued on.

"Mom, look, I don't want to hear about Ryker. Don't call me if that's all you want to talk about. When's the last time you asked me how I was doing? I'm the one who made the right decisions. I'm the one who finished college, graduated top of my class. I'm the one who closes multimillion-dollar book contracts."

This isn't the Bryce I know. This is the Bryce whose emotion has taken the best of her. I want to tell her to hang up the phone because I'm protective of her heart. But I can't. This isn't my battle to fight.

"I have to go, Mom. Millennium Falcon is beckoning me back."

I laugh out loud. Bryce shoots a look my way and smiles.

Bryce hangs up and shoves her phone in her bag, crosses her arms, stares me down. "Happy now?"

"You're right; you probably shouldn't have taken the call." I smile again.

She does, too, but the smile she gives isn't her best. Her most genuine. That smile, the genuine one, sat just before the phone call.

I think about the questions James has asked me in the past. Stupid, sometimes philosophical questions that have no bearing on my mental stability, but when he asks them, I always answer them.

"What makes you happy?"

Bryce is biting her lip. Stops. Turns her head to me. "I thought these were yes or no questions."

"What makes me happy," I start. "The woods at sunrise on an early morning hunt. A cold beer after a long, hot day. My job. A warm bed. And Cheetos."

Bryce laughs. "Cheetos?"

"Yeah." I adjust my hand on the wheel. "They don't have Cheetos overseas. Can you believe it? They have every kind of chip, except Cheetos. I guess I take that back. They do have some sort of cheese-puff chips, but they're awful. Your turn."

"Oh, let's see. The adrenaline rush I get when I sign an author. A hot bath. Watching puppies play on my Facebook feed. A hard workout—but only afterward. The rain."

Her last answer catches me off guard. "The rain?"

"I love it. That's probably why I paid Alex so many visits in Belle's Hollow. Do you know it rains there eighty percent of the time?"

"But you're in Los Angeles, California. They shut down that big freeway you all have after heavy dew, don't they?" I'm being sarcastic, and she knows it. "Do you like it in LA?"

"I guess I've stayed because it's the only place I know. It's my comfort zone. It's convenient. My family's there—albeit dysfunctional, but nonetheless my family." She pauses. "What was it like, growing up in Granite Harbor with a great family?"

I sigh. "No family is perfect." And I don't really answer her question because it's hard to remember those days. James says it's because of the PTSD. I'd like to blame it on something, but sometimes, I think it's an easy out. To blame PTSD for everything. I give her some of my truth. "I don't remember a lot. I have feelings that are associated with my childhood, which are good. It's just tough to remember what feelings are associated with what events."

Low hum of the tires.

"Why do you think that is?"

I give her another honest answer. "Sometimes, it feels like there's a freight train running through my head. Sometimes, it's loud, and I can't focus or hear anything but the train. Same with my memories. Sometimes, the train is just too loud." I pause. "I haven't shared that with anyone." Besides James. And I'm not ready to bring James up yet.

"Does the train ever stop?" She's staring at me.

"Yeah." *When I'm with you.*

"When?"

"During the important times."

"Do you have any memories at all of your childhood?"

"Sure. Just some are a lot hazier than others."

"Can you share one with me?"

I think about it. Not whether to share it or not, but if I have a good grasp on one.

"Aaron and I were about eight or nine at the time. We'd been downtown at Ring's Pharmacy, buying our weekly candy supply. We just paid Rick for it, and we were leaving when Irene Mathers walks in, pulling her husband, David Mathers, behind her. He ranted on and on, 'I'm sorry, Irene. I'm sorry.' Anyhow, she marched up to the counter, passing Aaron and me, and says to Rick, 'You need to give my husband something for his pornography addiction. It's the seventh time I've caught him this week, Rick. You've got to give him something."

Bryce starts to laugh.

"Aaron and I had no idea what the word *pornography* meant, so we ended up pulling out the dictionary and finding the definition. We laughed and ate candy and never looked at the Mathers family the same."

"Oh my goodness! Are they still married?" Her mouth is open, and her genuine smile is coming back.

"To this day." I nod. "I highly doubt Irene remembers seeing us that day because she was so mad." I laugh. I can do this with Bryce so effortlessly now, I realize.

Bryce stares out the window. "My brother called me six months ago. He'd been in his addiction for several years, and I almost wrote him off, ignored the call. But something told me I had to pick it up, so I did. He said he needed some food. But, for some reason, his voice was different with that call. He gave me the address of where he was. Didn't ask for anything specific—just food.

"I went to the grocery store and purchased four bags of groceries. I took them to the address he had given me. The sun was getting ready to set, about dinnertime. Ryker emerged from this bush, alone. I know that my brother loves me, and he'd never put me in an unsafe situation, no matter how bad it got. I handed him the bags of groceries, and he said, 'Thank you.' But it was the look in his eye that said so much more. It was like … it was like I had seen the old Ryker just for a split second. The grateful one. The unaddicted one.

"Anyhow, I got back into my car and shut the door, my keys in my hand, ready to start the car. Ryker though just stood there. Watched me. Contemplated maybe. I'm not sure. Then again, maybe he was waiting for me to leave. I started the car, and he started to walk back to the bushes, the way he had come. But before he made it, a little boy, no older than twelve, emerged. This time, Ryker didn't look back at me. Instead, he handed the boy some fruit and bread from the bags of groceries. Then, a woman emerged. Both didn't look homeless. They looked tired. The woman looked as though she'd been beaten down both physically and mentally. The boy just looked terrified." She pauses, maybe to keep her composure. Coughs to shake off the tears that might begin to fall.

"I drove away that night. Allowed my brother to be himself. Addicted or not, I knew he was helping the woman and her son. That my brother didn't cause the terror on the boy's face or the weakness in the woman—that had been someone else's doing. So, when I got home that night, I turned on the news and plastered across the screen was the woman's beautiful smile and the boy's sheepish grin with a man I'd seen before.

"Luke O'Connor is an up-and-comer, groomed for the political world. Luke's father and our father are friends. Luke is cocky and thrives off his father's wealth. On the outside, Luke has a smile that can negotiate a deal without a word spoken, and he has everything going for him. But, on the inside, he's far more sinister, far darker, and extremely smart.

"Ryker and I don't know Luke really well. On occasion, we'd be stuck at the same political function and have to endure him. He was tolerable. His ego would fill the room. So, we stood clear of Luke. As we got older, Luke began to bring women to events. But, when he brought Sandra, his fiancée, the look in her eyes told me, something wasn't right about Luke.

"It was reported that the wife, Sandra O' Connor, and son, Landon O'Connor, had gone missing in the early morning hours. That the husband, Luke O'Connor, was worried sick and prayed for their safe return. The problem was, he probably wasn't praying. And that Sandra and Landon were safe—away from him.

"I drove back to the address my brother had given me the day before. I brought clothes, toothbrushes, toothpaste, bottles of water, a prepaid phone just for emergencies, deodorant, sunglasses. I knew my brother needed my help. We had to keep them in hiding. Because that's what they were doing. They weren't kidnapped; they were trying to stay hidden." She stares out the window, never looking once at me. "Just outside of Los Angeles, there's a bus station that I'd found online the night before. It took an hour and four minutes to get there. I gave them cash and took Sandra's credit cards because she said she didn't want to feel compelled to use them during desperate times. It was when she quickly thanked Ryker and kissed the top of her son's head that I knew we'd done the right thing. I'm not sure why she was running, but I had a gut feeling the terror she and her son had lived every single day was what kept her going as far away from Los Angeles as she could."

"Have you heard from her?" I ask.

"No," she sighs. "Which brings me to why I told you this story." Bryce pauses. "Someone knows about what Ryker and I did, and he's not happy."

Twenty-One

Bryce

"We've received threats to our family. Nobody knows why, except Ryker and me. That's the way we'll keep it. We can't tell a soul where we put Sandra and Landon. Luke has too many links to law enforcement. Surely, they'll believe his charismatic smile, his charm—just as Sandra bought it on the day they met. And the reason no one knows where they are is because, if we talk, Sandra and Landon are as good as dead—or going back to the hell they lived in for years." I pause again. "The reason the black car ran us, your family, off the road is probably because of me. The car out front this morning? Probably because of me. I know I'm being watched. But there's no way Luke will make a move to where it's traceable. God forbid, he ruin his perfect reputation. I'm really sorry I didn't say something sooner, Ethan, especially after putting your family at risk like that."

Finally, I look at Ethan. His shoulders are tense, his jaw tight. He doesn't say a word.

I see a mileage sign—*Brookline ... 72 miles.*

"Are you mad?" I ask.

Ethan pulls his lip back and looks at me. "Why would I be mad, Bryce?" His tone is short.

"I put your family at risk. I didn't tell you."

"Did you drive the black sedan that ran us off the road?"

"No."

"I didn't think so."

I sigh. "There's more. I received a text message a few days ago. Somehow, he's gotten my phone number, which doesn't surprise me. I've tried to brush it off. Tried to reach out to Ryker, but he's pretty good at staying hidden. Sometimes, I think he stays loaded more than usual, so the fear doesn't come." I wonder, too, if he can gain enough clarity to realize the severity of the situation. I don't say this out loud.

Ethan nods.

My insides cringe. Turn to knots. "Please say something. Your body language is killing me."

Ethan's eyes dart to me.

"It's that obvious," I say.

He pulls his shoulder back again—a sign of nervousness— adjusts back into his seat, one large hand on the wheel, the other in his lap. "I-I'm angry."

"Look, I'm sorry."

Ethan reaches over and puts his free hand on my thigh.

Just friends, I remind myself.

"Not at you. At this situation. And this douche bag who thinks he can intimidate people. Hurt women. His child." Ethan shakes his head and stares out his window and then back to the road. "You and Ryker did everything right."

No, no, we didn't. Right to whose standards? My moral compass? Yes. The Ten Commandments? No. But what I do to rationalize my own behavior is tell myself that we aren't Catholic and the Ten Commandments only apply to Catholics.

What I don't tell Ethan is that Ryker and I lied to police. LAPD asked Luke's colleagues and their families if we knew anything about the missing persons, if we'd seen them. We told them no. And I don't tell Ethan this because I don't want him caught up in the shitstorm. I don't want police to get him. I don't want him to lose his job for some sort of conspiring charge. I'll tell the truth when I need to. But, for now, it will be a well-kept secret until I know Sandra and Landon are safe forever.

"Sandra and Landon are still safe?"

"As far as I know. I think there would have been a media storm if they'd been discovered." I don't say what knocks around in the back of my brain. *What if they were found and their bodies were hidden?* Because I wouldn't put it past Luke to kill and hide. Or have someone else do it. Pay them tons of money to do so. Luke comes from wealth; it's not something he's worked for. My brain starts to run. I should call Sandra. Just make sure they're all right. "I should call Sandra."

"Wouldn't be an awful idea." Ethan shrugs.

I'm not sure why I didn't think of this. Maybe the happy-ending woman wanted it to be just that. Sandra and Landon living in a quiet cottage off the coast of Florida or South Carolina, finally living a normal life after years of suffering.

Ethan sighs. "I guess this totally blows my Mathers porn story out of the park."

I give a half-laugh as Ethan pulls into a motel parking lot.

"Figured we could stay here for a few nights. I'll text Maria and let her know we'll be to her house in an hour."

A long line of motel rooms line up in a U-shape, and the parking is bare.

We both get out of the truck with our bags and walk into the lobby.

Ethan opens the door for me, his overnight bag over his shoulder. "After you."

"Thank you."

The doorbell rings as we enter.

"Brookline doesn't have much to choose from, so I thought this one would do."

We both look around the small lobby. A short, stuffy man with a bigger personality than life comes through the back door. It smells of old things and pot roast. Being that it's almost winter time, I assume many working families do a lot of Crock-Pot meals, and I also assume this man is a father and a husband with a side of the creep factor. Balding with a comb-over to suffice for the lack of hair, short and pudgy fingers, he pushes his strands of hair to the side.

"Folks, welcome to Garden Inn. Do you have a reservation?" the man says in a strong Massachusetts accent.

Ethan takes the lead. "We don't actually. Do you have any rooms available?"

I take in Ethan's scent as I stand close behind him—not purposely, but when he stepped forward to speak with the man behind the counter, he brushed against me, and I stayed put.

Staring at his back in his gray T-shirt, I try my best to breathe.

"Hmm. The only thing I have is a non-smoking room with a king bed," the man behind the counter says. Blinks. Stares from behind his thick glasses.

Non-smoking. That's weird. And I think back to a time when it was acceptable to smoke in restaurants, motel lobbies, airports.

I lean into Ethan and whisper, "We're friends now. Friends can share a room, right?"

"We'll take the room." Ethan gives him his credit card, and they exchange awkward words.

The man makes an odd humming sound as he waits for the credit card to process. It's between a whistle and a hum. The tune is familiar, but I can't put my finger on it. Maybe a scary movie. It makes the hairs on my neck stand at attention.

Quickly, once the exchange is complete, Ethan grabs an actual room key—not a card, a room key—and we set out to find room fourteen.

"It's the last room on the right," the man calls out behind us before the door shuts and hisses.

"Was that creepy?" I ask Ethan once we're out of earshot.

"He's harmless."

"How do you know he's not some sort of serial killer, and this isn't the new Bates Motel?"

Ethan laughs. "Are you sure you're a literary agent and not a writer?"

We reach our room. Ethan slides the key in the door and gives it a jiggle, and the door opens.

"I'll go in first, just in case there's a killer inside." Ethan looks at me, smiles.

"It's a good thing it's daylight, Ethan, or you'd better believe you'd be carrying my ass in this room right now."

We're both quiet. We don't say what we're thinking.

"Friends carry friends," I say to clear up the sexual tension before we enter the room. My breathing becomes labored.

In the room, we set down our bags.

"It's nice."

"It needs updating," Ethan says, setting down his bag and sitting on the edge of our bed.

Our bed.

He pulls out his phone. "Texting Maria."

I nod, sitting down next to him.

Breathe, Bryce.

The outside of our thighs touch. I run my hands along my jeans to clear away the sweat. The nerves. The residual effects of what Ethan Casey does to me.

I grab my phone from my purse and text Alex.

> *Me: So, Ethan and I are in Brookline, Massachusetts. I'll explain later. Just wanted to let you know in case we don't come home.*

> *Alex: What?*

> *Me: Staying at the Bates Motel. Only it's called the Garden Inn. :) Norman checked us in—though he looks a bit different.*

> *Alex: Your jokes are dumb. They aren't funny, just so you know.*

> *Me: Kidding. It was his mother, Norma. LOL!*

> *Alex: I hate you right now.*

> *Me: Kidding again. All is well. Fill you in when we get home. Ethan had to take care of a few things, and I decided to come along.*

> *Alex: Don't do anything I wouldn't do.*

> *Me: Trust me, Alex the Nun, I won't.*

> *Alex: Sigh. So not funny.*

> *Me: Love you.*

> *Alex: Love you, too. Call me later.*

I set my phone down and look at Ethan's screen. "Has she responded?"

"Not yet. Are you hungry?" he asks as I stand, looking up at me with his dark brown eyes.

"I can always eat. Are you?"

He shakes his head. "No, not really."

"Nerves?"

"No, I'm good."

"Liar. Do you know it isn't good to lie to your friends?"

"Scout's honor."

"Were you even a Boy Scout, Ethan?"

"I was."

He stands as his phone dings, our bodies into the dating space and not the friend space. A space I'm not willing to step back out of because I like the proximity of his body to mine. I like the fact that I can reach out and touch his stomach if I need to. What I don't like are the feelings associated with the touch, the ones that make my thoughts spin and my heart twist.

Ethan breaks eye contact with me and looks down at his phone, the saving grace that's now become the buffer between our bodies and our humanly needs. "She's with Robby at Brookline Hospital. We'll meet her there."

When he speaks these words, things change with our bodies, and between us, it becomes need-based. Meaning, I think he needs me just as I need him. The sexual tension from us is gone, and maybe it's more that he needs me to be there for his heart. I can also do that. Though these words aren't spoken, as if he's opened up the circle of trust, ever so cautiously, I want to be there when the pieces fall.

"Let's go."

Ethan locks the door behind us with the room key.

We ride in silence as his phone plays out the directions to the hospital.

"Arriving at Brookline Hospital," his phone says.

We get out of the truck, and when we meet at the front of the truck, feeling his tension, I stop him from walking into the hospital. I take my hand and put it to his chest. I don't ask him if he's nervous; I feel it. I also don't ask if this is okay—me touching him in this way; instead, I quietly slip my hand into his, and we walk into Brookline Hospital. There are no words that will take his fear. No words that will allow his heart to rest peacefully. Sometimes, we just have to feel through all the shit.

Ethan looks down at his phone in his free hand. "Room 424," he says.

We study the sign ahead that tells families and friends which direction to go—surgical unit, intensive care unit, patient rooms, MRI center.

Floor four is the last stop at the top. My hand in his tightens, trying to will the fear away. It takes forever to reach room 424. Before we enter his room, my stomach is in knots, but I don't let myself hesitate, for his sake.

There's a drawn drape that doesn't allow us to see Robby when we first walk in. Maria is sitting at his bedside, knitting.

"Oh, Ethan. I'm so glad you are here." Maria stands from her chair. Her smooth black-and-gray hair is tight in a bun. A small, simple gold cross hangs from her neck.

Ethan reaches out to hug Maria, and I gently pull my hand from his, smiling at her.

"Maria, this is my friend Bryce."

She takes my hands in hers. "It is so nice to meet you, Bryce." Maria's hands are warm, soft. "Ethan did not tell me he had a girlfriend."

Neither of us speaks to correct her. That we've had sex. That he's taken my body places in the dark and in the light that only warm my heart. I came along, so he wouldn't have to do this alone, as a friend, and if I'm being honest, so I could be with him.

"It's really nice to finally meet you, Maria. Ethan has spoken highly of you and Robby."

When Robby's name passes my lips, Maria's demeanor changes. Remorse? Guilt? Sadness, yes.

She leads us to his bedside, and we're not prepared for what we see.

I haven't seen Robby in person or in pictures. I've only been told stories. So, it doesn't completely catch me off guard when I see the head wrapping, the swollen eyes, the tubes going in and out of his body. His pale complexion. Immediately, I put my hand into Ethan's. But there's no outwardly reaction from Ethan when he sees Robby in this state. I know it's because of Maria. I know it's because of his military training; he's seen a lot worse. This is a snapshot of a life potentially saved. A healing body—not one in the field that's been left dead. Not one without arms or legs. Not a friend blown to pieces.

"How's he doing?" he asks Maria.

Maria is silent. She looks at Ethan and to me and then to her son. "Robby had just come home from seeing Madalyn." Maria looks at me. "His daughter. He had been over the moon about seeing her. It had been a while since he saw her last. I'm not sure what happened, but something did. Because, when I went to his room to tell him dinner was ready ..." There's an extremely long pause.

I want to reach out and touch Maria's shoulder to console her shattered heart..

Broken and put back together.

Broken and put back together.

Broken and put back together.

Broken.

Broken.

Broken.

Put back together.

Broken.

Again.

I know what that feeling is like.

"I found him, and there was a lot of blood." And that's all she says.

It is amazing what a mother endures when she has children. Maria is still here, by her son's side. Through his addiction, through loss of his own family, attempted suicide, she still stands. It makes me think of my mother's love for Ryker.

Ethan gently lets go of my hand and walks to Robby's side. The one he's stood next to during times I'm sure they'd rather have both died from than fought.

"Hey, Rodriguez," he whispers, trying to sit next to him, unsure of where to sit with all the tubes. He finds a spot. "You've done yourself in good, soldier."

I excuse myself from the room, so Ethan can have his time. Maria follows me.

Although it's midday, it feels like this day has lasted an eternity.

My eyes meet the cheap overhead lights in the sterile hallway. I rest my backside on the railing that lines the wall.

Maria does the same.

We stand here in silence. The lights flicker, giving us a much-needed distraction. It's past noon, but from the way the hospital feels, looks, the light, it seems more like the early morning hours,

156

before the rooster takes its perch or late at night. There isn't a busy nurses' station or traffic from family members paying visits to their loved ones.

The hospital is desolate, like this moment. I look at Maria and want to ask her if she's all right, if there's anything I can do, but I know what she's feeling. The answer will be no. The answer will always be no—unless you have a cure for addiction. Then, yes, please, come in and give him the medication, the treatment he'll need to survive this disaster, the tornado of wreckage he's created.

Please.

I speak, "One thing, I am tired of feeling was alone. A disease that wraps itself around happy families, disguises itself with casualness, with fun. Like a snake, it slithers quietly, sometimes unnoticed. Our family only wants to see the good and give well-thought excuses as to why they do what they do." I pause for a moment and stare at my feet. "It's the only disease that will tell your person, your family member, they don't have it. That their solution is to use. And then? The miracle happens; the solution stops working. Your family member can't get the high that they need to numb themselves. They will want an end. They'll want an end to the chaos they've created because they'll begin to see the wreckage they've caused. They'll try to numb again, and it won't work. Again and again and again, they'll try.

"Then, the jumping-off place—where Robby was or is. He'll want to die because he can't see his life as a good one. He'll see it for the train wreck he's become. He won't see the good in himself, just the war he's fought to get to where he is today. Life on life's terms seems too much." I pause again, only for a second or two, to pray that the right words keep coming.

"I feel bad. I wish my brother would just die. It would make his life easier. He'll have been out of pain, anguish. I feel like an awful sister for thinking that. My mom keeps making him sicker. Enabling him. Picking up the pieces when he falls. Giving him warm food, a bed, a shower. He needs to reach a bottom, and she isn't allowing him to reach it. Still. To this day. My brother uses on a daily basis. And, every time he calls, she's there to help," I sigh and stare up at the overhead light. "I don't know if any of this makes sense, Maria, and I'm not sure why this information is coming from me, but I guess it's information that I wish had been given to me early on in Ryker's disease." I nod.

"Where did you learn all this?" A single tear falls from her eye.

"Al-Anon. It's a program for family members who have addicts and alcoholics in their lives."

I see the anguish in her eyes. The worry, the hurt, the sadness. I'm not a mother yet, so I can only imagine what this feels like for her and my own mother. For some reason, I'm able to give compassion, empathy to Maria. Why can't I give it to Trudy Hayes?

"My heart is so sad. I try to put out a brave front, but it just keeps getting harder. I-I prayed Robby would find peace in whatever way he could." Another tear falls. "Even if he had to die." She bites her bottom lip, pulling at her gold cross, and closes her eyes.

Maria doesn't need an answer. She needs someone just to listen.

"In the beginning, after he came home from the war, I made everything for him. I did everything for him. I thought it was an easier way of helping him come back to life." She looks down at her cross. "Do you have kids, Bryce?"

"No."

Maria shakes her head. "It's a love I'd never known the strength of until the strength was put to the test. When my husband died. When Robby went to war and came home a different person. But, as a mother, you don't want to see things. You don't want to believe things. So, you tell yourself things like, *Maybe if I had just done this when Robby was little,* or, *If I had just been a better mother.* You try to blame yourself for his wrongdoings. Try to make sense of them. You still see the little boy, the toothless one, trying to figure out how to ride a bicycle." She toys with her fingers. "I feel responsible for his heartbreak. For his addiction." Her chocolate-colored eyes meet mine. "I created him. God gave him to me. Why can't I make him well?"

Tears start to well up in my eyes.

Don't you dare cry, Bryce. It's not your turn.

The sudden impact of what my mother has been going through with her own son hits me. My mother and Maria are both fighting the impossible.

"Your heart tells you one thing, and then your brain, even with reservation, follows the heart. Even if it's not the right choice. What feels good isn't the right decision," I say.

"Yes." Maria barely smiles. "I have faith that God has him. And, for whatever reason, I keep trying to interfere with that," she says, pulling on her cross again.

"Maybe," I whisper, "maybe faith wins."

Twenty-Two

Ethan

His mouth is barely open with a tube going down his throat. If Rodriguez could see himself right now, he'd be pissed. Mad that his mother has to see this. Mad at himself that he couldn't die right.

The one thing he's always cherished, before his daughter came along, is his mother. Talked about her. Told stories about his upbringing, proud of the hard-working woman she was.

Robby's face is so swollen; it doesn't resemble Robby at all.

We had to see this coming, I tell myself.

Toward the end, Robby lived recklessly. I'm not sure if he wanted to die, but I know living, for him, was much harder than most.

One of the machines he's hooked up to beeps.

One beep.

Two beeps.

Pause.

One beep.

Two beeps.

Stop.

I don't say anything, not sure if he can hear me or what my words might sound like in his head. But I think about our deployments.

We were moved from one area in Fallujah to another. It was our second deployment together. Off in the distance, we heard gunshots, which wasn't out of the norm. That was when Robby was starting to fade to black. He leaned back, and out of his fatigues, he pulled out a flask.

"What are you doing?" The M27 rifle—Lila, he called it—rested on his shoulder.

He took a long swig, watching me while seconds passed by. "Gettin' right." He screwed the lid back on.

We never drank and handled our weapons. I'd seen him drink hard outside the uniform, without the gun, in civilian clothes and wallet full of money. I'd even seen him get to the point of falling down but never this. This drew the line in the sand. It separated the heavy drinkers and the alcoholics. It separated the controlled drinkers and the uncontrollable drinkers. I wasn't sure Robby had a choice anymore—whether to drink or not to drink.

The shit we saw over there, we will never forget. Ever. Ingrained, imprinted on our minds like a tattoo amid the color of regret. Robby's best attempt at freedom was to drink it away. I must admit, from my own experience, the alcohol works for a while, and then it doesn't. The chaos gets louder. The desperation grows, and then you're stuck.

Another loud beep from one of the numerous machines sounds, and I'm brought back to the dark hospital room, alone with someone who resembles my friend Robby.

War. This—Robby—is what war looks like right now. Like a disease, it spreads, eating away at our unconscious mind in hopes that it will take us down to ashes.

I feel a hand on my back. The machine beeps again.

"The machine is beeping," I say to the hand on my back—or the human attached to the hand. It's hard for me to come back, to be coherent in the present moment.

The hand slides from my back and uses its fingers to coax my hand up, which is balled at my waist.

"It's okay," the voice says.

Slowly, my fist opens, and the hand gently slides in. The skin is soft in my palm.

The scent that surrounds me is familiar. It's a scent I associate with good feelings.

The beeping stops.

Thank God, the beeping stops.

The warm hand patiently sits in my palm.

"Ethan," the voice whispers, "we can go if you want. Maria went down the hall to check in with the doctor."

It's Bryce. She's here, and I associate the smell and her soft skin. It helps draw me back from the edge of nowhere.

My heart begins to pound—and not because of what she does to me, but because I'm not sure where I am or if this is all real.

"Bryce?" I whisper.

"Yeah?"

I don't respond. Maybe the question was to verify her identity since I haven't been able to take my eyes off Robby—or what represents Robby, which is a hollow shell of someone I used to know.

"Ethan?"

"Yeah?"

"Do you need some fresh air?"

"Yeah."

Bryce gently pulls at my arm, alarming my feet to move.

The white overhead lighting of the hospital hurts my eyes as we enter the hallway, as if the sun had risen too quickly.

Bryce keeps pace with my feet that move, though I'm not wiling them to; they're doing it on their own. I'm amazed at how well the human body works.

It walks.

Moves.

Breathes.

Pushes.

Stops.

Holds.

She takes me to the elevator and pushes the number one button. Soft instrumental music plays while we make our descent.

Her hand stays in mine.

I look down at her as she watches the light move to the number one position in the row of numbers. My heart beats against my chest as my breathing becomes shallower; it's harder to breathe.

My hand tightens around Bryce's hand. "Is that too tight?" I ask.

"No," she says, her eyes finally coming away from the lights.

163

The elevator doors open. She takes the lead, and I follow her out of the hospital to the fresh, cool air.

I suck in a big gulp of air, and my hands fall to my knees. I'm suddenly aware of the world around me.

Cars drive on the road out front.

I feel the drops of rain begin to beat against my face as I stand.

It's chilly, I think to myself as I suck in another mouthful of fresh air.

"Ethan?" Bryce asks.

What happened in there? I want to ask, but I don't want to scare Bryce. I like her a lot. I don't want anything to change between us, and yet I want everything to change.

I want to be the man who lifts her over the threshold of a new home.

I want to be the father of her children.

I want to be the man she's been looking for.

I want to be all that.

But something tells me I can't. She can't have a fractured man. She doesn't deserve a fractured man. She deserves someone who wakes up in the morning and doesn't have to deal with a closet full of demons. She deserves a man who is as good on the outside as he is on the inside. Solid. Well built.

"Yeah?" I say.

"Drink some water." She hands me a water bottle.

Bryce turns to me. Stares straight into me. Gently reaches up and holds my face in her hands. "Where'd you go?"

To a place I can't control. It's where I went after we made love for the first time in Los Angeles, I want to say but don't. *A place where time and space don't exist.*

I should answer her. She deserves an explanation, but I can't give it to her because I'm not really sure what happens either.

Snap the fuck out of it, Ethan. Answer the fucking question.

"Robby took me back," I lie. Back to the days where we measured another day served by the sunset and another day of living by the sunrise.

Bryce's eyes burn into mine. Fierce. With hope though and conviction. Her hands stay on my cheeks. Where most people would probably ask if I'm okay, she doesn't, and I like that. The truth is, I'm not sure I'm okay. I'm not sure if I'll be all right.

The only thing that is promised in life after birth is death.

She deserves more of a man, Ethan. You know that.

Undamaged goods. You could be that person, Ethan. You could be. With more work with James. You really could be.

She deserves more than you can give, Ethan. So much more. Let her go.

Something inside me tells me I can't.

"And what else?" she asks.

I try to pause this moment. She's touching me, not sexually. Touching me in a way that helps her heart and mind. Through the tips of her fingers. I feel this. She doesn't know this, but I do.

"Ethan, what else?" she asks again.

I don't want to tell her. I don't want to visit the dark places Robby and I spent too much time in. I don't want to tell her any of this. Because, if I do, will I look at her differently? Will I look at Bryce and attach the feelings of what we brought home from war to her? I can't have that. If anything remains of us, we have to be friends. I can't risk that. Or worse, will she look at me and think I'm an animal?

I pull my cheeks away from her hands that cradles them like a mother would her child. "I can't go there with you, Bryce. I won't."

Her eyes still on me, she moves with my every flinch, my every blink, my every breath. "Then, come with me." She takes me by the hand and pulls me to the truck. "Give me your keys."

I hand them over, and then we climb into my truck. "Do you know how to drive a stick?" I ask.

Bryce looks at me through the corner of her eyes. "Ethan, you underestimate a city girl. First, I drive a mean stick. Second, I milked cows on my grandparents' farm for many summers."

I listen to the low hum of the tires against the road and try to process what she's just said.

"Ethan, what can I do to help you feel better?"

I turn my stare to her. What I want and what I need are two different things usually, but right now—they're exactly the same. "You," I whisper.

Bryce doesn't smile at this. In fact, I'm unsure she's even breathing.

She says, "You're going to do what you need to with my body. If this is what you need to forget the current situation your friend is in, you will use my body to forget. Just for the night. Understand?"

What about tomorrow? I want to ask.

Bryce makes her way back to our motel.

Turns.

Bites her lip.

Smiles. Even if it lasts for only three seconds, I'll take it.

Turns again.

"Thanks for driving," I say because I think she knows this is important to me.

"You're welcome." Bryce pulls into the spot in front of our room. Turns off the truck. Pulls the key out of the ignition.

Nothing makes a sound after that.

A slow trickle of rain starts on the windshield.

"Come inside, Ethan," Bryce says.

Twenty-Three

Bryce

We both walk to the front door as the rain closes in on us. I know the difference of what I *need* to do and what I *want* to do. This is both.

I slide our room key into the door, Ethan close behind me, and I open the door.

Inside, Ethan takes his jacket off, and I set the key down next to the television. I go to the heavy, thick curtains and pull them shut, so all we see are the tiny splashes of light around the big front window. I can barely make out Ethan's figure, but I know where he stands.

I've never wanted anything more in my life. Not for him to make love to me, but for his heart to mend. Heal from the wounds. The scars.

I walk to him and place my hands on his hips. I slowly tug his shirt from his pants as he lifts his arms for me to slide it off. His shirt falls to the floor, and I run my hand across his chest, making sure this is real. That he won't leave. Walk out. Not like the morning in Los Angeles or the morning in the bathroom on Magnolia Road or in his bedroom.

Want rushes through my veins, and I feel my body go flush.

My fingers trace over the small ripples of his stomach as they work their way up to his chest. I run my hands through the small dusting of hair. You'd never know the body Ethan has. Women can only assume he's fit, but what's underneath seems only for me.

With his hands at his sides, I take his hips in my hands and pull him closer, placing my lips first to his nipples, wanting once again to know what they taste like. I hear the breath escape his mouth as I do this. I move my lips to the left side of his chest, where his heart is. I tighten my grip on his hips and slowly place my lips to his heart.

Ethan's always been able to exercise control. Restraint, from what I can see. In Los Angeles, he let me finish twice before he gave himself enough room to reach his climax.

As though I were in control, as if I had a say, I undo his belt and slowly push his jeans down to puddle on the floor.

Right now, my heart doesn't know how to fix him, how to make him okay, so my touch deepens as I slide my hands down his backside, inside his boxer briefs. I feel his breath against my cheek as I look up at him. His eyes closed. His hands still at his sides. His mouth slightly open.

With his erection against my stomach, I want nothing more than to peel off these layers of fabric between us and for us to join in the middle where our bodies aren't ours, but some sort of fate written in the stars.

That's when he loses it. Takes me by the shoulders. Squeezes. Turns and puts me down on the bed in one swift motion. Spreads my legs but leans back and yanks off my pants before he settles between my thighs. As if my top is as an afterthought, he gently pulls me up and slips my top off over my head. With my dark blue lacy bra exposed, he gently takes his fingers and pops it open so that my breasts pour out. He tosses it on the floor and leans back. The only thing left is my panties on my body as I ease back onto the mattress. Ethan marvels at my body as he sits back and takes me in.

He looks away. Shakes his head. Bites his lip.

I don't ask him what's wrong.

I know he needs me.

I know he needs this.

I reach up and pull him from the back of his neck as I whisper in his ear, "Take my panties off, Ethan."

Hastily, he rips them off me as his stare turns darker.

I lie back on the mattress and allow him to look me over as his hand slides against my inner thigh.

"Do what you need to, Ethan." My voice is raspy as I feel my body respond to his hands, his demeanor.

He gets down flat on his stomach but not before taking off his underwear, and he puts his face between my legs.

Without using his hands, his tongue slides between my folds, and my body begins to quiver.

I quietly call out as my legs move to the sides, and I watch him.

He pushes his tongue deeper into me, reaching my spot, and then uses his fingers to pull back my folds.

I don't dare look away as he probes me, taking his time with me, pushing his tongue deeper. I feel his finger slide inside me as he keeps pressure against me with his tongue.

I call out, getting lost in the feeling this brings.

He pulls his finger out and takes pressure off of my center. He leaves me on the mattress, breathless, legs shaking and spread for him.

Ethan watches me in the darkness for a moment, taking me in.

I reach down and take my breasts in my hands, needing him back. His touch.

"Get on your knees and face the headboard, Bryce," he commands.

I do.

With my backside exposed to him, I feel him finally settle onto the mattress. His hands are on my waist.

He settles between my legs and pulls me back.

We both call out because he's inside me now.

"Bryce," he whispers as a saving grace. That, somehow, maybe, I'll give him a break.

I move my hips because this feels too good, and he groans. "Oh my God."

He reaches underneath me and cups my breasts as I rock against him, feeling him slide in and out of me with each push.

Abruptly, he stops.

"Are you all right, Ethan?" My words are breathy. The weight they carry is heavy. Like waiting out a hurricane, waiting for it all to pass. I know Ethan isn't all right.

With his hands, he pulls me back to him so that my knees are at the end of the mattress. I'm still on all fours while Ethan towers above me, feet planted solidly on the floor. Gently, he reaches down and pulls me up so that my back is flush with his chest. Pushing my hair to one side, he trails kisses down the side of my neck.

"I have to pace myself with you, Bryce," he says as his hands reach around and take my breasts once again.

Feeling his erection against my back, I want to fall forward. I want him to touch me. But I don't tell him this.

I push my feet to the floor, making him step back. I turn to face him, walk around him, turning him with me so that we're facing each other. I push him to the mattress.

"Lie down."

He does. I climb on top of him.

Then I put my lips to his, but he stakes his claim when he grabs the back of my neck with his hand and deepens the kiss. Then, he pushes away from my lips, slightly pulls me up, so he can put my breast in his mouth.

I watch him.

He watches me.

Between my legs, I feel him. I gently use my body and maneuver him inside me as my middle meets his base.

"Bryce ..." His head falls back to the mattress, eyes closed this time, breathing heavily.

I rock back and forth, trying not to come just yet. "Lose it." I lean forward and whisper.

"Oh, God." He pulls his attention to where we're joined.

The bed begins to squeak as I sit up right and keep my hips right where they are.

As we rock and sigh and pant, his eyes say so much more.

They say, *I want, but I can't.*

They say, *I love you, but I can't.*

They say, *I'm damaged goods. You deserve more.*

But, in this moment, it's just Ethan and me. Separate yet joined. Two different people. Two walks of life.

As if this life were written and, finally, someone had gotten it right. But they forgot about one thing. Sometimes, damaged goods are the best goods. Our life experiences can either make us or break us.

Ethan has done both. He's been broken. And he's the best kind of broken. He's the type of broken that's putting himself back together. He's not the type of broken with missing pieces, irreplaceable pieces

In this moment, as his eyes bury into mine, I know I will love him for eternity. I know I'm meant to love him for the rest of my life. Whether he loves me or not, whether he allows me to love him or not, it isn't my job to convince him. It's my job just to be present.

We make love in spite of ourselves.

We make infinite love as he pushes me to my climax, eyes still boring into mine.

I'm reaching my limit as we rock.

"Ethan," I say breathlessly.

His arms around my middle, he gives me one last long look. I close my eyes and allow him to give me the release I need.

Stars explode as my entire body reaches its peak. I drop my head back and call out his name, grinding myself harder against him, taking in his scent as his arms tighten around me.

An explosion of broken and perfect and consequence erupts as euphoria settles in my body.

When the world stops moving and our bodies slow, I drop my head to look at him. What I expect to see and what I really see are two different things. I expected him to look more peaceful, like my body feels, but all I see is anguish. Quickly, he pulls out, sets me to the side, and stands.

He walks me to the wall, my backside to him, and places my hands against it. He isn't soft about this. He's desperate for an escape. In one swift motion, he pushes into me again and again and again.

My backside rocks against him with jerking movements.

"I'm sorry," he apologizes in my ear. "You need to see the beast that I am. This is how I need this."

His words both scare me and do something to my body that makes me want to give him everything. I do my best to remain steady as he uses me for protection against himself. He uses my body to rid himself of his thoughts, his feelings, his hurt, his fears.

"Bryce!" he calls out loudly as he gives one last hard push inside me.

Then, everything goes silent, except our panting. My body trembles in his wake, and I'm not sure if it's fear that he'll walk away once we're finished, just like the last time, or because my body is fully satisfied.

This time, gently, he pulls out. With my back still to him, my hands against the wall, our bodies stand against the darkness—not individually, but together.

"Bryce, you're shaking," he says, sliding his hands around my middle. "Come here." Ethan leads me to the bed, dragging the comforter back, exposing the white sheets. Then, he climbs between the sheets, puts me to his chest, and pulls the sheets over our naked bodies.

If silence had a name in this moment, it would be fear. Fear and darkness go together like smothered love—stifling, overbearing, and hard to overcome. But, right now, all I know is that I'd rather feel these things because I'm with Ethan. And I'll do it the way he wants. If that means as friends or lovers because living without him doesn't seem like a viable option. It's not something I think I can do. The strong, willful, never-need-a-man woman that I am has somehow changed, turned. Flipped.

This situation could have been avoided. Maybe, if I had ignored Ethan that day in Los Angeles, ignored his long legs and his dark brown eyes and long eyelashes, the vein that runs the course of his left arm, his big hands, maybe this moment wouldn't hurt so much, knowing it was the beginning of the end. Knowing I made a choice that would shatter my heart because what we did today wasn't love. We didn't make love. We didn't share our deepest secrets.

We put bandages on our wounds.

I lick my lips before I put my mouth to his chest for a kiss. "I know this is the end, Ethan."

Twenty-Four

Ethan

It has to be the end. And, if I tell her why, she won't give me a litany of excuses. Reasons this should work. Because she knows, too.

I have to right myself.

I want to tell her so many things.

I want to tell her what she does to my heart when I see her across a room. I want to tell her what she does to me when she smiles and tucks her hair behind her ears. Or the smirk that she gets right before she says something witty. I want to tell her that the broken pieces of me now live in a not-so-dark place and that life has somehow become brighter with her in it.

But I don't say anything. I just give her what I can in this moment, and that's my attention.

With the fear, anxiety, anger I had before we came to this bed, knowing that we'd right our wounds, I was full of hatred for myself, for addiction, for war.

Why Robby had to make the choice to enlist instead of going on to community college. Why Robby's ex-wife will have to explain to their daughter what happened and how war and suffering are what robbed her of her dad. All this heartbreak could have been avoided.

I don't want this for Bryce. I don't want to be Bryce's Robby.

I want to tell Bryce she deserves more than I can give her, so instead, I say, "You'll find someone who can treat you well." I stroke her arm with my fingertips, our naked bodies beneath the sheet of lies I've tried to tell myself.

Nakedness with Bryce is like feeling like the whole world is right. That every single thing has its purpose. Every moment. Every situation.

Twenty-Five

Bryce

"*You'll find someone who can treat you well.*"

My mother gave me some sound advice when I was seventeen when I thought Nathan Evans had broken my heart. She said, "Your heart will break, Bryce. Just make sure you pick up the pieces, so the evidence is gone."

That moment pales in comparison to the ache I feel now.

These words from Ethan make my heart break into a million tiny pieces. It's not because he doesn't care about me or love me. It's because he can't see what he's capable of, and no one can make him see that except himself. You can't force it.

The heartbreak is because nothing was done wrong. To love and not fall is rare, I know. To love and fall is almost always evident. Heartbreak is the consequence of love.

I can't convince Ethan that we will work. It's like waiting on my brother to get sober. He's not going to get sober until he's ready. He can't get sober for me, Mom, or even Dad. Because, when push comes to shove and life gets hard, he'll drink or use because it's what he knows. It's easier. It's easier than dealing with the awful situations of life. Like Robby. He tried to live with his own demons for a little while. He tried to cope. Tried to be good. But reality, it seems, slipped away and got stuck at the jumping-off place—where life is better lived either loaded or not loaded, and death is a very real alternative to that either of those options.

His fingertips trail across my back in an *I love you* sort of way, not in a way that says *I need to go*, and this hurts even more.

He pushes his lips to the top of my head.

Please don't do that, I beg as the tears sting my eyes. But I can't bear to bring the words to my lips.

After what he's lived through, he can kiss my head. I'll survive and not have long-term effects from it. Though my heart might not be the same, I'll survive.

What we tell ourselves, will ourselves to believe, the circumstances we create, the decisions we make, are indicative, I believe, of our hearts. What we're taught as children matters. What we're given in this life is a beginning and an end. That's it. There are no guarantees. No promises of a fruitful start, middle, and exit. How I choose to live my life today matters in the end. And, if it's lying here, naked, with a broken man who's fighting so hard to live without commitments, strings attached, promises of a future, I'll do it. I'll do it for Ethan.

"Biggest fear?" he whispers.

Ethan's big hand reaches the small of my back, and I feel the calluses of his palm against my skin.

Losing you. "Losing my brother," I lie. I've lost my brother already.

Ethan breathes in and out, my head following the rise and the fall.

"Yours?" I ask.

"Living."

There's an emptiness in the room, one that wasn't here before he said it. It's dark and heavy, and it resides on top of us like an elephant.

"Living?" I repeat, turning my head upward to look at him.

Ethan's staring straight ahead, and his hand still remains on my lower back. He's still. And then he says, "I don't want to end up like Robby, Bryce."

What I want to do is sit up, stare him straight in the eyes, and say, *You're not Robby. You're Ethan. And you won't, so stop talking like that right now.* That's what fear wants me to do.

But, instead, I remain still. Ponder in the quiet seconds that pass. The truth is, I don't know if he'll end up like Robby. I don't know the extent of his trauma. "Here's what I know about you." I bring my head down, so I'm staring at the same blank wall he is. "You'd rather break my heart than give me any less of a man you think I deserve. You traveled three hours to be there for Robby's mom while he lies in a hospital bed. You'd rather deal with your problems than run from them."

Ethan's head jerks back to me with a look like, *How'd you know?*

"Saw James's card on your floor in your house the other night. Must have fallen out of your wallet or something." I take in a breath, my lungs expanding against his side.

The truth is, I can't speak from experience when it comes to what Ethan and Robby went through. What they had to do. But what I can do is speak truth. Tell him what I know about him. Because, when we're stuck in our heads, we can make ourselves into people we're not. Both good and bad.

My phone vibrates in my purse. I try to move, but Ethan's grip tightens. I look at him, and he meets my gaze. Except it isn't Ethan. It's a man who needs his soul to heal. It's a man whose look has changed to reflect his insides.

And then he says something that makes me see him for the vulnerable man he's becoming, "Have sex with me again? Please, Bryce."

He doesn't ask to make love. He doesn't ask for anything else but my body. Not my heart. Not to have my toothbrush at his house. Doesn't give me a million reasons why I should. It's a simple question. I have a simple answer. I crawl on top of him, and we have sex one more time before we go back to the hospital.

"He's getting better," Maria says, a small tinge of hope in her eyes.

We're in the hallway light. This time, it's dark outside. A few of Maria's brothers have dropped in, but other than that, the rest of the family is distant. I get that. Understand it.

Everyone has left Maria here at the hospital, I think to myself, *and yet she remains vigilant. Standing by her son's side.*

A true test of a mother's love. A man who steals from you to feed his disease, yet you still stand for him. A curse and also a blessing. A blessing knowing you're still taking care of your son, so your heart can rest in ease.

I remember, when I went to an Al-Anon meeting, a man whose brother was addicted said that his brother finally got sober when their mother died.

He said, "Finally, our mother wasn't there to pick up the pieces anymore, and he was able to find his bottom."

The blessing part of this is, I've never seen a stronger love than a mother has for her child.

"He's going to be okay, Ethan. Go home. Take care of yourselves, your lives, Each other. I'll call you if anything changes." Maria smiles, touching my arm. "Besides, my brothers are here, so I'm not alone; I know that's what you're thinking, Ethan. Don't worry. I'm all right."

"You'll call me if anything changes?" he asks, but more as a reminder.

"Promise."

Ethan looks to me. "I'm going to go say good-bye to Robby."

I nod and smile. "I'll be here."

Ethan walks back into Robby's hospital room.

Maria's eyes fill with tears. "Thank you for coming here with Ethan. I prayed that he'd find a nice girl. Watch over him, Bryce, will you?" she sighs. "Ethan is such a good man. There aren't very many differences between Ethan and Robby, but the one thing I can see between the two of them is, Ethan has the ability to love with his whole heart. Robby did at one point, and maybe that's the moment when he started turning to drugs because it hurt too much."

"I will, Maria. I promise."

She wraps her arms around me, and I feel the tension leave my shoulders. Or maybe it's acceptance of the situation. I'm not sure. There's nothing awkward or stiff about this hug; it's warm and genuine. Robby grew up his entire life receiving these kinds of hugs from his mother. It also makes me think that, alcoholism or drug addiction, they don't care what kind of parents you have, what kind of car you drive, the profession you live. It doesn't matter. The disease doesn't care whose heart you break even if it is your mother's. It wants you dead.

Maria's phone rings. "Excuse me, Bryce. I need to take this." Maria puts her cell phone to her ear. "*Hola*, Jesus."

I walk down the hallway to the elevator and take the journey down to the ground floor. Ethan will figure out where I am. I'd hate to interrupt his time with Robby.

The elevator doors swoosh open, and I'm met with a sterile scent and the smell of rain. I look outside and notice the ground is wet from fresh rainfall. I pull my hood over my head and exit the hospital, making my way to Ethan's truck.

As soon as I slide into the truck, the rain starts again, bringing its fury. It's the calmness of the mood. The rain brings my tears maybe. Or the realization I've just discovered. My brother could very well die from this disease. I pitied my mother for wanting so badly to save her son. Looked down upon her. Gave her excuses why her help wouldn't work, only for those excuses to be thrown back in my face when I saw Maria's tired, sad eyes. Really what my mother has is hope. A hope she clings to every night before she goes to bed. Prays to God that he'll save her son. I shamed her. Gave her my wrath and a litany of reasons she should walk away. And all I was running on was fear. Trying to protect my own heart. Maybe hers, too, in some weird way.

I'm an awful daughter.

All my father wanted was for me to call my mom once in a while. Give her a reason to keep moving forward, and all I could do was give her hell.

My hands start to shake. Grow damp with nerves. Regret. Guilt.

The raindrops ting off the truck like bullets of vengeance.

How could I have been so selfish? How come I didn't see this before?

I pull out my phone. For the first time in a long time, I need to hear my mother's voice. I try to dial her number, but my hands are too shaky. Instead, I drop my phone to my lap, rub my eyes, and then slide my hands through my hair.

Fear is the root of anger.

"Regrets are for those who refuse change." Ethan's words sting my thoughts.

Regrets.

Are.

For.

Those.

Who.

179

Refuse.

Change.

Ethan's body pours into the driver's side, just like the rain. He fits next to me just like we've been doing this for years. He looks at me.

The rain falls, and yet the silence between us calls loudly.

"You okay?" he asks.

"I don't know."

Twenty-Six

Ethan

Our drive back to Granite Harbor in the rain creates some peace in me. One I haven't felt in a long damn time.

I look over at Bryce, who's staring out the window.

"Maine in the fall is better in the rain," she says.

"Why?"

"It gives me a sense of ease." She turns her head from the window to me. "Because it makes me feel like I'm home. Like there's no place else I'd rather be. Los Angeles is a commitment. You commit to the 405 Freeway every morning for stop-and-go traffic. You commit to trendy restaurants and size zero jeans. You commit to the fast pace. Convenience, which, also has its perks, by the way. But you commit to a lifestyle you've grown accustomed to. You try to convince yourself you're better suited for the convenience, pace, traffic, and the waistlines you'll never fit into. You try to convince yourself you're groomed for a life on the fast track."

She pauses and looks back out the window to the beauty I've seen for most of my life. Beauty that is somehow unappreciated or unnoticed now on my end, maybe because my perspective is tainted.

"I like how Granite Harbor has only one grocery store. I like how Lyn from Level Grounds remembers my name. How you have the Fall Festival and everyone comes together. I like how you're the reigning champ at the hot dog eating contest, and everybody knows it. I like how you still spend time with the people you grew up with, Ethan. And I also love how Granite Harbor begins to grow on you, even when you least expect it. I like all that."

"You know that living in a small town also has its disadvantages, right? Gossip spreads like wildfire. And you can't catch a break when you're eleven years old, and you're riding your bike down Main Street when you told your mom you'd be at a friend's house. Someone will inevitably rat you out." I smile.

"At eleven years old, Ryker and I would ride our bikes down Sunset Boulevard, trying to ditch our security team that Dad demanded we have."

"Did you succeed?"

She laughs a soft laugh. "No. Little did we know, they put tracking devices on our bikes after our first attempt to outrun them."

We pull into Granite Harbor. It's past eleven as the relentless rain pours down. We've had a long day, and I can tell Bryce is tired just by the way she's quiet. We pull up to her place, but something is off. Something isn't quite right. Maybe it's my military training. My instincts.

"Wait here." I undo my seat belt, hop out of the truck, and grab my gun from underneath the seat.

"What the hell is that for?"

"Stay put. And lock the doors once I shut mine."

"Ethan? What is it?"

"I'm not sure, but something isn't right."

Quietly, I let the door close on its own as the drops of rain meet my hair, face, neck, and clothes. I walk around to the other side of the truck.

I sigh when I hear breathing behind me. "Thought I told you to stay in the truck," I say through the rain that surrounds us.

"Guess I didn't hear that part."

"Liar. Stick close behind me, do you understand?"

"Yes."

We creep onto the porch, and the front door is ajar. Right now, I hate the rain because I can't hear a damn thing.

"Put your hand on my left hip and keep it there. Do you understand me?"

"Yes."

She puts her hand right where I asked her. This is reassurance for me that she's with me at all times, and I don't have to look down or behind me to know she's there.

I push the door open to a dark house and flip on the living room light.

My gun drawn, I survey the living room, which has been ransacked. The coffee table is overturned. Drawers in the entertainment system have been rifled through.

We quietly make our way to the kitchen and dining room where drawers have been pulled out, and cupboards have been gone through.

"He knows I'm here, Ethan." I hear the fear in her voice.

"Call 911."

After Granite Harbor Police are through, I shut the door behind the last officer.

"You're staying at my house tonight."

She smiles from the couch that she sits on. "I thought this was your house." She uses her wit in moments of fear.

"My other house." I sit down next to her. The rain has ceased somewhat.

"Nothing's been stolen. It's him, Ethan. I know it. He knows I'm here. Besides, when's the last time there was a break-in in Granite Harbor?"

"I'm sure it's documented in the newspaper somewhere." I try to smile.

She doesn't laugh. "I have to call Ryker to warn him."

"They dusted for prints, Bryce. Don't worry; they'll find him."

She shakes her head and bites her thumbnail. "No, you don't understand. Luke doesn't do his own dirty work, Ethan. He probably sent the mob or some crazy parolee looking for a quick job. Probably had him search for an address or something."

There's a knock at the door, and she jumps.

"Don't say anything about Luke to the police, please. Let them find him on their own," she whispers. "It's too much to risk."

"I got it," I say, placing a hand on her lower back as I stand.

I walk to the door, and it's Officer Lent.

He's pointing to the back of the house. "Were you—or did you, uh, drink coffee and smoke cigarettes in the area behind the house?"

"No. Why?" I say.

"You're going to want to come see this, Warden Casey."

I turn back to look at Bryce and motion my head toward the door, thinking there's no way in hell I'll leave her to sit by herself in this house. "Come on."

She takes in a big breath and lets it out as she stands.

In the dark and the drizzle falling from the sky now, with flashlights, we make our way to the back of the house that opens up to a wall of tall trees. We give space around the chair where the beam of light hits, so we don't destroy any evidence.

Officer Lent stands behind the chair and shines the beam straight into the bedroom Bryce sleeps in.

All of the air leaves me. I want to breathe, but I can't. I want to fucking punch something, but I can't. My stomach lurches forward. All the nights Bryce has changed in this room. Slept in this room.

"I take it, this is news to you both?"

"Yes," we reply in unison.

I feel Bryce's stare burn into the side of my face, but I'm too afraid to look at her, for fear she'll see my anger.

"As you can see, there are cigarette butts and three Styrofoam cups."

"This guy left in a rush. Why else would he have left evidence behind?" I say more rhetorically, talking to myself.

"Just what I was about to get at." Officer Lent is relatively new to Granite Harbor PD. He's younger. Probably trying to prove he's good at his job, though he is a nice guy. "I'll take this into evidence. See if we can get something from the cups and cigarettes. Gonna be a long night. Bryce, do you have somewhere else to stay tonight?" Officer Lent scratches the back of his head.

"She's staying with me," I say as if she doesn't have a choice in the matter. As if she were a child and I made the choices for her.

But Bryce doesn't do what I expect, like get irritated and explain she's a grown woman who can make choices for herself.

Save herself if need be. I know she is capable of doing all these things, so maybe it's more for my well-being; I'm not sure.

Bryce nods. "Yeah, sounds good."

I realize the shitstorm this will start. Bryce staying overnight with me. The whole town, I'm sure, is already talking. And I don't give a fuck.

I take Bryce's hand and lead her down the hill in the back of the house.

"I'll call you, Casey."

I hold up a hand to signify I heard him.

"Need a change of clothes?" I ask.

"No. Already have one packed, remember? We didn't stay as planned in Brookline."

I don't answer.

We reach the truck, and I open the door for her this time.

A slew of neighbors are outside, as Lent's patrol car still sits out front.

The Petes wave. I wave back as I hop in the truck, not wanting to engage. Explain what happened. I'll leave that up to the Granite Harbor PD.

We reach my house, and all is quiet. The outside lights welcome us, and my stomach grows uneasy. Who's to say Luke didn't come by my house, looking for Bryce?

I park on the street and pull my gun out from under my belt.

"What are you doing?" Bryce asks, staring down at my gun.

"Stay in the car. I'll give you the nod when the coast is clear." I stop before I get out, looking back at Bryce. "Seriously, stay in the car this time."

Bryce's tired eyes tell me she'll do just about anything. "Yeah."

It's hard to think that we drove six hours together, visited a friend, made love, and came home to a house turned upside down.

Quickly, I make my way to the front door, staying in the shadows. I test the knob on the front door. Still locked. A good sign. I reach in my pocket for my keys and look back at Bryce's silhouette. The door clicks when I unlock it. Leaving it open, I place my gun out in front of me and quickly clear my own house.

I walk back to the truck and take Bryce inside, grabbing her bag for her.

"Can I take a shower?" she asks when we reach the kitchen.

"Of course. I'll get you a towel."

I'm on the couch in the living room, scrolling through my phone, when Bryce comes out.

"Feel better?" I ask.

"Feeling like it was a Corvette that hit me now, not a semi. So, that's good."

She's got on a Bon Jovi "Livin' on a Prayer" T-shirt that hangs just above her knees, and I can't help but feel this in places I shouldn't.

She sits down next to me.

The rain has begun again.

She sees the glass of whiskey I've poured.

"Want one?"

"No, but if it's all right, I'll take a sip of yours." She reaches out and puts the tumbler to her lips. Allows the brown elixir through her lips and swallows. Sets the glass down. There's no reaction. No cough.

"You've proven yourself to be an experienced drinker." I pick it up from the coffee table and put her spot on the glass to my lips. Take a swig.

"No, my body just knows what it needs, Ethan." Her tone hangs on invisible notes in the air.

Her words make me want to do things that most friends don't do together.

Sex wasn't on the agenda today. And twice?

I set the glass down.

She's staring straight ahead, her elbows resting on her thighs as her arms stretch outward.

"Take my bed. I'll sleep here."

Her eyes slowly meet mine. She thinks. "I'd rather you sleep in your bed, and I sleep alongside you. If that's okay?"

The whiskey has exploded in my stomach. *Don't touch her, Ethan. Sleep next to her. Don't touch her.* I think twice about this because of the nightmares. I used to get them bad right after I returned home. Throwing punches. Strangling my pillow. From all the work James and I have done the nightmares have gone away for the most part. But now, with Robby's shit in my head, I'm not so sure they won't return. God forbid, I wake up from a nightmare, and I'm strangling her. This thought makes me grow ill.

"I can't do it tonight," I lie. Badly, I want her body next to mine. I want to be able to fall asleep with her, not worry about what my unconscious mind might do while I sleep.

"No, yeah, I totally get it." Bryce stands but not before reaching down and taking another sip of my whiskey. "That's smooth," she says as she sets it down for the last time. "Good night, Ethan."

She turns, and I think I can see her red lace panties through her T-shirt; it makes me hard.

The way she moved her body against me today. The way I took her in my mouth.

"Good night, Bryce," I groan, knowing I've made the right decision.

To deter my mind once she walks to my bedroom, I read a text from my mom. Something about dinner on Sunday, but I'm only two percent focused because I'm still thinking about Bryce in her red panties.

I walk to the kitchen and pour another glass, feeling the effects of the alcohol. Feeling the relief. Feeling my skin loosen. Just one more glass.

When I'm done, I feel really all right. I tiptoe into my bedroom and see the covers gathered where Bryce lies, sound asleep. I want to crawl into my bed with her. Show her, tell her how I really feel, but deep inside, I know I can't make that commitment. My head is still so fucked up.

She said she'd give me what I needed.

Her. That's what I need right now.

It's selfish, Ethan. You're a fucking selfish bastard.

She did say she wanted me in here.

It's the alcohol talking.

I take off my shirt, needing, just for a minute, to feel her body next to mine again.

But my phone rings from the other room.

Fuck.

Shit.

I walk back into the living room and see Maria's number.

My heart begins to slam against my chest.

This is a late hour for Maria to be calling.

187

Fear consumes me.

"Hello?" I say quickly.

There's no sound on the other end of the line.

"Hello? Maria?" I say again.

A broken, familiar voice sounds. "Ethan, he's gone. Robby's gone."

Twenty-Seven

Bryce

It's early, but I can figure out Ethan's coffeepot and make him coffee this morning. I pad down the hallway to the kitchen, but there's a silhouette in the darkness, sitting at the kitchen table.

"E-Ethan?" I whisper. My eyes begin to slowly adjust to the morning darkness.

It's him. And it's the stillness of his body that makes me break out in chills.

"Ethan? What's going on?" My stomach drops.

I see the whiskey glass in front of him from last night.

He stares it down.

Has he slept?

I can't bring myself to move.

"I tol' him, 'See you larer,'" he slurs.

My heart seizes. "Who?"

"I tol' him I'll be back to see him."

I try to swallow as my heart picks up pace. "Is it Robby, Ethan?"

His eyes meet mine. Hate and anger bleed across the table in my direction. "Don't."

"What? Ethan, is it Robby?"

Another piece of advice my mother gave me: "Don't try to convince a drunk person that you're right. Even if they're wrong, they're right for at least the next six hours."

I ask again, "Ethan, did Robby pass away?"

"Yeah."

He grabs the bottle and puts it to his lips, and I watch as the bubbles of air move from top to bottom.

Tears sting my eyes. "Ethan, stop." My voice is more than a whisper. "You're going to kill yourself."

He slams the bottle down on the table with so much force that the bottle and the glass crash to the floor.

Something inside me flinches, probably my heart, but I don't allow Ethan to see this.

"Ge' the fuck outta my house."

"What?" I say, taken aback. A piece of me wants to run. A bigger piece of me wants to stay. Take care of him. Heal him. But I can't do that.

"You prolly a slut anyway. Prolly sleep with whoever you wan'."

What? Who even are you right now?

My throat begins to ache with tears. I don't know how to respond. What he's saying can't quite compute.

Where'd Ethan go?

"You shoul' go. Prey on 'nother man with his own shit. Try save 'im. You 'n' me, we're different. You shop fur men at military bases, Bryce?"

Don't give him any satisfaction of seeing your hurt, Bryce. Take his truck keys and drive home.

Ethan can't even look at me. His forehead slowly drifts to the table.

I grab my overnight bag and his truck keys. I'll drive myself back to Magnolia Road.

Ethan can figure out how the hell to get his truck back.

Before I pull out of the driveway, I know it's early, but Alex will be awake with the baby or writing. I text Alex and ask for Aaron's number. Ethan's going to need him when he wakes up.

Alex: Sure. Everything okay?

Me: Yeah.

No. No, I'm not all right at all.
I don't have it in me to tell her that I'll fill her in later.

Alex: Everything isn't okay. Where are you?

Me: Home.

Alex: I'll meet you there as soon as Eli gets home.

I start to tell her it isn't necessary, but I stop myself. Because the truth is, I do need her right now. I remember how it felt to be there for my best friend when she lost Kyle and then almost Eli. I was there when she said she didn't need a friend.

I call Aaron.

"Warden Casey."

"Hi, Aaron. It's Bryce."

"Bryce?"

"Yeah." Tears come to my eyes.

"Is everything okay?"

When Aaron asks, the lump comes back. *Push it down, Bryce. Push it down.* "Not really. Robby died. I don't know much else, but your brother is hammered at his house. I think you need to check on him."

"Robby? Who's Robby?"

The lump grows when I realize Ethan never told his own twin brother about his best friend from the military. Ethan shared so many moments with both. He shared one life with his brother and another life with his best friend. I realize Ethan has so many walls up. He's so guarded that mixing the two lives that never meshed together, still so separate, meant opening up just a little, something Ethan wasn't ready to do with his own brother.

"Just stop by. He needs you." I hang up the phone and let the tears create trails down my cheeks as I drive.

As I pull up to Magnolia Road, the house seems quiet. Untouched. As if a stranger hadn't ravaged through it last night, looking for the one thing he couldn't find. It doesn't exist. The only thing that exists, the evidence, is in my head. The address. One I'll never give, no matter what happens. So, Luke can come back for me, but he isn't going to get anything.

I wipe my tears, sling my bag over my shoulder, head inside, and try to put my life back together.

The house, for the most part, is put back together. It's almost four in the afternoon. No word from Ethan or Aaron, but a car door shuts outside. I told Alex I just needed some time to think before anyone came over. Just needed to be alone to figure out how this all got so bad, so quick.

"Bryce?" I hear Alex say as the front door quietly shuts.

"Kitchen." My voice cracks as I try to figure out what I'll say to her.

She takes one look at me from the living room, and that's all it takes. She throws her purse down on the couch, and I place my hands on my face and begin to cry. I feel her arms around me, something I've felt a lot over the course of our friendship but not like this.

"Come on, let's go sit down."

We spend the next hour on the couch, talking, crying, laughing a little. I tell her everything. Ethan. Robby. My brother, Ryker, which she knows to some extent. I even include Sandra and Landon and Luke but only the necessary information—and not because I don't trust her, but because, if anything happens, I don't want her to take the blame for anything.

"When's the funeral for Robby?" she asks.

I shrug. "I don't know. I'm going to try to reach Maria, his mom, and find out."

Alex sighs and places her hand on my leg. "In the meantime, let's call for takeout."

I don't really have an appetite, but I know I need to eat.

"I'll call it in once I look at the menu online. Why don't you take a hot shower?"

I nod.

"Anything specific you want?"

"Just a salad or soup or something." I stand, looking down at my best friend, who's on her phone, looking into the menu. "Alex?"

She turns her head up.

"Thank you." My eyes burn. I'm tired. Emotionally drained. Exhausted.

"It's what you've done for me."

I bend at the waist and kiss her head.

Once in the shower, I wash Robby's death away. I wash Ethan's words away. I wash the fear away that probably still lives in pockets of my muscle memory. The heat from the water makes my body relax, except my mind. It still spins; it still goes, still moves with what-ifs and how-comes.

What if Ethan hadn't enlisted in the military?

What if he hadn't gone to war?

What if Robby had enlisted but stayed stateside? Would he still be here?

How come Robby died?

How come God didn't save him?

How come Ethan can't find himself?

How come this hurts so much?

Maria and I had exchanged numbers before Ethan and I left Brookline. I call her phone when I get out of the shower, but I get one of Maria's brothers instead. He fills me in on the details of the funeral, which will be on Friday. Again, I pass along my condolences. They say funerals aren't for those who've passed on; they are for those who are still here. What anguish Maria must feel. We all thought he was going to be all right. That he was going to pull through. I don't ask the brother what transpired in the last thirty-six hours, but something went awry.

"Dinner's here," Alex says through the door.

Then, I hear muffled voices.

I pull on a big T-shirt and pajama pants, brush my hair, and open the door to find Alex and Eli staring at me. Eli is still in his warden uniform, which tells me he's not yet off the clock, or he's just going home.

"What?" I say, as if my heart can take much more. As if I'm asking for another round of hurt. "Hey, Eli."

"Hiya, Bryce. So, I can take Ethan's truck back to him, so you don't have to deal with it," he says as if he's tiptoeing around my heart.

"Keys are on the kitchen counter."

Eli takes a to-go box, kisses Alex, grabs the keys, and leaves.

"Who's watching the girls?" I ask.

"My mom and Brand. When Eli told me he was running late, I called my mom." Alex opens her to-go box with French fries and beer-battered cod.

I sigh. "You didn't have to do that."

"Stop it. When Kyle died, who made all those trips to Belle's Hollow to assure me my grief wasn't going to kill me? You. When Philip died, who helped Mom and me plan the funeral? You. Bryce, you've always been there. So, stop with the *you didn't have to do that* stuff."

Smiling, I realize Alex is here for however long it takes me to feel better. "I should have gotten what you got. That looks delicious."

Alex shakes her head. "Best place to get fish and chips on the East Coast as far as I'm concerned." She dips a fry in her ranch and drops it in her mouth.

I grab napkins.

"Thanks," Alex says, taking one from my hand.

Alex's eyes search her food. I know she isn't searching for the ketchup or something to drink because it's all right in front of her.

"What?" I ask.

"It's just … you know Ethan is a good guy, right? Don't get me wrong; what he said to you was totally messed up and wrong, way off base. But underneath all the baggage is a really great guy."

"I just wish he'd let that guy come to the surface," I say. "I can't be the only one to believe it, Alex. He has to, too."

"I know." She dangles a fry above her box, still thinking.

"I'm driving back over to Brookline on Friday for Robby's service."

Alex nods. "I can go with you."

"Nope. You have two beautiful girls to take care of, Alex. And a beautiful husband." I crack a smile, my best attempt at lightening the mood.

"After the service, will you be going back to Los Angeles?" Alex gives me puppy-dog eyes.

I sigh, leaning back against the counter, crossing my arms. "My dad doesn't know anything about Sandra, Landon, or Luke. I'll stay here until they get everything sorted out. Besides, in the end, Luke will get what's coming to him."

Alex stops chewing. "Bryce, what if he comes after you again? I'm going to teach you how to handle a gun."

"I can't keep running, Alex. I knew, eventually, this would catch up to me. Don't worry, I can handle myself."

"Have you been able to get ahold of Ryker?" She takes a piece of fish between her fingers.

"No. Part of me is worried. Part of me isn't. Part of me knows he's smart, hiding out where no one will find him. He's good at that. But part of me thinks, *What if Luke got to him?*"

"I doubt that. Ryker's too smart for his own good."

My phone illuminates and vibrates across the counter. When I see the name, my stomach drops in both a good way and a bad way.

"It's Ethan."

"What are you going to do?"

I hit Ignore, and his name disappears from my screen.

Twenty-Eight

Ethan

Friday, Robby's funeral in Brookline, Massachusetts.

It's cold, and the wind has settled on east to west today.

The American flag is dropped over his casket. Robby lies inside in his dress blues. I brought them to the Holmes Family Funeral Services. Something Robby would have insisted on wearing.

One night, Robby said, a buzz settled in his eyes, "The Marines gave me structure. Gave me stability. Made me a man. *Semper fidelis.*"

I think it's the person inside that couldn't hide the awfulness of war even if he tried like hell.

I stand toward the back as more people begin to show and stare at Robby's picture up by his casket. My eyes burn from lack of sleep. My head is foggy. I pick at the calluses on my palm and wonder how many times I can pull the skin away before it begins to hurt.

The picture up front is of Robby smiling. It's the before. Before war. Before his addiction dictated his life. I look over at his daughter, who's in the front row, head burrowed into her mother. Death is harder for kids her age. She's eleven, I think. She knows she lost her dad far before his disease killed him, but nevertheless, she doesn't get to have the hope anymore that, someday, he might get clean. Someday, he might be accountable again. Someday, he might show up when he said he was going to show up for birthdays or Christmases. That, someday, he might walk her down the aisle on her wedding day.

All that's gone.

Numb, I guess, is how I feel. It's been three days since Robby died. Three days since Bryce left. Three days since I've had a drink. The thought of alcohol makes me want to vomit. Food has been a rare commodity, as I can't seem to get anything down. I called work, asking to come back early, and they willingly agreed. I'll start Monday. It will be a good distraction.

"Thank you for your service," a little boy, no older than six, tugs on my pant leg.

I forget what it's like to wear my dress blues anymore. Although snug in places it wasn't before, it fits okay. I bend down, stare back into the brown eyes of the little boy. The innocent eyes of a young boy so naive to the world. His long eyelashes slowly move up and down with each blink.

"You're welcome, buddy."

"I'm going to be a Marine one day, just like my dad was."

Was.

Was.

Was.

In this moment, it's so hard to tell the innocent child reasons to enlist. This is what war looks like. War is a byproduct of service. And this is what can happen to us. We become jaded. We become different people. Some become heroes, but we never can go back to who we were before. Not for our daughters, our sons, our wives, our husbands. We can't go back.

I can't say this to a six-year-old, so instead, I say, "You can be anything you want in life."

He nods and walks away.

I stand back up and adjust the uniform, checking the laces of my shoes, making sure they run parallel to the floor.

It's the blue bag, the black wool coat, and her auburn hair that catch my eye.

For a moment, I can't breathe. Seeing her right now feels like it's been weeks since I've seen Bryce last. Seeing her right now makes my stomach grow nauseous. What I said to her. I remember.

Pushing her away because of my hurt instead of running toward her.

"You really fucked up, Ethan," Aaron said to me after Bryce called him.

But she's here. And she's absolutely perfect.

I made several attempts to call her. I even explained to Officer Lent why the PD needed to keep extra watch on her house—of course, because of the break-in. I didn't explain further.

Bryce looks ahead as she takes her place in the crowd of people preparing to lay Robby to rest. She looks timeless and pale and stunning.

Two Marines stand off in the close distance, next to Robby's coffin.

Bryce reaches up and pushes a small piece of tissue to the corner of her eye, trying to dry what's left of her tears.

This movement alone rips me to pieces, and if I wasn't in my dress blues, I'd wither. I'm fucking tired of trying to hold my shit together. Fucking tired of being the person I'm not or the person I think I should be.

Tired.

"Taps" starts to play by another Marine. To the right of him though, I see another picture of Robby and me in our fatigues. One I didn't notice before. Why? I have no idea. But I see it now. We're smiling. Arms around each other. The smiles though aren't of joy, but of relief, gratitude, and sadness. We survived one more day in the desert. I remember distinctly what had happened the day prior to this picture. Our Humvee was ambushed. Robby and I were the only ones who survived. Sergeant Collins, Lance Corporal Peers, and Lance Corporal Santana were killed that day.

Survivor guilt is what James calls it every time I go back there in my head. I know something broke in me that day. I arm myself with a wall I use when my memories catch up with me. When civilian noise gets too loud. I go back to Iraq. Stay there in my head, live there. I've built a wall to protect myself. Made of all things hard. Bulletproof. It isn't over there that's hard. It's the coming-home part. We have to survive in a new manner of living. We're in constant battle with our minds.

Check the mail. Fight for sanity. Clarity.

Drink a glass of water.

Drive to the grocery store. Fight.

Kiss the love of your life. Fight. Because, surely, you don't deserve happiness, not when your comrades, your buddies, died for this country.

God.

Country.

Corps.

God forbid, I lose myself in Bryce. Fear takes over. Pushes me away. Fear of who I'll be if I allow myself to love her. Fear of what will happen to the man I've become and the old me I used to be. So, I try to suffer quietly, because that's what a good soldier does.

The picture I've seen several times before this moment suddenly feels heavier because, now, out of our Humvee attack, I'm the only one who has survived. I no longer share that experience with Robby.

Maria told me through her tears this morning about when she'd found Robby that morning he put a gun to his head.

He'd laid out his dress blues for her and left a note: *Ready and waiting.*

What Robby hadn't expected was to survive.

His brain swelled the night we left, hemorrhaged, killing him quickly while he slept.

"It was very fast," Maria, said. Her eyes puffy and red with loss.

I'm pulled from my memories to the Marines folding the flag and handing it to Maria as "Taps" plays again.

Bryce

In the picture of Robby and Ethan in their fatigues, they give smiles. As if Robby's grief didn't get the best of him. As if he didn't spend years trying to blanket what he had seen. What he and Ethan had had to do to save lives.

I realize, in this moment, that war is survivable, as I glance over at a grieving and broken Ethan. My heart aches. The real battle begins when they return home and run from the demons.

Ethan's tired eyes tell me he's spent days without sleep. I can't wish his sadness away. Take it away. He's got to feel through it, I know. As much as I was hurt by his words, I've also realized that I can't be the keeper of his wounds. I can't heal him. He's got to right himself.

Ethan

I catch her eye and feel the weight of her stare with the pain she feels for me, maybe for her own brother. Her own demons. We all carry them; some are just bigger than others.

I stare at James from the couch. He sits with one leg crossed over the other, his pen and paper on the coffee table. He never writes things down anymore when we meet.

"I can't be with her." I believe these words to my core.

James tips his head to the right. "You can't, or you won't?"

"Can't."

James shrugs. "Why is that, Ethan?"

I shake my head. "I can't hurt her."

"Oh, so you get to decide what she's capable of now? You're all-knowing? All of a sudden, you know what's best for Bryce?"

I sit back and let his words eat away at my skin. This is the first real time James and I have been able to talk about Bryce. Or rather, it's the first time I'm opening up about her really. About us.

"You don't want to hurt Bryce—you keep saying that—but the truth is, you don't want to get hurt. You don't want to lose another person you're close to. You aren't giving her the love or allowing yourself to be loved because of pure selfishness, Ethan. If I'm being honest."

Direct hit.

Like I've been punched in the gut.

"You can't control life, Ethan. The only things you can control are your attitudes and your actions. Everything else, you're powerless. You can't control how love works. You aren't that powerful."

James's words rain down on me like nothing I've ever felt before.

Ugly truth.

Bitter truth.

Painful truth.

And the longer I sit here, the more I am able to see just how right James is.

But, instead of lashing out and giving James all the excuses about why he's wrong, which is what I normally do before I see his point, I get up and leave. I drop a hundred-dollar bill on his desk on the way out without another word said.

Because the truth is, he's right, and my truth is that I'm not able to face that just yet.

I get in my truck. Sit with these emotions. Robby's grief still fresh. I have this huge fucking realization that I'm the asshole in the way of Bryce and me, that I've been so selfish. I slam my hands on the steering wheel.

Then, my own advice slams into me. *"Regrets are for those who refuse change."*

So, what? What happens from here?

My heart begins to pound, hands sweat.

You'll regret this one, Ethan.

You'll look back on this life and see where your missteps were made.

You'll see yourself in the mirror, alone, without love, because you weren't willing to change out of your own fucking ego.

I slam my hands on the wheel one more time.

And one more time, my conscience comes back. *You. Are. Powerless.*

Running my hands through my hair, I stare back at the set of eyes looking at me in the rearview mirror.

Let go.

I grab my key from the ignition and walk back into James's office.

"You're back?" James's taken aback and pushes himself away from his desk.

I stand at the door, fists clenched in my pockets. "How do I fix this?"

James motions me in. "Have a seat."

And this time? I listen.

Twenty-Nine

Bryce

It's been a month since Robby's funeral. I've gotten a lot done.

Shane Swenson and I worked tediously on fixing his manuscript to send out to editors at six different publishing houses. I paid a visit to our offices in New York. I paid the bill on Magnolia Road for another month. I received my trophy from the chili cook-off and displayed it on the front porch in its case, per the rules of the Fall Festival Board. Apparently, all winners must display their winnings appropriately. I'm still not sure what that's all about.

I also survived three calls from my mother. One call was to tell me that Ryker was back in another rehab. Another call to ask how I was doing, which was out of the blue and unexpected but welcomed. And the last to tell me she loved me. Also unexpected.

I've busied myself, so I don't think about Ethan.

I saw him in his warden uniform two days ago, which told me two things. One, he was back to work, and two, I really enjoyed seeing him in his uniform.

There's a knock at the door as I sit at my computer, welcoming the cold. A fire is burning, which I learned to build by myself—with the help of Eli.

It's three in the afternoon, and I'm not really expecting anyone, but maybe it's Ruthie sending over another cobbler.

To my surprise, it's an elderly woman in a blue housecoat with a heavy wool coat to protect her body from the elements.

My first thought is, *Why the hell is she out in the cold?*

My second thought is, *Doesn't she have kids who keep tabs on her?*

"Please, come in." I don't ask for her name. I just lend a hand and help her in the doorway.

She nods politely, a bright smile. "Thank you, Bryce."

She knows my name?

The woman hobbles into the kitchen and carefully eases herself into a chair at the kitchen table like she's been here before.

I follow her and sit down across from her. "Can I get you something to drink, Ms.—sorry, I didn't get your name?"

"Nana. And, no, thank you. I'm quite all right."

Her bright eyes explore the kitchen as she sits. They move to the dining room and then the living room, and finally, they fall upon me.

"Can I help you with something?" I ask.

Nana is quiet for a long moment and folds her hands into themselves. It reminds of the nursery rhyme of the church, the steeple, and all the people.

"I spent my whole life in Granite Harbor. Never once did I ever want to leave." Her eyebrows rise. "I suppose that was fear. Get stuck in a place too long, you get too comfortable." Once again, she looks around the room, untangles her fingers, and taps her fingertips lightly on the table. Her tone is soft, inviting, like a well-given hug. One you want more of.

I wait for her to speak again.

"I really like what you've done with the place."

"You've been here before, Nana?"

She smiles at this. "Oh, yes." Her eyes fall back to me.

"Where do you live now?" I ask.

"Not here." Nana shakes her head. "You're a beautiful woman, Bryce. Ethan is plumb stupid if he doesn't snatch you up and make you his wife."

I cock my head to the right, curious. "You know Ethan?"

She nods. Again, she takes her eyes from me and looks around the house once more.

"I love bright colors," Nana says. "Do you like bright colors, Bryce?"

I look around the kitchen, dining room, and living room. "They've grown on me."

Nana smiles, and my world grows a little brighter.

Her eyebrows rise as her smile fades. "Regrets are for those who refuse change."

My eyes narrow. *Wait. What?* My curiosity is piqued. "Nana, why are you here?" I don't believe she's here to admire my looks or the odd colors of Magnolia Road.

Her eyes stare straight into my soul this time. "Ethan was lost before you, Bryce." Tears well up in her eyes. She tries to smile through them. "You've changed him. For the better. You've changed him." She pauses. "Fear keeps us. It binds us. It doesn't allow for us to live our best lives because our hearts can be tender, raw—like in Ethan's case. But he loves you with all he has. I know it. Forgiveness is a tool we do not use often enough. We use the fear to fight forgiveness, and I'm not sure why." She ponders this for a moment. "What if we all lived life through forgiveness, Bryce? Oh"—she laughs a beautiful melody of a laugh—"what a life that would be. Hot dog."

My body starts to vibrate. Not in a way anyone can see, I'm sure of it. But in a way that everything makes sense. Chills spread across my skin.

"Well, I guess I ought to be on my way."

Please don't go, Nana, I want to say.

She carefully pushes the chair back from the table. I stand to help her, but she has it by herself.

Nana takes one last look around the house. "No, really, I think you ought to change the colors." Her eyes meet mine. "Change is good for the soul." She reaches out and touches my cheek. "Take care of each other, Bryce. Forgive one another. Give love. Don't live in fear; it's a waste of measured breaths that we don't get too many of."

"Please, let me walk you home or get you to where you need to go."

We walk toward the door.

"Oh, no, dear, I'm just fine. My husband is waiting outside."

"In-in the cold?" I gasp.

"Don't worry; he's a tough old Mainer."

Reluctantly, I open the door for Nana.

The chill nips at my face.

"Nana, I don't know if I can let you leave here. Please, do you have a person I can call for you at least? To come get you?"

Nana stands on the porch. "No, it's quite fine, dear."

An elderly man stands at the end of the walk with a dog. Like an Australian shepherd of some sort, I think.

This feels all wrong, allowing them to leave like this in the cold.

Quickly, I grab a jacket from behind the door. "Please, take this."

But Nana is already down the stairs of the porch.

"Oh"—she turns back to me—"Robby is fine. Tell Ethan that Robby is fine. He's finally free."

What? I'm so confused.

"Oh, and don't play cards with Ida on Friday nights. She cheats like a son of a bitch."

What? Ida as in Ruthie Murdock's mother?

"How do you know?" I call after her.

"Been watching her for twenty years," Nana says.

The man at the end of the walk gives me a wave and takes his wife by the arm, and they make their way down the sidewalk toward Main Street.

I watch until I can no longer see them, feeling uncomfortable—and not because of them, but because I let them leave in this weather.

Quietly, I shut the door behind me and rest my back against the door, thinking about Nana's words of forgiveness and fear. Regrets.

My phone vibrates in my back pocket. I pull it out.

Unknown number: You'd better run.

My throat begins to burn.

My hands grow cold.

My body begins to shake.

Somehow, I knew it would come down to this.

I walk into the kitchen, trying to dial one of Ryker's many numbers.

But, when I call, a phone starts to ring.

It isn't mine.

It's inside the house.

This house.

The house on Magnolia Road.

It rings again as I hold my shaking hand to my ear.

Ring.

I shake.

Ring.

The ringing gets closer and closer. Finally, I hear footsteps.

And, coming from the bedroom, I see boots. Big black hiking boots.

I trace the boots with my eyes, up to the black pants and black shirt, and I see Luke O'Connor's face staring back at me, the phone to his ear.

"I told you to run," he whispers.

My body runs cold. I try to swallow.

Find strength, Bryce. My voice, as if not my own, says, "I will not run from you, Luke. The world will know what an awful man you are whether I live or die. And I will never give you what you want."

He shrugs and casually leans against the doorframe. "That's not what your dad said when I went to his office to ask him, rather politely might I add, where you were. So, you know what I did, Bryce? I waited. I waited until the time was right. Clearly, the men I sent couldn't get the job done discreetly, so I had to do this one myself."

He grabs a handkerchief from his back pocket. Pulls a small, clear bottle from his pocket and dabs the handkerchief with it, dampening it.

Luke looks up and meets my eye. "Now, we can do this the easy way or the hard way. Really, it's your choice, Bryce."

Luke would be a handsome man, a real keeper, if he didn't have evil running through his veins. I can see why he'd be elected to office with his fresh smile, beaming white teeth, and a weakness for beautiful women. Layered beneath all the evil that takes away from his charismatic smile, his charm, beneath the mind of a criminal, I bet he's still a man, and I also bet he has a hard time saying no to a woman.

I don't allow him to see my fear but instead my confidence as I slowly step toward him. A seductive smile spreading across my face.

He's still. Doesn't move an inch, wondering what I'm doing.

"Can I tell you something, Luke?" I whisper as I get closer.

"What?" Now, he's curious.

I'm about ten inches from his face.

Before I answer, quickly, I take my knee and bring it up toward his balls with speed, hitting him where it counts as hard as I can.

"Don't ever underestimate a beautiful woman, asshole."

A high-pitched squeal comes from somewhere inside him as he drops to the floor.

I take off out the door, up behind the house, and into the trees.

Nightfall, I realize as my legs push me up the hill and into darkness.

My heart pounds against my chest. The trees fly by as I move. Just like my days of running long distances in high school. I smell the night—fresh soil and leaves from all sorts of plant families—but I don't feel the cold. My adrenaline is pumping too hard. My legs push further.

I don't realize I'm breathing hard until I reach the peak of the hill.

Then, I hear the thrashing behind me, and I know it's him.

Hide, Bryce. Take cover. Wait.

The thrashing gets closer, and while my adrenaline is still up, I begin to slowly panic.

Where? Where should I hide?

My eyes search frantically in the dark, my eyes now adjusted, able to make out shrubs, tall trees, rocks, but nothing close to something I can hide in or on.

Don't panic, Bryce.

And then everything goes quiet.

My heart pounds.

"Bryce, I just want to talk." I hear Luke say.

It's cold. It's now that I realize, if Luke doesn't kill me, the elements will.

I look up, and he's standing over me like a lion and its prey.

Thirty

Ethan

Something's wrong. Something doesn't feel right, I think to myself as I leave Ring's Pharmacy. The cold almost takes my breath away when I walk outside.

The town of Granite Harbor shuts down at dusk, except for the restaurants.

I had to work late, and Rick, living upstairs of the pharmacy, said it would be no problem if I came to pick up a prescription when I got off.

But something isn't right.

I look down the street toward the house on Magnolia Road. Bryce's house actually. Still, she hasn't taken my calls, and I understand why. I've got to give her time to heal. That's what James said after I marched back into his office and told him I needed help with this whole situation.

Instead of walking to my truck, I walk down toward the house on Magnolia Road, not because of my own needs, but because something doesn't feel right. I knock.

No one answers.

Lights are on inside.

Go inside, a voice says.

I hesitate. I don't want to invade Bryce's privacy. I don't.

What if she's in there?

What if she's with another man?

Jealousy begins to build, but I realize there's no way she'd do that.

Turning the doorknob, I walk in. "Bryce? It's Ethan. Are you home?"

Quietly, I shut the door behind me, set the prescription down on the coffee table, and slowly, cautiously make my way into the kitchen.

There's nothing out of place.

But Bryce's phone is on the counter, which is odd.

Don't look through it, Ethan. That's an invasion of her privacy.

Look through it, Ethan. What the hell are you waiting for?

I touch the home button, and her screen comes to life. On the screen, I notice a text notification from an unknown number.

You'd better run.

Fuck. My heart starts to pound out of my chest.

"Bryce?" I call out again, more panicked, leaving the phone where it is. That's when I notice the rather large boot print in the doorway off of the kitchen. It's a faint outline, and if I wasn't in law enforcement, I probably wouldn't have noticed it.

I walk over to it and kneel down to examine the print.

It's about a size twelve.

Wide foot.

I pop up and search the entire house for Bryce but to no avail.

Don't panic, Ethan.

The question isn't if Luke is behind this because the fucker is. It's if he sent one of his men to do a job he was supposed to do.

"Officer Lent?" I say into my phone. "I need your assistance at the house on Magnolia Road."

It isn't an issue of I will or I won't tell the story of the O'Connor family. It's a situation of life and death. I know Bryce, and I know she won't say a word about Sandra and Landon; she'll take it to her grave. This thought sends chills up my spine. A thought I'm not willing to explore.

Officer Lent is there within minutes.

"Watch where you step," I say to him as he walks into the house.

He meets me in the kitchen.

I proceed to tell him the story, the short version, of what happened with Sandra and Landon O'Connor.

He thinks on it. Sighs. Places his hands on his hips. "I don't want to poke holes in the story, Ethan, but this isn't evidence that he's been terrorizing his wife and child because they upped and left and stayed hidden."

"I haven't got time for this shit. I have to go find Bryce. She isn't here, and something is wrong."

I pick up Bryce's phone and shove it in my pocket, just in case Luke decides to call back. For all I know, he could have her. This thought almost sends me over the edge.

I stare at Officer Lent, dead in the eyes. "You're either going to help find her or contemplate whether or not the evidence is clear." I leave the house, shutting the door behind me. I run up to my truck and grab my heavy-duty flashlight, my gun already in my holster around my waist. I return to the side of the house to look for evidence.

Come on, baby, leave me something.

Carefully, I walk down the steps of the porch, turn back, bend down, and shine the light closely to see if I can see the boot tracks. I'm about to stand, but I see a small indentation in the dirt, part of a boot track, that is slightly turned to the right.

I stand now and turn my flashlight toward the wet soil next to the side of the house. I use my flashlight to navigate the tracks that I see.

Bingo. Boot tracks.

But I notice a smaller shoe, a slender sole.

A sickening feeling meets my stomach as I follow the small set of footprints because no longer do I care about the asshole in the boots; I only care about Bryce and what she was—is still—running from.

With each quick step, I trace the tracks of both boot and shoe to the base of the hill behind the house to the place we found the chair and the Styrofoam cups, which were taken into evidence.

But, with the leaves from fall, the tracks disappear.

Even though I want to yell Bryce's name at the top of my fucking lungs, I can't. He'll know I'm on his tail.

I pull my gun from my duty belt and quietly begin to creep up the hill, carefully listening.

I listen so hard until I hear sounds that aren't mine.

I hear sounds that belong to animals of the night.

Gathering myself behind a tree, I load my gun, my breaths reflected in the cold night air.

"Just wait for me, Bryce," I whisper into the night as I cock back my gun.

But then I laugh to myself. Bryce isn't the type to sit and wait. She's the type to protect. She's smart. I trust her to take care of herself. I trust her to do what she needs to. What I'm worried about is if she's backed against the wall and she has the option to protect the innocent or die. I know she'll choose the latter.

This scares the living shit out of me.

Again, I breathe in the cold night air.

What is Bryce wearing?

Is she cold?

Was she prepared to run for her life?

With each step I take, I'm one step closer to her and away from my old life. Because this moment right here is when I realize she's the person I need in my life. She's the one I want to spend the rest of my life with.

Fear is crazy. It pushes our limits. It pushes us as people. It forces us to see what we don't want to see. Make decisions that we should have made a long time ago.

I hear footsteps behind me. Not close behind me, but close enough.

An animal?

There are two types of animals. Ones that walk on two legs without empathy and a conscience, also known as cold-blooded killers, and those on four legs who just want to be left alone.

I'm hoping for the second option.

The darkness does things to us. Creates images in our heads. Situations that aren't real.

I quietly wait behind the tree, my head resting against its bark, gun cocked and loaded up at my ear, hands around the grip.

Once again, the footsteps.

I hold my breath and peer from behind the tree. Nothing. Only darkness.

Again, footsteps.

Fuck.

I peer one more time and see the badge.

The north woods of Maine is the game wardens' jurisdiction.

If someone goes missing, it's the game wardens who go searching.

Sure, we can have police help us search, but game wardens know the backwoods. Know the terrain. It's our job to find lost hikers or hunters or to recover a body.

"Ethan." I hear my brother, Aaron.

Thank God. I drop my head against the tree. Breathe.

I step into the darkness from behind the tree, so Aaron can find me.

Aaron and Eli approach.

"Officer Lent said you could use some backup."

I can't really see Aaron's face right now, but I know he's pissed I didn't call him first. I didn't expect to go chasing a madman up a hill tonight. If I had, I would have called him. But I don't tell Aaron this right now because I need to make sure we get to Bryce sooner than later.

"Did he fill you in?"

Eli and Aaron nod, their guns at their sides.

"Let's go find this asshole," Eli says, "but first, let's separate, drive him like illegal hunters drive deer. I'll come from the west. Aaron, you come from the north, and, Ethan, you stay put and come from the east." Eli holds his compass.

"If we get in trouble, you know the routine—two gunshots in the air," Aaron says.

We all nod in unison as the cold gets colder.

A woman's scream sends increments of pain through my body. Small, sharp pains.

"It came from the east," Aaron says, his compass in hand.

"Go," I say as we take off in the dark in our directions, still following our training on tracking, yet keeping a quick pace.

I don't allow my mind to wander. I stay focused, not allowing fear to interrupt my thought process, my concentration.

Now, the only sound left in the woods is the sound of our quiet feet against the leaves, the soil, the wet from the fresh rainfall.

I take out my compass and check my coordinates.

"I'm coming, Bryce," I whisper against the fear that's almost restricting my airway.

I push further up the hill, taking refuge along the trees.

Please, God, take care of Bryce until I can get to her.

The last time I prayed was when our Humvee was attacked in Iraq. The prayer was similar. A desperate call for help.

There are so many things I want to tell her, God. So many things I want to do with her. Please, God, keep her safe until I can reach her.

A shot is fired. It's a crack, like lightning through the sky, and I run east as fast as I fucking can.

I don't feel anything.

We reach the summit, and I see Aaron and Eli in their positions.

We stop.

Listen.

Muffled cries.

I know they hear it, too.

Heart pounds. My mind is taken in a million different directions of fear.

Aaron points down the other side of the hill as a red light moves violently.

Luke has Bryce.

Thirty-One

Bryce

Luke pulls me by my hair to a standing position.

I stand and realize I should be freezing, but adrenaline is pumping through my body like an open vein bleeds out.

"What are you going to do, Luke? You can't kill me. You'll never find your wife and son."

"That's what your brother said when I took my fist to his face."

My stomach tightens, clenches, at the thought of Luke hitting my brother. I've seen my brother's face bruised before. But it's the thought of whom he's protecting and why that makes my heart ache.

I go to a place where my current surroundings don't exist. I go there in self-preservation.

If I were to do my life over again, I'd have a better relationship with my mother. Try harder. Not allow my own hurt to get between us. Maria showed me what a mother's love should look like. I wasn't able to see it with my own mother because I, too, was too wrapped up in my own feelings. Too self-involved to just love for the sake of love.

I'd love Ryker for who he was, not what he did. I'd give him the same compassion I gave Robby as I watched the ventilator breathe for him.

And I'd tell Ethan Casey that I was in love with him. And that I didn't care what walls he had up. I'd push through them to get to his heart.

I see right now that what he said to me that night was to push me away, to protect me, not him. I know this because, right now, I'd do anything to protect him.

Luke drags me by my hair, and I stumble over the terrain of rock, wet leaves, and soil. I try to but don't dare scream because I don't want anyone to put themselves in a position to be killed, because if anyone find out I'm missing, it will be the Maine Warden Service who comes searching for me. They know the woods the best. They'll see my footsteps leading up here. I scream inwardly, manically, and replace the pain with questions.

Breathe, Bryce.

All it would take is the wrong footing to send my head to the jagged rocks below and succumb to my own injuries.

Would they consider it murder?

Would Luke go to prison?

Would Ethan get to him first?

If Ethan found Luke before other law enforcement, found my body, Luke wouldn't breathe to see another sunrise.

Fight, Bryce.

"Where are you taking me?"

I try to stand, but Luke yanks my hair again. I'm weak and tired, but I can see him as he searches our surroundings. He's got the gun in the other hand.

He's frustrated. I can tell by the look on his face.

"Luke, you're not going to find Sandra and Landon this way. You're just getting lost. The north woods is no place to get lost, especially with the falling temperatures." I let out a sigh because I can't seem to catch my breath.

"Just shut up!" He pulls me up by my hair once more.

Don't show him pain.

I inwardly scream.

Luke's eyes are crazed, paranoid almost, as he looks around in the darkness and then back at me.

Finally, he releases me, my hair, and I fall to the ground, relieved, trying to regulate my breathing.

"I should just kill you."

"What did you do to my brother?" Anger is now starting to fester deep within me.

"Fucking idiot." Again, Luke searches our surroundings with his eyes. "Fucking worthless piece of shit."

Anger gets the best of me. Searing anger. "That worthless piece of shit saved your wife and son a lifetime full of torture."

Luke stops searching. Slowly, he moves his head, so he's staring at me. Cocks his head to the right. Eerie stillness claims the north woods. Even the animals, the creatures, stay still. Quiet. They know evil when they smell it.

"What did you say?" His words are clear, full of madness.

I repeat myself. "That worthless piece of shit saved your wife and son a lifetime full of torture."

He walks toward me with purpose and shoves the gun against my cheek. He whispers in my ear, "You have no fucking idea what our life is like."

Is like?

Luke is using present tense as if they were still together. Still united.

Luke keeps the gun at my face and starts to laugh. He pulls back his face and brings the butt of the gun down hard against my face.

I call out.

He stands. "Tell me where my fucking family is, you stupid cunt."

My head aches. The blood that pools in my mouth, I try to spit it out, but everything aches. I can't see clearly, and my head begins to throb.

The truth is, I will never tell Luke where they are. I can't. If it means I have to die protecting them, so help me God, I will.

"I'd rather die than tell you. Men who hit their children and wives deserve to die a slow death." I spit out blood again, the ache in my face growing massively.

Luke points the gun directly at me as he stands not even five feet away.

I hope Ethan will understand.

I hope my mother won't blame herself.

I hope Ryker finds help, for his sake.

I close my eyes, blood pooling quickly in my mouth again.

Luke fires the gun.

It's warm when the bullet hits. Warm like flannel sheets on a cold winter night. The warmth spreads throughout my body, and my feelings grow softer. Lighter. As if this were just a dream.

Nana's words play in my head. *"Don't live in fear; it's a waste of measured breaths that we don't get too many of."*

Two figures emerge from the darkness.

Eli and Aaron, guns drawn.

I'm happy they're here. I'm really happy. I ease back to the ground as warmness continues to spread throughout my body.

They're yelling now, and I see their twisted faces.

"No!"

"Put the gun down!"

Then, shots are fired.

I stare up into the trees as my body rests on the terrain of the north woods. Somehow, it's comfortable and light and warm.

Finally, I see Ethan. He's over my body. I'm so glad he's here.

His face is concerned. Sad even.

"Don't cry, Ethan," I manage to say brokenly. "Don't cry."

I hear sirens in the distance, and I gently close my eyes.

Thirty-Two

Ethan

I gather myself and lie down next to Bryce, taking her in my arms, knowing I could make things worse, her injuries, but I can't help it.

"Bryce, you will hang on. Do you hear me? Help is coming." I bury my face in her auburn hair, not knowing where the blood begins and ends. "I love you," I whisper as I cling to her, desperately searching for where the blood is coming from.

I don't look over at the man's body, which lies not even five feet away, lifeless and without care. We knew he'd take himself out. He knew, if he took another shot at Bryce, he'd die instantly. Instead, he didn't want to die by our gunshots but rather his own. That's how some criminals work.

I hear Eli quickly say, "Isn't that the politician's son whose wife and son went missing?"

I curl into Bryce's body as she begins to shake.

"Aaron!" I scream. "Better get that ambulance here now! Her body is going into shock."

Aaron is pulling me away from her.

"No. No! I want to be here with her."

"Ethan, the EMTs are here. Please, you need to let go, so they can save her life, brother. Come on."

Aaron takes me by the shoulders and pulls me from Bryce. I reluctantly let go of her so they assess the damage to her beautiful body.

Quickly, they load her onto the stretcher.

"We need to get her to Portland. She'll be flown out," Randy, the EMT, tells Aaron as they brush past us with Bryce and down the hill.

By this time, almost all of Granite Harbor PD is here to help the EMTs down the hill.

I want to go. I get up, but Aaron catches me.

"There won't be enough room for you. Come on. You know that. With weight capacity, they need everything in the plane to take care of Bryce; you aren't part of that."

I gather my legs underneath me and run to Luke's body, but before I can kick the living shit out of it, Aaron comes up behind me and pulls me away.

"Brother, listen to me." His words are influential. "You kick him, it will only disrupt the actual picture of what played out tonight up here. Got it?" He breathes, still holding me back. "Besides, Ethan, he's gone. He'll feel no kicks or punches."

We stare down at Luke O'Connor's body, blood still oozing from the self-inflicted gunshot wound to his head.

Some things you can never unsee.

I shower at Aaron's in a trance. I sit down at his dining room table as he sets a bowl of soup in front of me.

"Not hungry."

"I know. Eat anyway."

"I want to go see Bryce."

Aaron sits down across the table from me, a bowl of soup in hand. He takes a bite. "As soon as you eat your soup, we'll go see Bryce."

Mom busts through Aaron's front door, my dad following.

"Oh my God!" She covers her mouth as she sees her boys sitting at the table. Running to me first, she throws her arms around me. Kisses my head. "How's Bryce?"

My dad walks to Aaron, putting a hand on his shoulder, kissing the top of his head.

"Just telling Ethan, as soon as he eats some soup, we'll go to Portland." Aaron nods.

My mom doesn't push the subject. Probably because she knows that those who are taken to Portland are taken for more serious injuries.

I take a few bites of soup. My mom and dad sit at the table with us.

"We'll drive you." My mom slides her hand across the table and touches my arm.

I know my parents have questions.

Who the hell is this guy?

Why would there be a psychopath in our little town of Granite Harbor?

What does Bryce have to do with this?

My brother flips on the television to break the silence in his kitchen.

"A small town where a crime rate doesn't exist and a town curfew isn't needed." It was a quiet evening in the town of Granite Harbor just a few hours ago. Just like every evening, the town shuts down, closing its doors for the day. The reporter from Augusta stands in front of crime scene tape. The house on Magnolia Road sits within the tape. "One person is confirmed dead, up this hill behind this particular house. Brian, we will keep you up-to-date as we receive more information. Back to you in the studio."

Dad says, "Boy, this will cause a political ruckus."

I look at him. "How do you know who it is?"

Dad looks to Mom, eyebrows raised.

"What?" she says. Rolls her eyes. Looks to Aaron and me. "Rick found out from someone on the scene. He told Todd down at the hardware store. Todd told his wife, Nancy. Nancy told Ruthie at the post office, and now, the whole town knows."

"And everybody has kept it a secret from the media?" I ask, both dumbfounded and partly proud of our community.

"What's that Las Vegas commercial, Bill? Do something in Vegas, and it stays?" She thinks. "No, that's not it."

My dad chuckles to himself. "That might be it."

Aaron gives me a *what* face. "Seriously?" Aaron says and looks between Mom and Dad and me.

If I could smile, I would.

"What happens in Vegas stays in Vegas," Aaron corrects.

"That's it!" Mom says. "What—now, what were we talking about?"

This reminds me of old times. Before the war. Before I left. It also reminds me of what Aaron did on the mountain before things got out of hand. Someone who knows me better than I know myself, and I him. Someone I pushed away when I got home. *He doesn't know what it's like.* I hid behind the fact that *I'm a different man now.* I allowed our experiences to get between us out of fear. Again, pushing people away.

I've erected these walls around me. It's time they come down. It's time my family has the old Ethan back.

My family has continued the conversation, and I return back to the present moment. See, they've grown accustomed to losing me in conversations. Made sacrifices.

I also realize now that it's my brother who knows me best.

When we heard the gunshot up on the hill, I took off running. It was Aaron's chest that I met, and his arms came around me like we were playing high school football all over again.

"You can't do this, Ethan," he told me. "You're running on pure emotion. You're not thinking with a level head. I will take care of her. You got me?" He pulled away, still hanging on to me though. "Do you understand?"

I stared straight into his eyes and gave him a half-nod. My heart pulsed against my chest.

"Once Eli and I reach them, you'll stay back. Let me do the talking. Do you understand?"

I nodded.

Aaron shook his head, a not-good-enough shake. "I need a yes from you, Ethan."

Anger shot through my body. Thinking of Bryce hurt, I uncontrollably nodded my head. "Yeah."

"Good. Follow me."

"Hey," I whisper as I pull up a chair next to her bed.

"Hey, yourself." Her voice is groggy, probably due to the pain medication.

"How are you holding up?" I want to reach out and touch her hand with the IV, but I don't. Instead, I lay my hand next to hers.

"I've been better." She coughs, holding her stomach, wincing. Her leg is bandaged and up in a sling of sorts, which is attached to a contraption that hangs from the ceiling.

"Sore?"

"Just a flesh wound." Bryce's eyes are still bright as she looks at me and tries to smile.

Machines beep at their own pace.

I had it planned out, what I was going to say to her. But, now, everything has left my head as I look at her.

"Look, Warden Casey, if you came here to break my heart again, let's get it over with already."

I reach out and push a strand of her auburn hair behind her ear. "When Blue died, I started to build the walls. As I got older and people left or died, the walls became bigger. When I went to war, I built a fortress around my heart. But the ugly truth about that is, I wasn't building the walls to protect you or anyone else. I built them to protect me. And, as much as I'd like to say it was me protecting you or me protecting them, it really comes down to me and my selfishness." I pause. "See, I didn't give you a chance to love me. Or give us a chance to start because I ended it before it began."

I look over to Bryce, and tears roll down her face.

"Don't worry," she whispers. "It's just the pain medication." She smiles and dries her eyes.

I laugh and then feel completely overwhelmed by her beauty, her wit. I shake my head. "No woman ever deserves to be talked to the way I talked to you that night. Ever. I was stuck. My back was against the wall, and I wasn't sure where to turn. While I'd like to hide behind the facts of the matter, the truth is, I can't. You deserve so much more, Bryce. I'm not here to make excuses. I'm here to love you for the rest of our lives. If you'll have me."

Tears fall from her eyes. "Stupid, stupid pain medication."

Her eyes meet mine, and I take her porcelain face with red-stained cheeks in my hands.

"I'd like to kiss you right now if that's all right with you?"

She nods.

I stand, lean in, and gently push my mouth to hers.

It's nothing like I've ever experienced.

Nothing. Not in the times we've kissed before. Nothing.

Her hands come around the sides of my neck as I ease down next to her on the bed.

I kiss her and see my brokenness.

I kiss her and see today, tomorrow, and the rest of our days together.

I kiss her and see how perfect two imperfect people are together.

I kiss her and see vivid images of color.

The truth is, I am at my best when I'm with Bryce.

She is love.

My love.

She opens her mouth and invites me in. I feel it.

"No, no. We can't do this here." I stop.

But I come back for one more kiss—this time, gently opening her mouth with my tongue. I get a taste.

Slowly, I pull away but linger near her lips, my eyes closed.

"Let's be clear, Warden Casey; I can do this. It might get awkward, maybe even a little ugly, but I can do this."

I laugh, and my head falls on the same pillow hers rests on. "I don't doubt you for a second, Bryce. Not for a second." I stare at her as she stares at me.

"Now what?"

"Well, first of all, we get your leg healed. Then, we'll spend copious amounts of time in bed, so I can show you just how much I love you. And then we'll go from there."

"Bryce?" A man walks into the room. A man who makes me question my own charm, good looks. He's tall with dark auburn hair. Clean-cut, clean-shaven, carrying two coffees. "Stopped and got some coffee." His eyes meet mine.

"R-Ryker?" Bryce says.

Thirty-Three

Bryce

My head is still not completely in focus with the pain medication, but it is enough to realize that my brother, Ryker—clean-shaven, clean-cut—is here. My sweet baby brother who's been through hell and back is here to look after his older sister.

"I'm going to give you guys some time," Ethan says, kissing me on the cheek. He stands at eye-level with Ryker.

"You must be Ethan Casey, Granite Harbor's golden military man. Several military awards. And the most hot dogs eaten at the Fall Festival for several years in a row now." He hands me the coffee, not Bryce. "Figured you might need this."

There Ryker goes, winning Ethan over. I roll my eyes and want to cry at the same time.

The boy I knew who was in there, waiting to get out. The boy who doesn't have poison running through his veins, and he's not his first thought, middle thought, and last thought, is here.

Ryker leans over and kisses me on the head.

"Brother."

"Thank you, Ryker," Ethan says. He looks at me. "I'll see you in a bit."

Ryker sits where Ethan sat.

The hospital machines do their work. Some quietly beep. Others just sit. There's silence between my brother and me as he sits next to me like we are kids again. I want this moment to stay, remain in my thoughts, and I want this memory—the feelings of goodness, wholeness—to wrap me up so that I can remember how this feels when the bitter pill of addiction returns and robs him, me, of time. My beautiful, handsome brother, the one I knew from years ago, is back. How long will he stay? I'm praying for forever. But, with addiction, it's just a game of seconds, of inches. It comes down to how badly you want it.

"Remember when we were kids and you fought Jacob Burges because he stole my lunch money?"

I nod. Smile. "Yeah."

"Remember when you told Tiffany Stallman that she could eat a bag of dicks when she broke my heart in the seventh grade?"

I roll my eyes. "Not my finest moment, but yes."

"Remember when you used to bring dinners to me down on Skid Row because you were concerned I hadn't eaten?"

I nod, trying to swallow my tears.

"Remember when you showed up at the hospital after I overdosed the first time and yelled at my drug dealer for dealing me drugs?"

I laugh only a little. I do remember.

"My drug addiction isn't my drug dealer's fault. You and Mom tried to pick up the pieces for so long, and when you stopped trying, I started to get closer to my bottom. I began to see fragments, missing pieces in my life. Like, why do I have to eat out of a dumpster to get dinner? Why do I sleep on the soiled ground next to a woman I don't know? Why don't I go to work or drive a car or have a place to live?" He stops talking for a moment. "About two months ago, I was sick. Tired. I wandered into the Midnight Mission. Heard of it?"

"No." I rest my head on my brother's shoulder as he tells the story.

"It was really late. I'm not sure what time. And I remember thinking, *I don't even have a watch to tell me what time it is.* Anyway, when I wandered in, I bumped into an old guy who was on his way out. He took me into his office and gave me some water. He began to tell me that I didn't have to ever use again if I didn't want to. That I didn't have to keep running. He shared his story of

228

hopelessness with me. I couldn't believe that this well-kept, old, white-haired man had lived the way I lived. He began to talk about hope." He chuckles to himself. "You know, I rehearsed this on the plane over and over in my head, praying it'd come out right. It feels like a fucked up mess."

I put my hand on his arm. "It makes perfect sense. Tell me more." I keep my hand on his arm.

"A moment of clarity came when I saw you drive away the last time. We were in a predicament with Sandra and her son, Landon. I knew right then that, if I didn't make a change in my life, I'd go on living this useless life and die right where I started. Another moment of clarity came when Mom caught me shooting up in her bathroom. It wasn't that she caught me; it was her reaction when I jumped, and blood poured from my arm. It was her trying to help me with it. She wasn't pissed that I'd done this in her house. She just wanted to help me. And I knew, in that moment, that Mom would buffer my disease, make excuses for me for as long as I needed."

The machines I'm attached to brew their secret recipe to assist my body.

All I can think about is how good my brother looks. Clean-shaven. Handsome. And I can't remember the last time I saw him look so well.

"Anyway, the old guy's name was Clancy. He gave me a job at the Midnight Mission once my withdrawal symptoms stopped—the nighttime floor sweeper. In hindsight, I don't think Clancy needed a floor sweeper." Ryker laughs. "I think he was just giving me something to do with my time."

"Are you staying with Mom and Dad?"

Ryker shakes his head. "No, still at the Midnight Mission. Helping others. Sweeping the floor at night."

"You don't want to go home?" I ask.

"No, I'm not ready. I used for a long time, Bryce. If anything, I have to make an investment in my recovery. When I'm at the Midnight Mission, I stay up late to do the floor and wait in the lobby for the Rykers of the world to come in. I want to remember what it was like out there. I never want to forget the incomprehensible demoralization I felt when I walked into the Midnight Mission without a shower in weeks. Without a watch.

Not knowing what day it was. I want to remember what it felt like because I never want to go back to that way of life."

Again, the tears start to come. I'm not sure if it's the pain medication this time or the fact that my brother, my beautiful baby brother, is back.

His hand tightens around mine. "I'm sorry I couldn't get to you before Luke did."

I jerk my head up to look at Ryker. "Why is that your problem? How were you to know he'd find me? Didn't he find you?"

"No. Never did."

"Really? He said he did. He had one of your phones."

"Unless he stopped by the Midnight Mission while I was in withdrawal"—he laughs—"I don't remember seeing him."

A machine is out of juice or not getting a good read because it begins to beep.

"How do you sleep in this place?" Ryker looks at the many machines and then looks back at me. "I'm so sorry, Bryce, for all the worry I caused you, all the sleepless nights. All I can promise you is today. I'm clean. I'm sober. And I'm finally free."

I reach up and touch his face. The face that used to be filled with sores. "Have you talked to Mom and Dad?"

"Yeah, they're out in the hallway. I told them I wanted to talk to you first. Alone."

"Shit. Mom's here?"

"Yes, I'm here, dear. My daughter got shot in the leg by her father's colleague's son, who's apparently a total lunatic, and you thought I wouldn't show up?"

My mom and dad come around the curtain of the hospital room.

My dad rushes to me, trying not to look too eager. Regret and pain cover his face, his wheels turning like twisted metal. "Why didn't you tell me? I could have—I could have—"

"Robert, no. Not now." My mom pats my hand as he retreats, so my mother can hug me. "How are you feeling?"

"Like I was shot in the leg." I roll my eyes. "Come here, Mom."

She leans in, and I wrap my arms around her neck, thankful for her. For the first time since I was a little girl, I show my mom how much I do love her. No sarcasm anymore. No need to deflect my pain onto her. Maria made me see a mother's love. The truth is, my mom would walk through hell and back for Ryker and me. She has. Our family—so fragmented, like shrapnel splayed against a white background—we've danced around our issues for years. Never discussed them. Just kept moving forward because that's what the Hayes family does.

Dad stands in the corner now, leaning against the wall in a polo, jeans, and loafers. Pensive and hurt and heartbroken. He doesn't say this; I see it in his eyes.

"Dad?" I ask.

"I just didn't see it, Bryce. How could I let my family around a man who would try to kill you?" He's at a loss for words, shaking his head, trying to pinpoint the exact moments where he should have noticed but didn't.

"This isn't on you, Dad. You and Mom raised Ryker and me well enough to stand up for what we believe in. Know right from wrong. Protect those who need protecting. So, instead of beating yourself up, why don't you come over here, so I can say thank you? Because God knows I can't get out of this bed right now, and Ryker's smashing the crap out of my hip."

My dad laughs only a little. Smiles. Walks over to us on the hospital bed.

"We might be broken, but we're still the Hayes family. And I can't think of any three other people that I'd rather have in my life," Mom says. "I'm just happy to have our family back together."

"Hello?" I hear a familiar voice.

"Alex?" I say.

After hugs are exchanged with my family and her, Alex reaches in and buries her head in my shoulder as we hug. "Oh, God. I'm so thankful you're all right," she whispers softly into my ear, so no one else can hear her fear.

"I'm glad Eli was there."

"Me, too." She slowly pulls away, giving my hand a squeeze, her eyes filled with tears as she looks down at me.

"I'm not dead, Alex, for Christ's sake—at least, I think I'm not." I give her a smirk. "Hey, really, I'm all right. Okay?"

"Yeah." Alex gives my hand another squeeze.

Ethan appears from behind the curtain, and I melt. He walks to me, kisses my forehead, and whispers, "I'm sorry. I didn't mean to interrupt. I just needed to see you again."

I look up into his eyes.

The same eyes I saw in Los Angeles for the first time.

The same eyes I saw when we first made love.

The same eyes I saw before they carried me off the hill.

I want forever in those eyes.

"Dad, Mom?" I say, still staring at Ethan. "I want you to meet my boyfriend."

My brother gives me one last kiss on the forehead before he stands from my bedside and walks to my parents' side.

"We've met," Ethan says, glancing in my mom and dad's direction.

"You'd better snatch him up quick, B. I'm not sure he'll be on the market too long with those beautiful eyes and that hunky body," my mom says.

My face turns a shade of pink. "Mom, did you just use the term *hunky?*"

The room erupts with laughter, a good, wholesome laughter.

I grab Ethan's hand, who's leaning into the bed, facing the group.

Eli, Ryan, Merit, and Aaron show up, too, each reaching in and giving me a hug.

I take an extra-long hug with Aaron and Eli. "Thank you for saving my life and for watching over Ethan when I couldn't."

"Just remember, we love home-cooked meals on late-night shifts," Ryan says with a wink.

I look around the room at my group of friends. My family. My brother. The love of my life.

Life is hard. Sometimes, really tough. At times, we can't see the light through the middle of the storm clouds or feel the sun on our faces because of the rain, but we can always hear the truth that invariably leads us to where we need to go.

Ryker and I knew what we had to do to take care of Sandra and Landon. We knew, no matter the price, that truth would prevail even if this was a different outcome.

The truth is, Luke didn't win. The truth is also, people lost a husband and a father tonight.

Thirty-Four

Bryce
Six Weeks Later

"The storm is about to begin," Ethan says. "We'd better get back to the house."

Ethan's arm tightens around me, and he kisses the top of my head. The cold makes my now-healed wound still ache but not enough to ruin this moment.

We pass Level Grounds and pop in to say hi to Lyn and get a cup of hot chocolate. My hand falls into Ethan's as he takes the lead.

But it's dark inside, and the only light comes from the fireplace that projects a warm glow against the brick walls that line the coffee shop.

There's no one behind the counter.

"Lyn?" I call out.

Ethan looks around and then back to me. He turns and takes my hands in his. "In a million years, I could never have imagined finding someone like you. Someone who makes my hands sweat. My heart beat fast. Someone who's patient. Cares for others before herself. In a million years, I don't think I could have found someone so perfect unless you were planted in that convention center in Los Angeles for me to find," Ethan says.

"I might not have gotten it right the first time, but you'd better believe I'll get it right the second time, Bryce Hayes. I don't deserve you, but if you'll have me, I'd love to wake up to you every single morning for the rest of our lives. I'd love to be your person, to confide in, trust, to love.

"Maybe it was divine intervention that brought us together, but perhaps it was two people who couldn't walk away from love, no matter the cost. No matter the expense. I'm in love with you, Bryce, and I'd love for you to become Bryce Casey."

Ethan gets down on one knee in front of the fire, in front of God, and in front of me and says, "I think life is full of missed opportunities. I think we all deserve to be the happiness on book covers, calendar pages, postcards. And I think it comes as long as we're open to it. That we pay attention to all the small signs along the way. Bryce, you were almost a missed opportunity. The biggest missed opportunity of my life. I see it now. That whatever you want to call it—God, divine intervention, destiny, fate—kept pushing our paths together. I was too wrapped up in myself to see it. I see it today.

"You deserve coffee every morning and to be made love to every night. You deserve soft kisses when life gets tough because it will. You come first in my life, Bryce. You always will. Please tell me you'll spend those nights and mornings with me for the rest of our lives."

I knew Ethan was the one from the first moment I laid eyes on him. I knew the first time when we made love. When I watched him at Robby's funeral. I know I'm not the one who's supposed to fix his heart, make him well, but I believe I'm supposed to be Ethan's love, his life partner, his best friend, and I'm supposed to give him love. Hold him when he wants to break. Free him of the confines of his mind when the memories get to be too much.

I know he'll take care of me. Be gentle with my heart and love me for the rest of my life the way a woman deserves to be loved. I don't just see it every time he looks at me; I feel it. But my wit gets the best of me.

"On one condition."

Ethan smiles, kneeling in front of me, the fire crackling behind him. "What's that?" he whispers.

"That, all the nights we get to go to bed together, I get the left side of the bed."

"I can arrange that." Ethan smiles a big, beautiful smile. A smile I didn't know his mouth, his lips, was capable of.

"That, if you make the coffee, I'll pour it, and we will sit and enjoy it together."

"Can do."

His hands slide down around my hips, and my body breaks out into chills. My eyes close, and I begin to lose focus.

"You haven't agreed to be my wife yet, Bryce."

"I did a long time ago, Ethan. I just never told you." I pause, pull back, and look him in the eyes, so I can see his ruggedly handsome face. "I would love to be Bryce Casey, Ethan. I would love to be your wife."

The smile that touched his lips only moments ago is back, and this time, he has a box in his hands. Opens it. Pulls out the ring and slips it on my finger. It fits absolutely perfectly.

"How did you know my size?" I stare back at Ethan, smiling.

"When I went over to ask for your hand in marriage while your parents were here, your mom gave me your ring size."

My heart begins to thunder against my chest, and tears start to build. "You asked my dad?"

"I can't ask this beautiful woman standing before me for the rest of her life without asking her father first. He loved you first."

I push my lips to his and enjoy the sweet mint his mouth brings. I pull away just so I can stare and marvel at the man who was brought into my life not once, not twice, but several times.

"Why did you choose Level Grounds to propose? I mean, it's perfect. I love Lyn, love this place."

Ethan looks around at the dated brick walls. Pictures of old Granite Harbor.

"My grandparents used to own this building. It's where they built their future together. They were married seventy years before they died within two weeks of each other. I figured we could start where they left off." Ethan takes my hand and leads me to a picture hanging on the wall. He turns on his phone flashlight and scans the picture. "See, here they are."

It isn't fear that causes the bottleneck in my throat. It's disbelief. It's the feeling you get when faith in something bigger than you turns into reality, but your mind can't quite catch up.

My words are lodged in the bottleneck, too.

"Bryce, what's wrong?"

I try to speak, but all I can do is stare back at the woman who told me to call her Nana and her husband who came by my house six weeks earlier.

"Bryce?" Ethan's tone is more worried.

"Where's—where's the Australian shepherd?" is all I think to say.

"What Australian shepherd? Bryce, are you all right?"

"Uh, the dog was black, white, and brown. Big face, sweet eyes." I describe what I saw on the walkway that night, sitting next to the old man as he waited for Nana.

"Blue?"

My head whips to him. "Your dog that passed away?"

Ethan nods. "But, Bryce, what's going on?"

I swallow. Drop my head and try to wrap my mind around this. I think about Nana. It was her house. That's why she kept looking around. Asking about the colors.

"Ethan, I—can we sit down?"

Ethan takes my hand and leads me to a table.

"The night Luke came, a woman—that woman"—I point to the picture—"Nana is what she told me to call her—stopped by the house on Magnolia Road."

He cocks his head to the right and leans back in his chair. "But—"

I take in a deep breath. "I know." I shake my head. "She said, 'Don't live in fear—"

Ethan cuts me off and finishes the sentence, "'It's a waste of measured breaths that we don't get too many of.'" His eyes grow big, and he leans forward, elbows resting on the table, staring at me.

"She started to talk about you and how much you loved me. She said, 'Forgiveness is—"

"'A tool we do not use often enough,'" Ethan whispers the rest of the sentence.

"Yeah." I measure my breaths by keeping count.

"My grandfather was with her?"

I nod. "And Blue. They waited for Nana outside. I walked her out, trying to convince her to allow me to take them somewhere. I didn't want them walking in the cold." I laugh at the realization that spirits or whatever probably don't get cold.

"I still can't wrap my head around this, Bryce."

"I can't either, and I saw it with my own two eyes."

A knock at the door startles me but not Ethan.

"Oh," he says.

"What?"

Ethan stands and takes me by the hand. "Well, I was hoping you'd say yes to my proposal, so I invited a few friends to come help us celebrate."

"You hate parties."

"But I love you. I'll break for you. Even if it means you see my dead grandparents."

We both laugh, but secretly, I know we both feel their spirits here tonight. Standing, watching the love.

We walk to the door and open it.

It's Ruthie, Milton, and Ida first. I remember Nana saying that Ida cheats at cards, and I giggle to myself and make a mental note to tell Ethan that when we go home.

"Well, is it a yes?" Ruthie's eyes are big with excitement.

I hold my hand out.

"Hot dog!" Ida yells and throws her arms around Ethan and me. "Now, where's the cake?" She steps inside.

Ruthie rolls her eyes and gives us a hug. "I was pulling for you two."

Milton shakes Ethan's hand and gives me a hug. "About time, Warden Casey. Thought you'd let her slip away again."

"Not a chance." Ethan's hand tightens around mine.

Then, my parents appear with my brother, and tears start to flow. They're smiling, laughing. My dad has his arm around my little brother, who kisses the top of his head.

I am so grateful for the gift of time. I'm grateful for forgiveness. I remember Nana's words.

"What if we all lived life through forgiveness?"

My mother embraces me, and I feel her tighten her arms around me. Feel her breath against my cheek. And I bury my face into her neck and tell her how much I love her.

Ryker and my dad each shake hands with Ethan.

"We had a backup plan in case she didn't say yes, Ethan. Because, no matter what, we wanted you in the family," my dad says.

I give my dad the same big hug I always have.

"I love you, baby girl." I hear the break in his tone, and I know it's a happy break.

"Love you, too, Dad."

Ryker swings his arms around me. "I'm so glad I didn't miss this," he whispers in my ear.

"Me, too." I kiss him on the cheek.

"Which way to the food?" he asks.

"Food?" I look at Ethan, who looks back at Lyn behind the counter.

My head drops to the side in thanks. I mime the words, *Thank you*, to her.

She beams back, unwrapping food trays.

Next are Helen and Bill.

After that is Aaron and Lydia, who owns Rain All Day Books.

I side-eye Ethan and wonder what's going on with these two.

I hug Aaron and whisper another, "Thank you," in his ear.

"Just doing my job, sister-in-law," Aaron says.

I hug Lydia. "Thank you for coming, Lydia."

"I wouldn't have missed it."

She quietly follows Aaron in.

"Is there something you're not telling me, Mr. Casey?"

"I am just as shocked as you are," he whispers.

We greet Eli and Alex and their girls, Emily and Noah. I sweep up both girls in my arms and give them kisses on their cold, red noses.

"Hey, matron of honor." I kiss Alex on the cheek. "I hope my girls are ready to be flower girls." I look at them both.

"I wove you, Auntie," Emily says and kisses me on my nose.

My heart explodes.

"Come on, girls. Let's let Auntie and Uncle Ethan get back to their guests." Alex takes the girls but not before leaning in and telling me how much she loves me and how happy she is for us.

Ryan and Merit show up with Hope, and again, I have to hold her because kids. It makes me wonder if Ethan wants kids. Not a question we covered before we got engaged. I guess, if he doesn't, I'll have to bend. Because I can't *not* have Ethan in my life. But, knowing him, he'll want kids just because I do. I think he'd be an amazing father.

Brand, Eli and Merit's father, and Meredith, Alex's mother, come in next.

Meredith grabs me by my shoulders and pulls me in. "You know I'll always have two daughters—one biological and another by the gift of friendship."

I rub her back. "Always."

Brand reaches in for a hug. "I thought this old boy would die in his work truck on a hunt rather than settle down with a beautiful woman. I'm real happy he chose the latter."

"Me, too, Brand."

And the guests keep pouring in. Apparently, you can't have a party in Granite Harbor without the village and its people. Because it takes a village to raise children. Just like we're doing with Hope, Emily, and Noah.

Pharmacist Rick shows up with a plant. Why a plant? I'm not sure, but I take it with a smile.

Tom Sullivan and Mayor Thissel show up, too.

Before I know it, Ethan and I turn and stare at the room full of people who are all here for us.

"We can live in Los Angeles, if you'd like?" He looks back at me and grins.

"Not a chance, babe. Not a chance. We're staying here. Granite Harbor will always be home."

I put my arms around his middle as his arm goes around my shoulders.

He kisses my forehead. "Okay, let's mingle."

After the gathering, Ethan and I bundle up in our coats for the short walk back to Magnolia Road. It's cold. Maine cold is a whole lot different than California cold—well, at least Los Angeles cold. A cold day in Los Angeles is a seventy-degree day. Maine cold should come with some sort of warning label.

I still walk with a bit of a limp. The doctors say that will go away with time. I'm half a second slower these days.

My hand tightens around Ethan's. As he serves as the robust protection from the elements, I curve under his shoulder as we walk.

"I didn't know you were missing in my life until you weren't there, Bryce. I didn't know I needed you until I couldn't reach for you," Ethan says.

We reach the porch of Magnolia Road.

Ethan goes in first, gently leading me inside.

Oh my goodness.

Candles are lit everywhere.

My first thought: *Is the power out?*

My second thought: *No, this is all for us.*

I look up at Ethan, whose eyes are on me. He doesn't say a word. He just removes my coat and drops it on the sofa. He removes his own coat and drops it on the couch on top of mine.

Ethan places his hands on the sides of my jawline but doesn't kiss me. He just stares.

"What?" I whisper, impatiently waiting for his mouth.

"I want to spend the next sixty years making up for the yesterdays I missed with you." He runs his fingertip down my neck and across my chest, lingering in the space near my breast, against my top.

On my tiptoes, I reach up and kiss his jawline, one of the most distinctive characteristics about Ethan Casey that makes my heart beat quicker than I'd like. I feel his chest against mine, and I sigh.

"Make love to me tonight?" I say as I kiss him again, this time on his neck.

"Not yet." A devious smile spreads across his mouth.

He takes my hand and leads me through the living room, the kitchen, and into the bathroom. A bath is drawn, candles lit. Rose petals laid.

I look back at Ethan and drop my head to the side. "I hope this bath is for two."

Ethan lifts his arms, tugs at the bottom of his shirt, and slides it over his head.

His beautifully broken body. The scars you can't see, the ones that lie on the inside, stroking his body with madness.

His beautifully broken body. The damage that doesn't sleep.

His beautifully broken body that somehow found its way through the darkness and to the light to be saved.

I run my hand over the ripples on his stomach as I feel his quick breaths in my ear. My heart pounding in my chest, I try to slow my heart with my thoughts.

Slow down, Bryce.

You have this man for the rest of your life.

Taking the top button of his jeans, I release it and slowly ease down his zipper. I hear his groan in my ear.

My groan. The one that I get to hear every time I do something that he can't control.

Sliding his jeans down, I make sure to get them to his ankles.

I take his boxers and do the same, allowing him to spring to life.

"Step out," I tell him as I pull his jeans and boxers out from under him.

He does so with a smile, and I come back up to meet his mouth, but he denies me.

"Not yet," he says.

I feel the walls between my legs weaken, drawing out the wetness.

Carefully, he lifts my top but not before taking his hand and sliding it around the inside of the waist of my pants. With my top off, my black lace bra is exposed.

He slides his hands down my shoulders and reaches the button of my jeans, pops it with one hand, and slides just my jeans to the bathroom floor.

Ethan stands back and admires my body, but he doesn't touch me, and I see that it almost kills him.

"Touch me, Ethan."

He whispers under his breath, "Not yet." He takes a step closer, and I feel him against my stomach. "But you know what I want to do to you at this very moment?" he breathes in my ear.

"What?" I turn into him, allowing my breasts to rest on his chest.

"Slide your panties to the side and see how wet you are."

I stifle a breath. "What's stopping you?"

"Time." He takes his fingers and slides my panties down.

He stands back and marvels at my body again. The body I grumble at. Pick apart in the mirror and in my head.

Ethan stands, so our bodies are touching. The ache between my legs begins. An ache that only Ethan can take care of.

He steps in the warm drawn water and sits down. "Between my legs," he commands.

I step in, ease into the bath between his legs, and lean back against his chest.

Ethan's hand slides down my hip and across my stomach, and right before reaching my breasts, which I'm praying he'll do, he stops short.

"You're a tease, Mr. Casey. Has anyone ever told you that?"

He laughs a low, throaty laugh. "Among other things."

And it dawns on me that I don't know how many people he's slept with. Who he lost his virginity to. Who his first kiss was. But what I know about him is so much deeper.

"Tell me something good, Bryce." He pulls his knees up, and I rest my arms around them.

This, I think to myself, *is intimacy*.

"Good. Well, there's this beautiful man who just asked me to marry him. And you know what?"

"What?" I can hear his smile through his word.

"I said yes. I said yes for a million reasons. But two that stand out."

"Yeah? What are those?"

He draws his fingertips up and down my arms, slowing my heart.

"His heart, for one. He's got this damn heart that tends to draw people near him even if he doesn't see it, and it's the fact that he doesn't see it. And, two, he's the handsomest man I've ever met—that, too, he doesn't know. And that makes him all the more beautiful."

Ethan laughs again, still running his fingers up and down my arm. He's quiet though. The warm water feels good against my body.

"There was time overseas that I didn't know if we were going to make it home." His words barely linger in the warm steam that surrounds us. He's quiet for a moment. "I'm so glad I did. I don't know how I got so lucky with you, with life, Bryce, but instead of asking why anymore, I'm going to accept what's in front of me."

I run my fingers along his thighs and feel him harden beneath me.

"It's time to go to bed, Ethan," I say.

Thirty-Five

Ethan

She stands so gracefully from the bathwater, and I follow her lead, grabbing a towel for her first and then a towel for me.

Barely dry, she takes my hand and leads me into her bedroom, where I lit one candle and put it on the dresser. The curtains are already pulled closed because there's no way in hell I'll risk that shit again—some sick fuck looking through her window.

Bryce turns back to me and kisses my chest, sending chills up and down my spine as I watch her. I take her chin and tip it back. I put my mouth on hers, trying not to act too hungry for her kiss. But I am. Our kiss deepens as our worlds, although different, blend together once again. Creating a world of our own that consists of love and making love and trust.

She pulls back to breathe, and I allow it but take her hips into my hands, knowing the inevitable, the outcome. That I'll get to be inside her again. I'll get to watch her come unraveled at my touch.

Gently, I turn and lift her onto the bed, watching her body relax into the mattress.

I see her before me. Her dark red hair splayed against the neatly made bed.

She reaches up and cups her own breasts in her hands, and her legs fall open.

Fuck. But I don't say this out loud. I don't want her to think I'm all hard up because of her naked body. I take in her milky-white skin and the tiny patch of hair that sits between her legs. Her long, beautiful legs that are open just for me.

"We're not lucky. This is life giving us a second chance to get it right."

I climb on top of the mattress and sit between her legs, my legs folded underneath me.

I run my hands over her hips and her breasts, pinching her nipples, so she calls out just a little.

My hands slide down from her breasts to her hips, reaching her soft patch of hair.

"I will try to be gentle, Bryce."

"Don't." Her words are terse. "I don't need gentle right now, Ethan. Gentle can come later."

Oh, fuck.

Using my finger, I pull back her layer of protection to expose her beautiful pink folds.

"Oh, God," she whispers as her back arches against the mattress.

"You're really wet, Bryce."

I push against her top notch and slowly open her up with my finger, sliding in to reach the center of her body.

She's breathing harder now. "Oh, Ethan." Her back arches again.

Carefully, I pull my finger out, get down on my stomach, pull her folds back, and press my tongue against her middle, probing and flicking.

I look up, and she's watching me, panting. Her legs relax around me and completely go limp.

She takes her hands and holds my head, pushing me deeper into her. Watching me. Making a face of ecstasy.

I'm about to come unglued. My dick aches for her, but I can't stop watching her get off on this. I could watch her reach her limits forever. Holding her folds back, I flick her top notch again and push deeper on it.

"Oh, God, Ethan."

Her hips rock against my mouth, and I take her in.

But I stop because I know she's reaching her limit, and I'd also like to slowly make love to her tonight.

Her body relaxes once again on the mattress, but I move up her body and slam my mouth against hers. I don't allow myself to slide into her yet, so I flip her and take in everything about her. From behind and on our side, I put my length against her backside as she moves her top leg to where it's in the air. She turns on her back, so we're like the letter T.

Her opening is against me.

"Inside me now, Ethan," she begs.

I don't even think twice. I can't. I feel the head of my length between her folds. "God, Bryce."

"Inside me, Ethan," she pants.

I do.

With one swift movement, I push inside her until I can't reach a place further.

She calls out as I push and pull, and she stares into my eyes. She holds one of my bent legs between her legs as I press into her, something to hang on to. With the other hand, she grabs at her breast. I watch her as her eyes close, and she bites her bottom lip.

This feels way too good. She's way too wet.

"You're too wet, baby. We need to switch it up. This feels too good."

I pull out, and this time, she climbs on top of me. We join again, putting her mouth to mine.

With a hooded look, she rocks against me. I push her hair back out of her eyes, grabbing the back of her neck. Then, I slide my hands to her ass, slowing her because, with what she's doing to me, no doubt, I'll blow it before she does, and that's not happening.

I sit up and take care of both breasts with my mouth, probing, kissing, giving each one equal attention.

"Lie down," she says.

I do.

I slip my finger between us, so every time she rocks, my finger meets her notch.

She picks up pace, her eyes on me. "I'm going to come, Ethan."

I don't answer her. I just stare back and keep my finger in its place.

She shakes her head, rocks harder and faster. Closing her eyes tightly, she drops her head back and allows the pulse through her body to take over.

Once I know she's deeply satisfied, I pull out, flip her on all fours, and slide inside her.

I take her hips in my hands and push and pull in quick succession.

Stars.

The bright full moon.

Her face.

I explode.

Carefully, I pull out, scoop her up in my arms, and pull her to the pillows. I push us both under the covers and lie here, trying to put the world back where it belongs, trying to catch our breaths.

Bryce turns toward me, my arms still protectively around her.

"We need a couch in our living room. Two chairs for guests, but just one couch that we can watch the evening news on. We'll also need this house, not your house up on the hill. And you'll need to wear your uniform home every day. I'll cook dinner in the nude."

I smile, pull her closer, and allow her scent to seduce me again. "Yes, ma'am."

"I'm kidding. I mean, wouldn't that be awkward if Nana and Grandpa stopped by again, and there I was, in just an apron?"

We both laugh.

I agree, "Yeah, that would be a little awkward. But so are two ghosts showing up at our door." I stop talking, taking in our future together. "We can build a house together, Bryce. We don't have to live here. It's old. Really old."

Bryce shakes her head. "No. This house is the house on Magnolia Road. It has memories, history. Memories that aren't mine yet, but I'd like them to be. This is where we're meant to be. Besides, where will Nana and Grandpa come when they want to pay us a visit? Surely, there are no directions in heaven to find the living."

"I'm sure they'll know where to find us." I kiss the top of her head, smile, and ask God how I got so lucky with this beautiful woman in my arms.

And these words come to my head: *grace* and *forgiveness*.

"Do you want children, Ethan?"

"Four."

She freezes but quickly realizes I'm kidding—about the four part.

"Let's start with one."

"I hear it's best to start trying early and quickly," I say, bending to kiss her already-swollen lips.

She breathes me in. "The sooner, the better."

And we make love again.

"So, how are things with you and Bryce?" James asks, setting down his bottled water on the coffee table between us.

"Real good."

James knows me and knows that *real good* means real good. I don't have to emphasize words or explain.

James nods, setting his paper and pen next to his water. My hands grow sweaty.

The rain starts to tap against the window of his office.

"I think you're ready, Ethan. I think you're ready to move on. It's been three years, and while I will never tell anyone they're healed, because your PTSD will always be a part of you, you've learned to live with it, not against it. I'm not sure we need to meet anymore."

I knew this conversation would come. I, too, know it's time. But I have one question for him. "Why do I get this beautiful life, James? Why me?"

James sighs. "Grace."

I nod. "Yeah. That word just keeps coming up in life it seems."

"Trust it." He pauses, almost apprehensive of the words, but he continues anyway, "Look, this is James, not James Rector, Ph.D. A friend. Not your therapist. This is my belief, not something you'll ever read in some textbook. I believe nothing happens in this world by mistake. Nothing. We're given this life to live, and grace comes. We might not think we deserve it but recognize it. Timing is everything. Think of it this way: you might have been ordered to come to counseling, but the military didn't order you to see me in particular. You randomly chose a name based on your Google search and called. I think there was a reason you dialed my number and not anyone else's. You met Bryce three years back, but again, timing is everything. You weren't ready, and maybe she wasn't prepared for the love you two shared. Grace. Maybe one of you would have screwed it up then." His eyebrows rise. "Just my opinion, of course."

I sit here, wide-eyed. James is quiet most of the time. I know he's got opinions, and when he's ready to share them, he does. And, most of the time, he's right.

"Thank you, James." I stand and stick my hand out to shake his. I want to say, *There's no way to repay you for what you've done for me, but maybe, someday, I somehow will.* But I don't say any of this. I hope, through my handshake and the look in my eyes, he'll read it.

"It has been my pleasure, Ethan. Thank you for your service to our country."

I leave James's office and get in my truck, and it's freezing-ass cold outside. I rub my hands together for a minute and start my truck. I sit here for a minute.

Maybe our lives are already planned. Maybe we have this predestined plan to work out. Maybe all we have to do is just show up for life every single day and let grace do its work.

My phone rings, and I smile at the number.

"Hey," I answer.

"Hey, yourself. How'd it go?" Bryce asks.

"Well."

"Good. Come home, baby."

"On my way."

"Is everything all right?"

"Yes." *Yes, it is.*

"Good. Now, get home. I made a fire." I hear her smile.

"You did?"

"Alex says I can't survive a winter in Maine without learning to make my own fire since you guys will be out saving lives and all."

When Bryce says "saving lives," I think about how she saved mine. How she came into my life, opened my blackened heart, and turned it to a tone of pink again—with the help of James, too.

Grace.

I pull out from James's office for the last time and make the drive home.

Thirty-Six

Bryce
Six Months Later

I admire my beautiful wedding ring as I look through the stack of mail in the house on Magnolia Road. How Granite Harbor helped us pull off a wedding in two months, I'll never understand. Maybe Nana had something to do with it. But we were married in Level Grounds Coffee Shop for two reasons:

1. It was the dead of winter.
2. It just felt right.

And, in true Granite Harbor fashion, the whole town showed up. Somehow, everyone fit. Lyn helped with food. Mayor Thissel married us. And Nana and Grandpa's picture hung on the wall.

A postcard in the mail catches my attention. On the front side of the postcard, there's a picture of a beautiful bride, like out of a magazine. She's laughing, looking into the camera, and I'm mesmerized by her eyes. Familiar eyes. A boy has his back to the camera, and the two of them are holding hands. There's no location on the front, so I flip over the card.

Some sort of advertisement, I think to myself.

But there, on the back, is a woman's handwriting.

Thank you.

Love,
S.

Sandra. I put my fingers to my lips and smile through the tears. A postcard telling me she and Landon are okay. Happy. Content. I turn the postcard back over and look at Sandra again. It's her. A smile I've never seen on her face in person because it was shrouded with sadness and fear.

Ethan comes up behind me. Puts his hands on the counter on either side of me, so I can't move. He kisses my neck.

"Who's that?" He pulls his lips from my neck.

I flip over the card, and he sees the writing.

"Sandra and Landon?"

"Yeah."

I turn to face Ethan. "How do you get sexier in that damn uniform every single day, Warden Casey?"

He bends and kisses my lips softly. Pulls away and looks into my eyes. "Behind every strong man is an even stronger woman." He leans down to my growing belly. "You hear that, Emma? Strong like your mom."

I laugh and pull his mouth to mine. "Go take off that uniform, and let's watch a movie by the fire."

Staring into my eyes, he says, "*Steel Magnolias*. Again? Is this because you're pregnant?"

I shrug. I have made him watch it a handful of times. "Come on. I'll even pop the popcorn while you change."

Ethan nods, walking toward our bedroom. "All right. Since you said popcorn."

I'm on the couch with the bowl. An opened beer for him and water for me. Ethan sits down next to me and pulls my legs over the top of his, and we watch the movie together.

Grace.

Love.

One day at a time.

The End

Acknowledgments

It takes a lot of work, not just on my end, to get a book to into readers' hands.

I want to thank my editor/formatter, Jovana Shirley. Your countless hours spent on my manuscripts, and your attention to detail never ceases to amaze me. Your patience and your grace give me room to fly.

I want to thank my proofreader Julie Deaton. You not only have a beautiful southern accent, but you have an unbelievable eye for detail.

Hang Le, your incredible book covers always blow me away. Thank you for making my books shine.

I want to thank Michael Beas at ebook Marketing Solutions and Nazarea Andrews for the promotion, marketing and time you both put into my books.

Big thank you to the book bloggers. You spend many hours promoting our books for fun and for free. Please know that I appreciate each of you so much.

And, lastly, to my readers—thank you for buying this book. Thank you for taking a chance. Without you, indie authors wouldn't be able to do what we love.

J. Lynn Bailey

To my husband and children, I love you three more than you will ever know. Thank you for always giving me a soft place to land.

A Note to the Reader

THANK YOU FOR READING MAGNOLIA ROAD.

If you enjoyed *Magnolia Road*, please leave an honest review on Amazon and Goodreads. By leaving a review, it makes the book more visible to more readers. The more reviews, the better promotional opportunities for the author.

Get the latest information on book releases, sales, and more.

Sign up for J. Lynn Bailey's newsletter at http://eepurl.com/db34Iv.

You don't want to miss out on the next book in the Granite Harbor Series, which is Lydia and Aaron's story. Want to know when the book releases?

Connect with J. Lynn online:

Facebook: https://www.facebook.com/AuthorJLynnBailey/

Instagram: https://www.instagram.com/jlynnbaileybooks/

Twitter: https://twitter.com/authorJLynn

https://www.jlynnbaileybooks.com/

About the Author

J. Lynn Bailey has loved to write since she learned to read, around the second grade. When she isn't running after her children, watching *North Woods Law* or *COPS*, or on the hunt for her next Laffy Taffy joke, you can probably find her holed up in her writing room, feverishly working on her next book. She lives in Northern California with her family.

OTHER BOOKS BY J. LYNN BAILEY